Summer dreams are sun-kissed adventures waiting to happen. . .to you!

The days seem to linger under cloudless skies, while the nights are filled with exotic fragrances and caressing breezes. Summer's here and so is love.

Summer Dreams is the beach book you've been waiting for all winter. Four never-before-published inspirational romances, all served sunny side up. The temperature's rising as four of the most highly acclaimed writers of the genre—Veda Boyd Jones, Yvonne Lehman, Tracie Peterson, and Kathleen Yapp—spin dreams of love to last all year.

Summer dreams that come true can ripen into a lifetime of love!

Summer Dreams

Veda Boyd Jones

Yvonne Lehman

Tracie Peterson

Kathleen Yapp

A Barbour Book

Published by Barbour & Company, Inc.
              P.O. Box 719
              Uhrichsville, Ohio 44683
              http://www.barbourbooks.com

 Member of the
Evangelical Christian
Publishers Association

Printed in the United States of America.

Summer Dreams

Summer Breezes

Veda Boyd Jones

Chapter 1

Melina Howard had been cleaning on the sailboat for two hours. She'd brush-scrubbed and hose-rinsed the outside, vacuumed the inside, charged the battery, packed sodas and ice in the built-in cooler, and stowed sandwiches and snacks in the small galley drawers.

Where was Chad? He said he'd be here by eight to help her, and it was already past nine. The race would start at ten.

The wind was perfect for the regatta—probably fifteen miles an hour. She hoped it would hold. Oklahoma weather in June was subject to sudden changes. The wind could die down one minute and then switch to an entirely different direction the next.

"Melina," a male voice called from shore. "Phone at the clubhouse."

Muttering to herself about her late cousin, Melina hurried across the steel footbridge that connected the multislip docks to the shore. She waved to other members of the sailboat club who were preparing their boats or gathering under the huge picnic shelter to discuss the race, then grabbed the dangling receiver on the outdoor phone and leaned beside the clubhouse door. "Melina Howard," she said in her normal no-nonsense voice.

"Now don't start yelling, but I won't be able to make it," Chad said.

"What's wrong?"

"Nothing. When I said I'd crew for you, I forgot that the Wilsons and Bladows were coming over for dinner. Mary Lynn says we can't call them up and uninvite them, and she needs my help getting stuff ready this afternoon. Sorry," he added with a sheepish quality in his voice.

Melina counted to ten three times. She was a true redhead with the temper to match, but she also had the good sense to control her emotions.

"Know anybody else I can get?"

"There are usually hangers-on around the club. Maybe one of them would crew."

"I'll look around. Talk to you later," she said and hung up. She could have been more gracious, but she was ticked and didn't mind him knowing it. If he'd phoned her earlier, she could have called another cousin to help her out. It wasn't as if he were her only cousin. She had forty-three first cousins, and most of them lived around Crossland.

The last few days had been hectic. She'd graduated from law school, closed her apartment in Norman, and transported all her earthly possessions back to her old room in her parents' large home. The bar exam was scheduled for the last week of July, and she needed to spend every spare minute studying for it. After that she'd decide where to get a job.

Today was a gift to herself. She'd missed sailing and had planned on this treat before hitting the books hard. Oh, she made it home from time to time, but between visiting with her folks and her legion of relatives there was rarely an extra few hours for sailing. She'd made it back for the annual blessing of the fleet in April, but that had been a one-day trip, and foul weather had not been conducive for sailors taking their boats out.

The clubhouse door banged beside her, and she straightened from her leaning position.

"Tom Brown," she exclaimed. The crusty old-timer was one of her favorite people at the sailboat club.

"Well, howdy, Melina." He touched the brim of his faded ball cap. "When'd you get back? Come for the big race?"

"Moved back Thursday. And I'd planned on racing, but Chad just bailed out on me. Are you taking your boat out?"

He shook his head. "Not this time."

Tom was the most seasoned sailor around. If he would crew for her, she'd surely win.

"I need a crew. Interested?"

Tom grinned. "Hate to turn down the chance of spending the day with a pretty girl, but I'm shooting off the starting gun and keeping times."

The aluminum screen door on the clubhouse slammed again.

"Hey, Blake," Tom said. "You on a boat?"

Melina looked up at a tall man whose tanned complexion told her he spent a great deal of time outside. Of course, that golden color could have been the result of a tanning salon, but his muscular build belied that scenario. She couldn't see him lying still for an artificial tan. Odd, she'd just seen him, and she was making judgments on his personality.

He was shaking his head. "Everybody's already crewed up. Need help with the start?"

"Nope. This here's Melina Howard, and she needs a crew."

"Oh? Blake Allen," he said and held out his hand.

Melina shook hands with him and noted his firm grip that would be an asset on a boat.

"I'm a pretty good hand," he said. "And willing to take orders."

Tom guffawed. "Blake's been teaching people to sail for five years. I'd like to see him take orders."

Melina looked from one man to the other. Blake grinned at Tom's kidding, and the older man patted Blake's shoulder.

Obviously they were friends. Tom wouldn't have offered her a crew who wasn't trustworthy. But should she consider taking a stranger on board?

Tom must have sensed her unease. "Blake's been in and out of Crossland several times a year teaching for that sailing school. Now he's moved here full-time. He joined our church last Sunday." As if that wouldn't clinch Melina's opinion, he added, "And he's looking to buy his own boat."

"You're the captain," Blake said. "I'd just like the opportunity to get out there today." He motioned toward the lake. "Good sailing weather."

An experienced sailor, one who was willing to crew for her, and a good-looking man on top of that, although she didn't want to admit that had any bearing on her decision. She'd be a fool not to take him on.

"Do you like to race?"

"I'd rather sail for pleasure, but a regatta now and then stirs up the blood."

Exactly how she felt. She welcomed the competition on occasion, but mostly she liked the peacefulness of being on the lake without the roar of an engine, and with the only sounds the lapping of the waves and the wind in the sails.

"I've got her cleaned up and ready," she said and nodded in the direction of her parents' boat. "Let's go."

"Thanks, Tom," Blake called over his shoulder as he followed Melina across the footbridge to the dock.

"It's a Catalina 25," Melina said and pointed to the last slip in row D.

"A sturdy boat," Blake said. "I've sailed Catalinas before."

While Melina climbed on board, Blake walked around the boat, studying it, then he disconnected the lead lines and climbed on board.

He silently inspected the masts, looked over the

engine, and disappeared into the cabin for a moment.

"Familiar with it?" Melina asked. She knew a good sailor wouldn't take a strange boat out without locating emergency equipment and making sure the engine was clean and the tank filled with fuel. "Oh, the sink water's not drinkable. It's laced with a tiny bit of bleach. The cooler with the spout has ice water."

Blake helped Melina with the sail cover and fed the lines to her as they prepared the mainsail. Together they connected the jib sail and left it crumpled at the front of the boat.

"Ready to cast off, Captain?" Blake asked.

Melina nodded. She pulled the chord on the outboard motor. It sputtered once, then caught. Satisfied, she nodded to him, and he threw the dock lines off. She backed the boat out of the slip, then manned the tiller as they slowly cruised out of the cove toward the two buoys that marked the starting line.

This was going to work out. The man knew sailing, and they were communicating with glances and nods, just like a crew who had worked many races together.

When they reached the invisible starting line, Melina killed the motor and Blake raised the mainsail. They sailed in circles, staying as close to the starting line as they could, studying the other two-member crews, and waiting for the starting gun. A few moments before the race was to start, they raised the jib sail.

From an anchored boat, Tom Brown called, "Ready!" and the shot of the gun signaled the beginning of the

Grand Trophy regatta.

Nine boats vied for position and zig-zagged across Cherokee Lake. For the first few minutes, Melina called out various commands, "Prepare to come about, hard alee, trim that jib," while Blake pulled on lines, cleated them, and smoothed puckers out of the sails.

Fifteen minutes into the race, they settled into a comfortable routine, holding their own in the midst of the boats.

"So, you taught sailing," Melina said to make conversation. "Here and where else?"

"All over. I worked for a marine outfitter and sailing school from Houston, and I flew to wherever necessary to give lessons. Mostly I covered the Gulf area and Midwest inland lakes. On occasion I've sailed off the East coast."

"How'd you get a fun job like that?"

"I studied maritime skills in college. My degree's in engineering, but I got hooked on sailing and took an extra year to cram in maritime classes. Teaching sailing was a great job, but like Tom mentioned, I've decided to retire from the traveling life and settle right here in Crossland." He tugged at the brim of his baseball cap that shaded eyes as blue as the Oklahoma sky. "I'm tired of motel living and fast food."

As soon as they changed tack, then changed direction one more time, they popped the tops off sodas, and Melina continued with her questions. She was interested in this man. He was a natural sailor, but there was more in those intelligent eyes, and she wanted to find out all there was to know about him. And she had time for that. The race course was a direct route past Governor's Island to Two Tree Island, then circled it, returned to circle Governor's Island, back to Two Tree then home to Dillar Cove. Hard to say how long it would take. With a good wind, probably six hours. With any doldrums at all, it would take longer.

"So, now that you're settling down, what will you do for a living? Continue with sailing lessons, but in a permanent location?"

"Maybe a few on the side, but I've been hired by the Great River Dam Authority. I've been learning the ropes for the last week at Gossard Dam."

"So you'll be making the calls on when those flood gates are closed and raised. That's a lot of responsibility." She didn't add "for someone so young," but she thought it. He was probably in his late twenties, maybe early thirties.

"Yes, it is. But don't forget, the sailing was a temporary sideline, not just a frivolous way for a single guy to have fun. I'm an engineer."

She nodded. "Why here? Why this lake when you've been all over?"

"I'm an Okie. There's something in the blood, don't you think? Some fierce, unexplained loyalty to the state. What about you? Are you a native? Oh, are we ready to tack?"

She hadn't been watching their direction; she'd been

watching his deep blue eyes and fascinating expressions. Now she turned all business and they changed tack. Sixty-two feet down. Melina glanced at the depth meter. Right on target—sixty-two feet. She knew this area and she knew it well.

"I'm an Okie, all right. Born in Crossland. Want to take the tiller?" she offered. He took her seat and she climbed on the cabin top to check the main halyard. "Where in Oklahoma are you from?"

"Is this an inquisition?" he asked with a teasing note to his voice and a grin.

"Maybe a cross-examination," she answered and grinned back. "I just graduated from law school, and I have occasional relapses into legalese." She doubted he objected to her questions. After all, didn't men like the conversation to revolve around them?

"I was born and raised in Oklahoma City, but my roots go back to this area." He looked around and chuckled. "And I mean this very area. My grandfather's house was right below this boat."

Melina gasped and glanced at the shoreline again.

"You're not one of those Allens, are you?"

"I don't know about those Allens, but I'm Claude Allen's grandson."

With that bombshell, she almost lost her footing. If she hadn't grabbed hold of the mast, she knew she would have fallen overboard.

17

Chapter 2

"Claude Allen's grandson!"

"Why is that so startling?" he asked. "You couldn't possibly know my grandfather. He died before I was born."

"He's dead? My grandpa's still alive." She hurriedly made her way off the top of the cabin and climbed down into the cockpit to sit opposite him. He offered her the tiller, but she shook her head.

"I think you'd better explain why our grandfathers are important."

"How much of the history of the lake do you know?"

"I know President Roosevelt approved funds for the dam and the formation of the lake in 1937. It's the largest multiple-arch dam in the world, and workers poured concrete twenty-four hours a day for twenty months until it was finished. Can you tell I've been reading pamphlets? I also know there's a ghost town right down there." He pointed to the watery grave of Gossard below them. "Grandpa owned land in the Great River valley, and he had to sell it when the dam was built to make the lake."

"Had to sell it? Ha!"

He raised his eyebrows at her. "Did I use a wrong

word? What is it, Melina? What's going on?"

"I don't suppose you've heard of the Howards?"

He looked thoughtful then shook his head. "No. I don't know any Howards, except you."

"My Grandpa Howard and your grandfather were neighbors. Grandpa owned a great deal of the Great River valley on both sides of the river. He also owned the general store in Gossard, the town that was drowned when the dam was built. The Allens owned several acres, but they never had much luck farming it, even though the soil was good. Grandpa ran cattle. Look up there." She pointed toward the bluff above them. "From this angle you can barely see the roof through the trees, but if we were over there you could see Grandpa's house. It was impossible to move the old homestead out of the path of the water, so he built a new one way up on the hillside, out of harm's way."

"So both our grandfathers owned land and sold it. And that's a problem?"

"The Howards have owned this land since 1851."

"They were Sooners?" The way he said it wasn't complimentary.

"No, they didn't break the law. Besides, this land wasn't even in the land rush. My great-great-great-great-grandmother was Cherokee. So, the Howards were allowed on Indian lands. Generations of Howards were born in the old homestead house. Then it was destroyed when the lake filled up in 1940, the lake your grandfather lobbied for."

"But my grandfather lost his home, too."

"Claude Allen sold his land for a big profit. Grandpa lost his business!"

"So, there's some feud between our families that's sixty years old, and I didn't even know it existed." He removed his cap and ran his hand through his wavy brown hair in an exasperated movement.

He made her sound silly. Melina counted to ten then counted again. The feud might be silly, but Grandpa Howard wouldn't deem it silly. He'd fought Claude Allen tooth and nail for the land and his store, and he'd lost part of his heritage. Okay, if she were being fair, she'd say the Howards lost to the state. Allen hadn't proposed the lake; he'd merely raised support for it.

"I've got to think about this," she said. She was a logical person with an analytical mind, perfectly suited for law, her professors had told her time and again. But when it came to Grandpa and his land, all logic escaped her and her emotions and years of hearing Grandpa's stories took over.

"What's to think about?" Blake asked in typical male fashion. "Does this affect us?"

"Us?" As if there were an "us." Oh, she'd let a thought flicker through her mind about the two of them becoming friends, maybe more than friends. He was a very handsome man with his quick grin and dark tan. And he was obviously a very responsible engineer if he was working for the GRDA. According to Tom, Blake had joined their church the Sunday before, which headed the list of qualities she found necessary in a man she was interested in.

"Us. As in today. This regatta. Shouldn't we come about?"

Melina could have screamed. Not only because she had associated a more important meaning to "us," but of course, they needed to tack again. She glanced at the depth meter. No problem. Thirty-six feet. She manned the lines for the jib and pulled hard after Blake shouted, "Hard alee!" The jib sail moved smoothly to the port side of the boat and filled with wind. Soon they were in the main channel of the lake.

The other boats were already around the bend. Had she actually started this race confident they would win because she had a sailing instructor aboard? Of course, no one could fault her for not concentrating on the race when she'd discovered that it was a Howard and Allen crew. That was synonymous with Hatfields and McCoys or Montagues and Capulets.

Maybe that last analogy went a bit too far. After all, they were no Romeo and Juliet. His "us" that she'd jumped on referred only to their partnership in the race.

"I'll take over the helm," she stated. They changed positions and Blake manned the jib lines while Melina called out orders. They paid attention to the wind, to their speed, and to the other boats. They came upon one and passed it, then met the others who'd already made the circle around Two Tree Island.

"Should we tighten the mainsail?" Blake asked.

She glanced at the bowed shape. Of course they could increase their speed if they pulled it tight. She nodded to him and watched the arrow at the top of the mast. They were listing, but that didn't bother her. She didn't mind being on a slant, but she was on the listing side. Blake had wedged his feet against the opposite bench seat and kept himself upright.

She didn't care if he fell on the floor.

What was wrong with her? Had years of hearing about the wrongful use of their land colored her view of an innocent person?

Or was he innocent? Those lines on his forehead told her he was plenty concerned about the feud now. Maybe he'd known about it all along.

"How does your grandfather feel about you sailing on the detested lake?"

She was surprised at his question.

"He says it's the only way we'll get to use our land."

He pursed his lips, evidently in thought.

"Are we part of this feud? I had the impression you were a smart woman who wouldn't be tied to the past."

Now, how could she answer that? She couldn't say she wasn't a smart woman. She stared at him.

"Why don't we declare a truce until we can sort this thing out?" he suggested. He held out his hand.

Would it betray her grandfather if she shook hands with the enemy and became his friend for a day?

She reached for his hand. It was more a hand-holding than the businesslike shaking of hands they had done when they'd met at the clubhouse.

"Friends," he said, then turned loose of her hand.

"Friends for today," she answered.

She let him take over the tiller when they reached Two Tree Island. He cut a sharp arch around it and headed back toward Governor's Island.

"Why Two Tree? There's only one."

"The other tree died sometime back. When the water level's high, before your department opens the flood gates, the island can be underwater. The big tree has survived annual submersions, but the other one was weaker, and it died."

"Did the Howards survive the submersion? What became of them?"

"I thought we were going to forget about the feud."

"We're not going to participate in it. But I'd like to know a little about your family. You've already asked me a lot of questions about my job. What about yours? Where do you work?"

Melina explained about the upcoming bar exam. "I don't know where I'll work. There's the obvious—Oklahoma City or Tulsa—but I could stay here and go to work for my dad. I'd learn a lot under him. He's a dynamite lawyer, quick on his feet, and he knows the law backwards and forwards. But would that be too much family?" Now, why had she confided in him? She'd never even voiced that concern aloud.

They changed tack for a more direct route to the big island.

"So, your dad didn't suffer any ill effects from not having the land." It was a statement, not a question.

"No. Probably it did him good. Grandpa sold everything in his store and didn't set up shop again. He also sold most of the cattle, so he didn't need my dad on the ranch. Grandpa still has some livestock, but Uncle Jim and his family live near him, and they take care of the cattle."

They came upon another boat and passed it. The wind was creeping up, probably approaching twenty miles an hour.

"Look at that squall line," Blake said.

They were listing at a sixty-degree angle, but Melina, who was now the one bracing herself against the tilt, knew no fear. The strong wind blew her hair around her face, but it was exhilarating, and she felt safe with Blake at the helm. He was almost at one with the tiller, his hand vibrating on it.

She glanced at the sky. The clouds had been building, but she'd thought they were harmless cumulus clouds. Now they had turned dark and were racing across the sky.

"Lightning," Blake said. "It's not close yet, but we'd better find shelter."

"There's a cove over on the east shore," Melina shouted over the wind.

They tacked once more, this time sailing with the wind behind them, the most dangerous way to sail. Still Melina trusted Blake's expertise.

She couldn't explain herself. One minute she was impressed by him, the next she wanted to push him overboard, and the next she trusted him. What a gamut of emotions and all toward one man.

She took orders from him, lessening the tension of the lines and watching the shore rush toward them.

"Right there," she yelled. It was a tiny inlet, not twenty yards across, but it was deep enough, and it was heavily wooded on both steep shores. Their mast wouldn't be the highest point around. As they sailed in, the hills blocked some of the wind, slowing them down.

"Take the tiller," Blake called.

She relieved him of the steering while he uncleated lines and climbed to the front of the boat and pulled down the jib. Then he brought the mainsail down, roughly securing it with bungee cords.

A tiny cove branched off to the left, and Melina steered the craft toward it. She started the engine to make the turn, then killed the motor once they were in the tiny safe harbor. Blake threw out the anchor, which caught and held them in place only ten feet from each shore.

"How deep?" he asked.

"Plenty. Twenty-four."

Rain began, at first huge drops spaced inches apart. By the time they had taken shelter in the cabin and secured the hatch, rain pounded the roof above them.

"Are you wet?" Blake asked.

25

"Not bad. We had pretty good timing." Her last words were drowned out by close thunder.

"Good thing we got off the lake," Blake said. "There wasn't a thunderstorm watch when I checked the weather this morning. That front shouldn't move in until tomorrow sometime."

"Oh, well. It'll pass. How about lunch?"

It was already after twelve, so this storm merely meant a delay in the race, and they could eat in peace without balancing drinks and sandwiches while sailing.

While Blake unfolded the table from its secure position on the wall, Melina unpacked sandwiches, chips and sodas.

"We can dine in style," she said and took a seat at the table. Blake sat opposite her and reached for her hands.

"Grace?"

She held his hands and bowed her head.

"Dear God, thank You for giving us shelter from the storm and for this food. Amen."

"Amen," she said and looked up into his eyes before she withdrew her hands. She'd never had a date share grace with her before, unless they were at a family dinner. Not that he was a date. She didn't know where that thought had come from, but here was another aspect of a multidimensional man.

"Good sandwich."

"Thanks. Chad loves subs, so I indulged him."

"Chad?"

"My cousin who was to sail with me today. His wife

had other plans for him."

"I'm glad," he said softly.

The hostile atmosphere she'd felt earlier was replaced by an entirely different air. Even with the rhythmic pounding of the rain above their heads, sounding like the drums of long ago Indian tribes who once roamed these hills, there was contentment and peace.

Chapter 3

Forty-five minutes later, the Howard-Allen crew hauled up the anchor and motored out of the inlet. Once they cleared the small cove, they raised sails and once again harnessed the wind for speed.

Sun sparkled off the wet deck of the boat, and a rainbow gleamed in the distance.

"See any other boats?" Blake asked from the stern where he manned the tiller.

Melina, who stood in the cockpit looking over the bow, called back over her shoulder, "Not a one in sight. Think we're way behind or way ahead?"

It had still been sprinkling when they had donned rain gear, which Melina supplied from under the cabin seats, and reentered the race, but she had agreed with Blake that it was safe. There had been no chance of lightning, the bane of sailboats. The boat's aluminum masts served as lightning rods.

"We'll have to sail as if we're behind, but believe that we're ahead," Blake said.

Melina followed his odd logic. Confidence gave them a sailing edge, but they couldn't get sloppy and go too long on one tack and not be aware of the subtle changes in the wind.

Now that the sun was drying the sails and the deck, Melina shed her rain gear. Although she couldn't see it, she felt as if steam were rising around her.

"Sure is sticky now," Blake said, voicing her thoughts.

The wind had died down to around five miles an hour, so they were still moving, but not making much time.

It took an hour to reach Governor's Island and circle it, and they chatted the entire time. Blake asked Melina questions about law school and the bar exam.

"Do you have a system for studying law?" Blake asked.

He obviously knew someone who had taken the bar before, Melina thought. "I'm going to cover contractual law first. Outline the book, decide on possible questions, and write the essays. That's my weakest area. I only had one class in it, and it was a sleeper."

"I had a friend who studied one hour, took a fifteen-minute break, then studied another hour, break, an hour, break, from eight until six, six days a week."

"I'm afraid it will take it," Melina said and wondered which gender his friend was, but didn't want to ask.

"He passed with flying colors, so I guess it paid off."

Melina was relieved his friend was a male. She was beginning to worry herself. She couldn't remember a time when she was so enamored, bewildered, fascinated, and confused over a man she'd just met. What was it about him? That grin was charming, of course, and his

29

eyes reflected an intelligence that looked into his soul. Polite, considerate, Christian. What was not to like? His ancestry! She had almost forgotten he was an Allen.

"Portside—a boat," she announced. "Must be headed for Governor. We're ahead of at least one boat." She strained to read the name, then recognized the *Morning Sun*. "That's the Robinsons' boat. Have you met them yet?"

"No. I've known Tom for several years, and I've met a few others, but mostly the sailors who would be around during the week."

"They're good sailors and loyal members of the club. My folks own *Wrinkle in Time*." She pointed to their boat. "But someday, after I pass the bar and have a paying job, I'd like my own boat."

"I meant to ask about the name."

"Actually I named her. I feel as if time stands still when I'm on the water. Contractual law, real estate law, all disappear from my mind when I'm out here. No cares, no worries, just wind and sun and peace. God's world at its best. So, it's a *Wrinkle in Time*. I borrowed the name from the book I read as a kid."

"I like it," Blake said, and Melina felt as if she'd done something quite clever in naming the boat.

"I'll introduce you around when we get back. Oh, are you staying for the barbecue? It's tradition after the awarding of trophies."

"If I can. I'm not a member. I don't have a boat yet."

"You can be my family's guest," Melina said, remembering the new rule that wouldn't let people join the club who didn't have a boat. After all, a sailboat club needed members to pay slip charges and dues to keep up the clubhouse and the restrooms which were equipped with showers and lockers.

"Thanks. I'd love to stay for supper." He propped his feet on the opposite seat and leaned back. "I love sailing," he said with a contented sigh. "I could do this for weeks on end."

"I've always wanted to spend the night on this boat, but I never have," Melina said. Now where did that come from? He seemed to drag thoughts from her before she knew she'd had them.

"I once sailed for three weeks up the coast from Florida to New York with some friends. Best sailing of my life. There were four of us on a 35-footer, but we were organized and didn't get in each other's way. Our jobs were scheduled, so everyone had break time and on-time. We docked for food and supplies as we needed. Most of the time we were fifty or more miles at sea, so going on land was a treat. Once we passed a huge yacht and asked if we could buy a head of lettuce." He laughed. "They gave it to us in exchange for some spaghetti. It was almost like having neighbors at sea."

"Sounds great. Someday I'm going to try something like that."

"You ought to take time out from your studies on a clear summer night and sleep on the boat. You'd be lulled to sleep and wake up after sweet summer dreams. Nothing like it. Ready to tack? Wind's up a bit."

The wind gusted up to ten miles, sending them slicing through the water.

Around the bend they saw several more boats sailing toward them.

"Do you think they're on the way home or heading to Governor's Island?" Blake asked.

"Hard to tell. They're all bound to have taken cover when the storm hit. None of them is foolhardy. But we're either way ahead or way behind."

"One more tack," Blake said, "and we'll reach Two Tree."

After they circled it, they were on the home stretch, on a long tack headed back to Dillar Cove. The afternoon sun blared down on them. Melina went below and fetched a couple of sodas.

"If the others are racing behind our time, we should see them coming at us after we round that bend. If not, we could come in last place," she told him as she popped the top off a soda and handed it to him.

"We were pretty close to cover when the storm came up. Maybe the others had to go out of their way to reach safety."

"Or maybe we stayed in the cove longer than they did."

"A possibility. We didn't watch the weather while we ate. But it was an enjoyable picnic," he said and grinned. "Couldn't ask for better."

"I think we have our answer," Melina said. She gazed toward the bow and saw only motorboats in that part of the lake. "I wonder if there's a booby prize for last place."

"What about *Morning Sun*? We passed it," Blake said.

Melina shook her head. "I've been thinking about that. I don't think they were in the race. It looked like several people on board, and this is a two-person regatta."

He lifted his eyebrows as if to ponder the situation, but kept a hint of a smile. "I've never come in last in a race. It'll be a new experience."

For ten more minutes they cruised along, then the wind died down and only the merest trace of a summer breeze stirred. They tightened the mainsail until it was vertical, without so much as a curve in it, trying to catch a hint of wind.

"Do you have a bigger jib?" Blake asked.

For an answer, Melina went below and opened the hatch to the fore compartment where the sails were stored, then she returned to the deck.

"While I take the jib down, can you get the pole from under the cockpit?" Melina asked. There was no need for either one to control the tiller. They weren't going anywhere. Too bad this wasn't a spinnaker race. They could use the extra-large sail to catch any movement in the air.

Working in tandem, they lowered the smaller jib and

raised the larger one. It helped, and they now made forward progress.

Another hour passed before they saw the buoys that marked the finish line. But even the timing boat was gone.

"You think Tom gave up on us?" Blake asked.

"If they were all back but us, I don't think they'd wait around. Last is last."

They lowered and put away the sails, again without needing to steer. Blake started the engine and guided the *Wrinkle in Time* into the cove.

"Hey, you finally made it!"

"Where have you two been?"

"Sailing," Melina shouted back at the folks under the picnic shelter who as a group watched their slow progress toward D-dock.

"I'll bet," someone called. "What else?"

Melina turned beet-red, and it wasn't from a sunburn, although she knew she was probably a bit pink from that. These people were big teases. What did she expect from them? She'd have probably joined in if it were another young couple who turned up late.

"Do you want to jump or you want me to?" Blake asked. He guided the boat in a big arch, preparing to park her in the slip.

"Would you? Right now I'd probably miss the dock and land in the water," she said. They traded places, and Blake jumped off the port side onto the dock, ran to the helm, stopped the boat from running into the dock, and secured the dock lines.

In silence they worked. Melina handed the trash sack and a bag full of uneaten snacks to Blake who remained on the dock.

"Anything else?" he asked.

"That's it." She closed up the cabin and locked it, then turned to find Blake climbing back on board.

"Did you forget something?" she asked.

"Yes." They stood facing each other in the cockpit. Blake reached for Melina, pulled her into his arms, and kissed her with such tenderness that she tingled all the way to her toes.

When the kiss ended, she let him hold her a moment longer before she pulled away.

"Why?" she whispered.

"Since they all think I've already done this, I figured I ought to know what it was like," he said huskily. "And, wow! I should have done it earlier."

She laughed. And what could have been an awkward moment passed with her feeling like a co-conspirator in crime.

He helped her off the boat, and they each carried a bag across the footbridge. Melina stowed the bag of snacks in her car, and Blake tossed his sack in a trash barrel. As they walked to the picnic shelter, Blake rested his arm around her shoulder.

"Might as well give them something to talk about," he said. "Otherwise, they'll make it up. Besides, I like this."

She liked their closeness, too.

The other sailors were gathered in groups chatting with each other. A few men stood around the barbecue pit where a large fire burned too hot for hamburgers.

Tom Brown sat at a picnic table with charts and trophies in front of him.

"So you decided to come back," he said when they reported in.

"How could we possibly be so far behind?" Melina asked. "We took cover from the lightning, but didn't the others?"

"Sure, but that storm moved through in about ten minutes, so it didn't delay the race much. The others sailed in the drizzle."

"Oh," Melina said. She glanced up at Blake. "How long did we take for our picnic?"

"Picnic?" Lewis Rossiter said. His sailing partner and he moved closer to Tom's table. "We hugged shore 'til the clouds blew over, then we wore slickers and ate soggy sandwiches. And you all had a picnic during a race?"

"Maybe we could have left the cove a little earlier than we did," Melina said.

"And maybe not," Blake said. "We had a pleasant meal."

Lewis hooted. "A pleasant meal?"

"Yes," Blake said. "We enjoyed the sail, and that's the important thing. Melina's a good captain."

In a strange way, Melina felt that Blake was defending

her honor as a sailor and a lady.

"That's why we sail," Tom chimed in. In a loud voice he called the sailors together. "Time to award the trophies."

Blake led Melina to a table at the end of the shelter.

"Thank you," Melina said.

He raised his eyebrows in that way he had of questioning or pondering.

"For being so gallant."

"My pleasure. And I meant it. You're a fine sailor, and I did enjoy the day."

Melina enjoyed the evening as well, as they sat on the edge of the group, being part of it, but being enough separate that they could talk.

And they talked and talked. What was it about Blake that made her share her deepest secrets? She told him about the worst moment of her life. She and her high school boyfriend had argued on the Saturday afternoon of her senior prom. That night he stood her up. She was decked out in a new dress with her hair elegantly styled on top of her head. She'd waited an anxious hour before she knew he wasn't coming. She'd jerked pins out of her hair, changed into jeans, and fled to Grandpa. They'd played checkers until the wee hours, and Grandpa had told her she was the prettiest and smartest girl in Oklahoma.

"I agree with your grandpa," Blake said when she'd finished her story.

He told her about his worst moment, too. His dog

Freckles had died when Blake was ten, and he'd never gotten another dog because he didn't want to go through that grief again. As an only child, he'd poured his heart out to Freckles, and his loss was overwhelming for a young boy.

"Do you think you'd like a dog now that you're settling in one place?"

"I don't know," he'd answered. "I'll think about that."

He'd kissed her good night right there by her car, and it affected her in the same manner as that kiss on the boat. It made her dizzy, made her happy, and she wanted more.

Alone in her room she thought about Blake Allen and his kisses. She'd never felt such a strong attraction for a man in her twenty-six years, and she'd only known him for a few hours. There was a special rapport between them, a special kinship. Oh, no. Once more she'd forgotten about the black mark against Brett Allen. She prayed for wisdom about the old Howard-Allen feud and what to do about loyalty to her family or to her new friend. For she knew Blake could be a very good friend and maybe more. She'd never believed in love at first sight before, but something she couldn't explain was afoot here, and she prayed for guidance on that, too.

Chapter 4

The next morning she dressed with care for church, knowing Blake would be there, but she didn't see him when she walked into the sanctuary with her parents. She fidgeted through the service with the bulletin and half-listened to the minister. When he mentioned a garden of friendship, she raised her head and looked at him. He'd already moved on to making friends of your enemies.

"Matthew said, 'Love your enemies and pray for those who persecute you.' Don't hold a grudge. Even in our church family we have those who talk before they think. The best way to get even with someone who has said something that hurt your feelings is to forget it."

"What's he talking about?" Melina whispered to her mother.

"Oh, there was an incident in the women's circle. A little misunderstanding. I'll tell you later."

Melina nodded. Of course she'd heard you should love your enemies, but that part about the best revenge is to forget was a thought she wanted to remember.

Could she apply that adage to her life? She couldn't think of an enemy. She'd had arguments, no, discussions, with people, but nothing serious. She'd even made up with the old boyfriend who'd stood her up for the prom. They'd never gone out again, but they hadn't been enemies.

"Psalm 141 says, 'Set a guard over my mouth, O Lord; keep watch over the door of my lips. Let not my heart be drawn to what is evil. . . .' Sometimes that can be a struggle," the minister said.

That must have been some incident in the circle, Melina thought, to warrant an entire sermon on the subject. Reverend Miles moved on to gossip.

Now that was something she'd been subject to just yesterday at the lake. She was sure the sailors' tongues had kept wagging, speculating about her relationship with Blake, long after they'd left the barbecue. But that was minor stuff, and those people knew her. Their teasing wasn't malicious, just in good fun. She wouldn't let that bother her.

She hoped Blake had taken it in stride, too. It didn't seem to have bothered him last night. Where was he?

She shifted in her seat and glanced over her shoulder. Oh! Not only was he seated in the next to last row, he was looking straight at her. She smiled, he smiled, and she turned back toward the front of the pew.

"Kindness is the ability to love people more than they sometimes deserve," the minister was saying. "We all make mistakes, and Christian hearts seek forgiveness for their mistakes. Just as we need forgiveness, so we should also forgive others."

What had happened at that women's circle?

"Join me in the Lord's Prayer," the minister said.

Together the church members' voices raised to the Lord.

"Amen," the minister said.

After the service, Melina turned to her mother. "I have an inquiring mind. What happened at the women's circle?"

"We'll talk at home," she said.

Several of Melina's relatives greeted her as they all walked toward the back of the church.

"Did you find a crew yesterday?" Chad asked. "Sorry about letting you down."

"Good morning, Melina." She'd know that deep voice anywhere.

Melina smiled up at Blake, then introduced her parents, a few of her cousins, and a couple of aunts and uncles.

"So, you're the one who sailed with my daughter yesterday," Don Howard said.

"She's a real sailor," Blake replied.

"Yes, she is. But I understood she came in dead last for the first time in her life."

Chad hooted, and Melina nearly choked. She hadn't told her dad about that. Her parents had come in after she'd gone to bed last night, and this morning she'd told them about meeting Blake and about his new job. She'd mentioned that they hadn't won the race, but she'd not said they were last. Nor had she told them that Blake was Claude Allen's grandson.

"Tom Brown told me about the race in Sunday school," Don explained with a chuckle. "He mentioned something about a picnic, but I didn't make the connection between it and that brief thunderstorm."

"Blake, would you like to have Sunday dinner with us?" Suzann Howard asked. "Melina told us you're new here, and we'd like to welcome you to the community. A few family members will be there, but not the whole clan."

"Thanks. I'd like that. It sure beats the hamburger I was planning on fixing. Melina, want to ride with me and show me the way?"

"Sure," she answered. She was surprised her mother would ask Blake without consulting her, but this time it was a pleasant surprise.

When they arrived at the Howards' large ranch-style home, Don took Blake out to look at the horses while Melina helped with the finishing touches of dinner before her two brothers and their families arrived.

"So, what happened at the circle?" Melina asked while she laid out silverware and plates on the buffet.

"It's too stupid for words. And it's something that's been building. I don't think you've met Lorrene. She moved here last year. When Mildred was ill, Lorrene took over the altar decorations. She thought we should have something different, so she didn't follow Mildred's directions about a purple tablecloth for the altar table. She used green."

"Oh, no!" Melina said in mock horror. "Not green!"

"I know it's silly. Anyway, she also put fresh flowers on the table and moved the Bible to the altar. Mildred was furious because it's always been done her way, and Lorrene thought it was time for a change. It's split the circle down the middle. The traditionalists versus those who prefer change."

"And where do you fit in?" Melina asked.

"Somewhere in the middle. If there's a reason for the church tradition, that's fine. If it doesn't have a theological purpose, then I don't see why we can't have some variety."

"And Reverend Miles? How does he see it?"

"He's tired of the bickering and pettiness. Thus today's sermon. Did you notice all the squirming women? And some men. It may have started in the circle, but it's spread."

Actually Melina hadn't paid much attention to those around her. She'd been thinking of her own situation with Blake.

"Do you think it will do any good?"

"It better. Reverend Miles is at the end of his rope. Now that it's out in the open, this feud had better end today."

At the word "feud," Melina dropped two forks that clattered noisily to the floor. She should get the old feud out in the open, too, then maybe it could be laid to rest, and she could enjoy her new friendship with Blake.

"Blake Allen is Claude Allen's grandson," she blurted

out. No further explanation was needed.

Suzann Howard let the oven door slam shut and turned toward her daughter. Her eyes widened and her hand covered her lips.

"Does he know?"

She didn't have to explain who "he" was to Melina.

"I just met Blake yesterday. I haven't seen Grandpa since to talk to him. But don't you think it's the same feud as the traditionalists versus those who want change?"

"I don't think it's quite the same. Although Grandpa wanted his land because it had been in his family for generations, that's a little stronger than a tradition of a certain color tablecloth."

Melina heard the men come through the back door into the mud room.

"Let's wait to tell your father until after dinner," her mother suggested.

"Wait to tell me what?" Don asked.

"How could you hear that?" Melina asked, trying to stall the issue.

"Cherokee hearing," Don said proudly. He turned to Blake who had followed him into the kitchen. "I have Cherokee blood in my ancestry. It goes back quite a ways."

"Yes, I know," Blake said. "I think they wanted to wait to tell you about my ancestry."

"Oh?" Don looked from Blake to the women and back again.

"My grandfather was Claude Allen."

Don stepped back.

"His grandfather is dead, and it has no bearing on Blake at all," Melina said quickly. "He didn't even know about the Howards."

"Does Dad know?" Don asked.

"No, but I'm going there this evening and tell him," Melina said. "It's time this whole thing was forgotten. We can't change the past, and there's no sense in ruining the present worrying over it."

Car doors slamming outside arrested the tense group's attention.

"Let's discuss this later," Suzann said, and Melina interpreted that to mean "don't tell the others yet."

Four adults and five kids noisily entered the house with several conversations going at once. Melina finally got their attention and introduced Blake to the relatives. He shook hands with each one as Melina said each name.

"This is Jennifer." Melina pointed to her eight-year-old niece.

"Hi, Jennifer," Blake said and extended his hand.

"Are you Blake Allen who took Grandpa's land and made him lose the store and should never be allowed to live in the great state of Oklahoma?" Jennifer asked.

"Jennifer!" Melina's brother's voice held rebuke. "Of course he's not. There are lots of Allens in this world."

Melina counted to ten as an embarrassed silence stretched out. "Been spending time at Grandpa's?" she asked.

45

"I can beat him at checkers," Jennifer said, "almost every time."

"I'll bet you're good," Blake said. "And yes, the man your great-grandpa didn't like was my grandfather. But that has nothing to do with me."

"Oh, okay," Jennifer said in an accepting manner, but Melina's brothers and their wives stared at Blake.

Melina quickly introduced her nephews and wondered how life could get so complicated so quickly.

"Dinner's ready," Suzann called. "Don, will you carry the roast to the buffet table?"

Conversations started again as the group moved to the dining room.

"You're lucky there wasn't a big family dinner today," Melina told Blake as they entered the room with its extra-long table. "Did I mention I have forty-three first cousins, and most of them live right here in Crossland or close enough to make it to a Howard dinner?"

"No, you didn't mention the extent of your family. I think it's a topic we tried to forget yesterday."

"And one we should forget today," Suzann said from behind them. "I'll say grace."

Melina glanced at her mother. Normally her father said grace, even if it were fairly repetitious. Suzann Howard said grace when she had something to say.

"Dear Father, thank You for today. Please nourish this food to our bodies that they may be strong and serve You better. And nourish our minds so that they can make good decisions and know what's important

46

and what's best forgotten. Amen."

"Amen," echoed around the table.

Not another word was mentioned about Claude Allen as the Howards filled their plates from the buffet, but Melina knew that later she'd be called on to explain.

The kids sat at the round table in the area right off the kitchen while the adults sat in the formal dining room.

Through dinner Blake entertained them with stories about his sailing experiences.

"We've only sailed on Cherokee," Don said. "I'd like to tackle the Great Lakes sometime."

"I have a friend who keeps his boat on Lake Erie, and that would be a good one to start on," Blake said. "I won't have time off this summer, but next summer I intend to go up for a week's sail. Maybe you'd like to come along."

"I'll keep that in mind," Don said and nodded his head.

It wasn't a firm commitment, but it was a start, Melina decided.

After dinner, Blake suggested he and Melina go for a drive. Melina jumped at the opportunity to get away from the group. They'd been polite enough to Blake, but there was a reservedness about them, as if they were waiting for a pronouncement from the Howard patriarch before they could be sociable.

"You can show me all the important places in Crossland that I should know," he said. "And I'll treat you to a hamburger for supper."

"Sounds good. Sunday night supper at the Howards is find what you can in the refrigerator and eat it before someone else lays claim to it."

As soon as they were in his car, Blake said, "You seem to have come to grips with this Allen-Howard feud. Why the change?"

"I'm working on it," Melina said. "It's like Reverend Miles said today—the best revenge for hurt feelings is to forget whatever the other person said. I know there's more at stake here than hurt feelings, but what good comes of remembering it? Turn here, and I'll show you the high school." She didn't know why he'd want to see it, but she figured he had already found Wal-Mart and the hospital in the two weeks he'd been in town.

Last night she had prayed for understanding of the feud and today's sermon, if she interpreted it for her situation, gave her the answer. Bring it out in the open, then forgive, then forget. She hoped Grandpa would understand. Tonight she'd tackle the old man.

Chapter 5

Melina pointed out areas of interest from the tag bureau, so he could get a new license for his car, to the library. They walked in the park and watched kids playing on the monkey bars.

"Now I have a place to show you," Blake said. He drove them straight to the Dairy Queen. "Can't beat a chocolate dipped ice cream cone on a Sunday afternoon."

"Yes, you can. I like strawberry dipped," Melina said. They strolled hand-in-hand to the side door and entered.

"Oh, no." Melina turned pale.

"Are you all right?" Blake asked.

"Hi, Melina."

"Hey, Melina, what you doing here?"

Grouped around the counter were another bunch of her relatives, and this group included Grandpa.

"Hi," she finally managed. This wasn't how she intended to introduce Blake to the old man. But maybe she wouldn't have to tell him the connection here. "Blake, here's another batch of Howards." She laughed self-consciously. "Uh, you'll never remember these names, but this is Steve, Uncle Ernie, Aunt Esalie,

49

Tammy, Sue Ellen, Bobby, Goldie, Ken, and Grandpa."

She pointed to each one as she said his or her name, much as she had at the house. "This is Blake," she said, purposefully not giving his last name.

Blake waved his hand in greeting.

Grandpa leaned heavily on his cane and took a couple of steps to reach them. He held out his hand to Blake.

"Hello, Blake. So, you finally brought a young man home."

If Grandpa could have stood up straight, he would have been the very same height as Blake. He'd always been a giant to Melina when she was young, and he still was. But eighty-five years had taken their toll. It was only in the last few years that Grandpa had resorted to a cane. He'd seen arthritis as another challenge to beat, but now there was usually pain in his eyes and his crusty manner had taken a bitter turn. Grandpa and Blake shook hands.

"Actually, Blake lives in Crossland. He moved here a couple of weeks ago." Besides his last name, she thought she'd hold his job in check for a moment, too. Referring to the dam always brought the homeplace back to Grandpa's mind.

"Oh," Grandpa said. "This line is sure slow. We want to get our ice cream before the storm hits."

Melina glanced outside. She hadn't noticed a storm brewing, and the sun was shining bright, but she knew better than to question Grandpa. He had an uncanny sense about weather, as did most men who lived off the land. If he said it would rain, it would rain.

"Melina and I sailed yesterday in the regatta," Blake said.

"I saw the boats out there. Did you win?" Grandpa asked.

"No. But we had a good time," Melina said. "Blake has taught sailing lessons for several years. He may take Dad up to Lake Erie next summer." She wanted to establish a family connection before she told him tonight about Blake's relatives.

"You say you just moved here?" Grandpa asked.

"Yes. I'm working as an engineer for the Great River Dam Authority."

So much for her plan to keep that under wraps for a while. She turned her attention to Blake's words.

"Melina pointed out your place. I'll bet you've monitored every foot that lake level raises and falls."

Grandpa chuckled, not the reaction Melina expected. "I've been watching that lake for over fifty years. I can tell you every time they should have raised those gates at the dam and every time they didn't. The last few years, they got a problem with flooding in Seymour. You need advice on raising those flood gates, you come to the right source."

"I'll remember that," Blake said.

"Where you from?" Grandpa asked.

"Oklahoma City."

"What'd you say your last name was?" Grandpa asked. "You resemble somebody I used to know."

Melina stepped in front of Blake as if to ward off a blow. She hadn't counted on this. She hadn't thought about Blake looking like his grandpa.

"Allen. Blake Allen."

"You any kin to. . ." Grandpa's voice trailed off as if he couldn't even say the name.

"Claude Allen was my grandfather."

Grandpa stared right through him. Melina's relatives all turned from their places in line and stared at Blake, too.

"Melina Howard! Are your forgetting your heritage? How could you be out with an Allen?" Grandpa asked. His was a controlled voice, but the pitch was getting higher with every word. He swung his cane at the air and turned and stomped out of the Dairy Queen.

"Grandpa," Melina called after him. But the stooped old man walked purposefully out with as much dignity as his arthritis would allow. He gave the impression that there wasn't enough air in the Dairy Queen for an Allen and a Howard to breathe.

"Now, Melina, what'd you go and do that for?" Uncle Ernie asked her. "We'll have a hard time getting him settled down."

"Claude Allen has been dead for forty years. Blake didn't even know him. How can Grandpa hold him accountable for something that happened that long ago?"

Uncle Ernie didn't answer, and Melina didn't wait for him to think up a reply.

52

"Let's go, Blake. I suddenly don't feel like ice cream."

"I'll be right there," Blake said.

She marched out the side door to Blake's car and climbed in without waiting for him to follow. Through the windows of the Dairy Queen she could see to the other side entrance where Grandpa sat in Uncle Ernie's car. She couldn't see his expression, but she knew it would be one of betrayal. He'd always told her she was his special granddaughter. She'd flown to him for understanding in times of need and in times of triumph and in times of pain. Now she had hurt him. The logical side of her told her that Grandpa was wrong to hate a dead man and to hold his actions against his grandson. But the emotional side of her, the side she had almost denied existed for the last three years while she studied law, wanted to run to Grandpa and tell him that she was sorry. That she wouldn't see Blake again. That she would hate Allens for as long as she lived.

"Here," Blake said and handed her a strawberry dipped ice cream cone through the opened car window.

"Thanks," she said. She waited until he climbed inside to apologize for Grandpa's behavior. "I'll talk to him tonight."

"Maybe you should leave him alone for a while. He'll come around. He just needs time."

"Maybe you're right," she said. "I'm not sure how I expected him to take it." Maybe she'd thought he'd explode, then settle down. That was the way she used to handle problems before she'd wrestled with her temper and won. Now counting to ten usually worked.

As Blake drove the car around the Dairy Queen to the exit, she glanced at the solitary figure huddled in Uncle Ernie's car. He had been her problem solver, her confidant, her advisor. She sniffed back tears.

"Melina? Are you all right?"

"I'm okay. You're right. He needs some time."

They drove in silence through a winding residential section. Melina rolled up her window. Fat raindrops pelted the car as Blake turned into a driveway.

"Run, before the downpour starts," he called.

They dashed for the porch, and he unlocked the front door and hurried her inside.

"Home, sweet, home," he said and made a sweeping gesture of a nearly empty room. Lawn chairs served as living room furniture. A TV sat on the floor with a VCR on top of it. Cement blocks and boards formed a bookcase that held books, speakers, and a CD player. A set of barbells rested near one wall.

"You lift weights?" That didn't surprise Melina.

"I try to keep in shape." He waved his hand at the room. "I've always rented a furnished apartment because I traveled so much. It's going to take some time to find furniture."

"There are lots of second-hand stores around. If you like to refinish wood, you can get some quality furniture pretty cheap."

"Actually, I've saved quite a bit of money over the years, so I could buy furniture, it's just that it takes time to shop for it, and that's pretty low on my list of priorities. I've been wanting to learn my job first." He waved to some books and pamphlets on the floor beside one lawn chair. "And ahead of furniture on the purchase list is a sailboat."

He picked up a newspaper and showed Melina the want ads. One was circled in red ink.

"I've located a boat that might be just what I need. It's in Seymour, and I'm driving up there tomorrow evening to look it over. Want to come? Can you take time from your studies?"

"I'd love to see it."

Blake fixed a couple of glasses of iced tea, then they settled in the lawn chairs to watch a video he had rented. Rain beat on the roof, and an hour and a half later when the movie was over, it was still coming down hard.

"How about that hamburger I promised?" Blake asked.

"If you don't mind, I think I'll pass. I may go spend the night up at Grandpa's. I used to do that a lot, and he may feel like talking now."

Blake reached for her hands and pulled her out of her chair and into his arms.

"I'm sorry I've caused so much trouble for your family. From the moment I first saw you scrubbing on that boat, I wanted to know you. Now I want to know even more. But, I don't want to cause you pain."

So, he had seen her even before she'd met him at the

clubhouse. That thought pleased her, and she smiled.

"It's all right. You've done nothing but make us face a situation that's had too many years to fester and grow, and it's time it was treated and allowed to heal."

Blake leaned down and kissed her. But instead of the kisses of yesterday, this one was long and lingering. Then he kissed her again.

"I'd better be going," Melina said when they finally drew apart.

"Yes, I guess we'd better," Blake agreed.

He took her home and gave her a brief peck when he left her at her front door. "I'll pick you up tomorrow around six-thirty."

"I'll be ready," she said and watched him run back through the rain to his car.

Inside, she explained to her parents about Grandpa's reaction to Blake's heritage. "I'm going to spend the night up there. I think he needs a friend."

"He's already called for you," her mother said.

"I'll be back early tomorrow," Melina said. She packed a backpack with a few essentials and drove to Grandpa's.

At the top of the hill stood the house Grandpa had built in 1939. Gossard Dam, which was being built that year, destroyed the old homeplace and the town. Part of his home was made of fieldstone from the old house. So, it wasn't as if all of his heritage was gone. He still had chunks of rock that his ancestors had touched and loved. Now if only she could make him forget the feud and not let the bad aspects of the past destroy her future.

She ran from the car to the front porch. Many times in her childhood Melina had sat here in the rocking chairs with Grandpa. As they rocked he looked over his old land and told her what it was like before the Great River flooded the area. Today the rain obscured the view of the lake.

"Grandpa," Melina called. She knocked twice on the screen door, then opened it.

She walked through the front living room. Many feet had worn a path across the flowered linoleum floor. On each side of a two-foot strip the linoleum bloomed bright colors, but from the front door to the door to the middle room, the colors were dim.

"Grandpa," Melina called again. She found him in the middle room staring at the huge map of the lake that had been thumbtacked on one wall.

"Ernie says I'm a bitter old man," he said instead of a greeting.

"No, you're not," she said. "You're a man who's taken life in stride, adapted to it, even if you resented it, and made the most out of it. No one could blame you for carrying a grudge. You're a normal human being in that respect."

"I know every inch of this part of the lake," he said and pointed to the old homestead site. "Right here is where your father was born. It's under forty-five feet of water. My store was right here." He pointed to another area. "Over here was the pasture where we kept the cattle. Great River ran too swift and deep there for them to get water from it, but there was a little creek that fed into the river right here. My cows would stand in it on hot July days, trying to beat the heat. I can see them now, swishing their tails over their backs to keep the flies off."

"Some things have changed since then, but some have stayed the same," Melina said. "I've seen your cows over on the pasture by Uncle Jim's barn. They still swish their tails to keep off the flies. They may be standing in a pond now instead of a creek, but they still act the same."

"Cows don't change and people don't change," he said.

"People can change," Melina argued and remembered the church circle's feud. "Just because they get used to a purple tablecloth doesn't mean they can't like a green one."

Grandpa looked at her, his brows drawn together. "What tablecloths?"

"Oh, it's nothing." She didn't want to explain about something so trivial. Grandpa attended a country church where he'd gone all his life. He never liked the town churches and their organized ways. He preferred singing on Sunday and a preacher stopping by every other week. He liked religion simple. He liked it straightforward, black and white. He didn't see life as shades of gray.

And now he was faced with a situation that didn't fit

into his definition of right and wrong. All he knew was he had been wronged by a neighbor all those years ago. She'd heard his tirade against Claude Allen many times. He and Claude had been friends, and then they were enemies.

But what about now?

"What are you going to do about Blake, Grandpa?"

"I don't know that I can like him, Melina. He's an Allen, and there's been too much water under the bridge."

Chapter 6

Too much water under the bridge. Melina was sure Grandpa wasn't aware of the irony in his simple statement. He was merely repeating an adage he'd heard all his life.

What could she do to change his mind? Or was there nothing? How did that affect her relationship with Blake?

It wasn't as if they actually had a relationship, although she was going with him to Seymour tomorrow. That was an official date. Their other encounters had been happenstance: his crewing for her in the regatta, her mom asking him to dinner. But now she had made a choice to see him again. Was she being disloyal to Grandpa?

Honoring her elders had been part of her upbringing. It wasn't just behavior based on biblical precepts; it was based on her love and respect for her relatives. And she would do nothing to hurt Grandpa. But what could she do to change his mind?

Nothing more was mentioned about Blake or the lake or the Howard-Allen feud. They spent the evening huddled over the checker board, as they had done countless times before.

Later when she climbed in the four-poster bed in the front bedroom, Melina listened to the rain on the roof and wondered again what she should do about Grandpa and Blake.

When she left the next morning, it was still raining, and she was no closer to a solution to her problem than she had been the night before. But one thing was crystal clear in her mind. She couldn't hurt Grandpa anymore.

Melina spent the day reading and taking notes on contractual law. What a bore. She hoped working in a law office was more exciting than this sentence by sentence interpretation of fact and intent.

That was another decision to be made. Where would she go to work? Head to the city or stay in Crossland? Well, she'd get through the bar exam first, then tackle employment. She was lucky her parents were allowing her to stay with them for a couple of months while she prepared for the test. Others in her graduating class had taken jobs as law clerks and were putting in eight hours at an office, then studying at night.

On one of her breaks, she turned on the TV to The Weather Channel. The rain would continue through the day and into the night, sometimes heavy. At least they weren't under a tornado watch, which was a normal part of an Oklahoma summer. But would Blake want to look at a sailboat in a downpour?

He didn't call to cancel and showed up on her doorstep promptly at six-thirty.

The windshield wipers kept time to the songs on the

radio as Blake drove them to Seymour. Melina hummed along with a song by her favorite country singer, Trey.

As if he could read her mind, Blake said, "The sailboat is in dry storage in a converted barn, so we can still climb all over it."

It was a bigger boat than she'd expected, a 35-footer. The cabin was arranged differently than her parents' boat, but it still economized on space, much like a camper. This boat even had a captain's chair and chart table.

"Could you sail her alone?" Melina asked, then thought better of her question. He'd taught sailing, so he'd probably encountered every possible sailing obstacle.

"Not as easily as a smaller boat, but I think I can handle her," he said. "If Joshua Slocum could sail single-handed around the world in a 36-foot sloop, surely I can sail alone on Cherokee Lake. But most of the time, I'd sail with a crew." He looked right into her eyes. "Picnics on the water are so much more fun when there are two aboard."

"You'd have room for a house party," Melina said, "but that would be fun, too."

Blake and Mr. Garrison, the owner, talked price while Melina explored the boat. It was luxurious inside, definitely designed for comfort and for sailing in bigger waters than Cherokee Lake. He'd mentioned sailing on the Great Lakes. This boat could go in the ocean, too.

Imagine sailing to Bermuda or the Bahamas in something like this. She was off in another world when Blake called her name.

"Ready?"

He was smiling, which was a good sign. The owner was smiling, too.

Blake didn't talk about the boat until they were back in the car.

"She's a beauty. A bit more than I was hoping to pay, but she's in excellent shape for a ten-year-old boat. Looks brand new. Sails are strong; lines have been maintained. Of course, I'd want to take her out before I bought her."

"Of course," Melina agreed. "And you'd need a crew for that, first time and all."

"Was that a hint?"

"No, that was almost a plea. She's a beautiful boat. I'd love to be on her when she plunges into the water."

"Good. Can you meet me at the sailboat club at five tomorrow? He'll have her in the water by then, and we can give her a try."

"Melina peered at the rain outside her window. "Will we have good weather?"

"Mr. Garrison's desperate to sell her, so he said he'd bring her up, rain or shine. If we dress for it, it won't be bad. Besides, how long can it rain? It's bound to stop by tomorrow."

Instead of following the highway to Crossland, Blake detoured and followed the Janos River, then took the road that paralleled Seymour Creek.

"I've been reading past reports of the flooding in this area and studying maps. I see part of the problem. These houses were built on the flood plain, and there's too much concrete and asphalt. Not enough drainage. That runoff has to have some place to go."

"The water's high just from the last day of rain," Melina said. "We're lucky it's been fairly light most of the time. If we had steady downpours like we had last night, there could be problems."

"I think we're safe." He jotted down the water level from the flood gauge that stuck out of the creek. "The weather service says this won't last too much longer."

"It's odd that Seymour floods. It's at the head waters of the lake, at least thirty miles from the dam. Wouldn't you think that it would flood at the other end?"

"That's what doesn't make sense, but it'll be fine." He dismissed the topic, but the worry lines stayed on his forehead. "Tell me about your evening with your grandpa," he said as he turned on the highway toward Crossland.

"We played checkers. He's hurt by my disloyalty, and I'm not sure how to convince him to forgive and forget."

Blake nodded. "I talked to my dad last night. He remembers very little about the building of the dam. He was only five years old at the time. And he knew nothing about the Howards. But he said my grandfather worked hard to bring hydroelectric power to this area. He even went to Washington, D.C., to talk to congressmen about it, and he was proud of his efforts. But he wasn't the only one who lobbied for it."

"I know it's been good for Oklahoma," Melina said. "But I don't know that Grandpa will ever admit that."

When they arrived at her home, Blake kissed her good night at the door, after declining to come in for coffee.

"I've got some sailing magazines at home, and I want to read everything I can about that boat. See if there were any design problems, that sort of thing, before we sail her tomorrow."

His methodical approach to buying a used boat didn't surprise her, but she wanted to spend more time with him. She wished he'd asked her to go home with him and help with the boat research.

That line of thought did her no good. She'd spent time with him the last three days and still didn't have a solution to the problem with Grandpa.

Maybe the real problem was how much of a problem she would allow Grandpa to be. Would she let Grandpa keep her away from Blake? Or would she just not tell Grandpa about her dates with Blake?

And what about the rest of her family? At church Blake had met several of her cousins and a few aunts and uncles. At the Dairy Queen he'd met more, and via the grapevine, the rest of her relatives knew about his ancestry. Her mother had told her some of them had been quick to recognize the Allen name. Melina chastised herself because she hadn't immediately associated Blake with Claude Allen. But she had known several Allens in school, and had grown less suspicious about the name. Her relatives were walking on eggshells around Blake. Although individually they might not think the feud should be continued against a person who had nothing to do with the dam, collectively they were Howards, and that meant they would follow Grandpa's lead. And Grandpa was a sentimental man with a stubborn streak and a grudge he wasn't willing to let go.

Normally a decisive person herself, Melina reminded herself of Grandpa's rule: In an odd situation, either fish or cut bait. Participate or get out of the game. But was it all her decision to make? What if Blake got tired of being blamed for something for which he was not responsible?

The rain stopped by Tuesday afternoon but a coolness stayed in the air. Melina dressed in layers to accommodate the evening chill and arrived at the sailboat club early in time to help Mr. Garrison launch the boat and tie it up in an empty slip.

By the time Blake got off work and arrived at the club, the place was full of sailors who'd been sidelined long enough by the weather. The white sails of several boats already dotted the water. Melina stood on the dock watching Blake walk down the hill toward

the water. Mr. Garrison met him at the footbridge
to the dock.

"Hey, Melina," Chad came up behind her with a couple of other cousins. "Want to race? Ted and John and
I are taking out *The Windsweeper*."

"Sorry. Blake and I are trying out this boat."

"Oh, still seeing that guy, huh? Maybe we ought to
go out with you. Get to know him a little better. Check
out his intentions."

"I don't think so," Melina said.

Chad and the others walked along the sides of the
boat, looking her over, as Blake and Mr. Garrison
approached the slip.

"What a beauty," Chad said. "But she's big. Wonder
how she'll handle?"

"Want to find out?" Blake asked. "We're taking her
out for a sail."

"I'll go," Chad said with a knowing look at Melina,
who shifted her gaze to the water. She hoped her cousins
would leave Blake alone and not embarrass her with
inappropriate questions.

Ted and John didn't have to be asked twice. They
climbed on board with the others. With many hands
working, the sails were connected, dock lines thrown
off, and the boat was off on an adventure within ten
minutes.

"How do you like a wheel instead of a tiller?" Melina
asked Blake.

"Doesn't vibrate. Much like a sports car compared to

a luxury sedan. There's a specialness about both."

"Definitely luxury," she said.

Under full sail, the boat sliced through the water.

"This is living," Chad said. The three cousins had crawled all over the boat and given it six thumbs up.

"You could live on this boat," Ted said as he came up from the cabin.

The crew tried different moves with the boat, changing directions, coming to a complete stop, turning in a circle. Once Blake dropped the safety pillow in the water and timed how long it took them to maneuver the boat back to pick it up.

"Now, you all enjoy the ride. I'm going to sail her by myself," Blake said. He pulled lines, changed tack, and anchored the boat in a cove.

The smile on his face grew wider and wider.

They watched the sun sink to the horizon before they turned the boat back to Dillar Cove.

For a moment, Melina and Blake were alone in the cockpit.

"What do you think?" she asked.

"I love it. I can handle it, and it's seaworthy. I've been saving for a boat, and it's exactly what I want."

He looked like a little boy in a candy store. His eyes sparkled, and his grin was infectious. Melina grinned back.

She looked over the familiar lake which gleamed with the glow of the sun's last rays. The boat was right over her ancestor's lands, right on top of the old store, right on top of her heritage. Against her will, she glanced up at the bluff. There, silhouetted against the dusky sky, stood Grandpa, looking down at them.

Chapter 7

He couldn't know it was them. Without binoculars, he couldn't know four of his grandchildren were sailing with the enemy. Since the big boat wasn't one that normally sailed on Cherokee Lake, it would draw Grandpa's attention. That was all. But Melina couldn't shake the guilty feeling that clutched at her heart.

She glanced at Blake and knew he'd seen Grandpa, too. He reached for her and she sagged into his arms.

"Blake, I. . ." She couldn't finish the sentence. Her gaze went back to the bluff where the old man stood. Together they watched him wave an arm in dismissal, as if shoving them and the boat down into the water, down with the ghost town of Gossard. Grandpa turned and walked back to his house.

Melina fought a sob that welled up in her throat and anger that threatened to overwhelm her. She counted to ten, then again. This time her struggle to overcome her temper failed. She pushed away from Blake.

"How can he do this? How can he force evil feelings on me? On all his offspring?"

"Was it evil before you knew an Allen or did you parrot back what he taught you just like your little niece?"

"Does it matter?" she snapped.

"I think it does," Blake answered. "Let's get this boat in, and then we'll sort this out."

The wind had shifted and picked up, and they were among several boats that headed back for the safety of the dock.

"Ready to take them down?" Chad called from the bow. "I thought this next go round wasn't to hit until later tonight."

Blake had thought the same thing. The weather forecast he'd heard on the radio assured a breather from the rain, but predicting weather in Oklahoma was far from an exact science.

"Pull them down," he called back.

The crew lowered the sails, tied and covered the mainsail, and stuffed the jib in its bag. Blake fired the inboard motor and guided the boat into the cove. Getting the boat loaded on the trailer would be a feat.

Fast moving storm clouds roiled above them.

"Mr. Garrison," Blake called the man to the cockpit. "I'd like to buy your boat. Can we leave her here overnight instead of loading her and go somewhere and talk? It'll be tomorrow before I can get the money to you."

The owner glanced at the sky then back at Blake. He held out his hand and they shook, sealing the deal. "We can leave her here. No need to cart her back and forth again."

Blake maneuvered the boat into a slip, and Melina's cousins jumped off and tied her down.

After making sure the boat was secure, Blake, Mr. Garrison, and Melina climbed off and hurried to the clubhouse as the first raindrops splattered them.

The one large room was furnished with tables and chairs, and behind a counter were a couple of refrigerators and a stove for the convenience of the club members. The place was deserted now as other sailors scurried to tie up their boats and run for their cars.

Blake used the inside phone to call the caretakers and make sure his new boat would be all right docked at the club overnight.

"No problem," he told Melina and Mr. Garrison. "Although I have to apply for club membership in order to get a permanent slip. I need a club member to vouch for me."

"I imagine we can find someone," Melina said. "I'll ask around." She smiled at him, and he laughed. Teasing him made her feel much better than letting her temper shout at him. Why couldn't she have controlled that outburst on the boat? Grandpa's attitude was her problem, not Blake's. She didn't need to take it out on him.

Blake and Mr. Garrison settled down to talk business. Melina offered to leave, but Blake insisted she stay. They hammered out an amicable agreement, and Blake arranged to deliver a cashier's check the next day.

As soon as Mr. Garrison left, Blake turned to Melina. "I think it's time we played face your fears."

"How do you play that?" Melina asked.

"You tell me what you're afraid of, and we discuss it

and decide on the solution to your problem."

Melina got up from her chair and paced over to the wall of windows on the lake side of the clubhouse. Rain poured down on the deserted boats below. Lights on the docks cast an eerie glow that pulled her mood down. She turned back to Blake.

"Shouldn't we forget problems tonight and celebrate your new boat?"

He shook his head. "Not yet. What's your fear, Melina?"

She hugged herself, as if that would protect her from the pain of exposing her thoughts. It was too early in their relationship for her to bare her soul, but once she looked into his eyes, she knew this was the moment of truth. It was as if he willed the words out of her.

"I don't want to choose between you and Grandpa."

There she'd said it. She watched for his reaction.

"You shouldn't have to choose."

Oh, no. Did he feel nothing for her? Was that special longing she experienced for him a one-sided emotion? She looked down, not wanting to see the pity in his eyes.

"Your grandpa shouldn't transfer his dislike of Claude Allen to me. He's the one making you choose, not me. He should love you enough to want you to be happy."

Melina searched his eyes for a clue to what he was saying.

Blake drew her into his arms and rested his chin on

top of her head. "There's something special between us. I feel it, too. And we should have the right to explore that feeling without being torn by guilt."

Her voice was muffled as she hugged his chest. "So now that I've faced my fear, how do I solve the problem?"

He drew away from her so they could look at one another.

"We care about each other, so we face the problem together."

"I've prayed about it, and I feel God wants me to know you and put this silly feud behind us. But how do we change Grandpa's attitude?"

"We should pray for guidance on how to do that. I feel certain that Grandpa will come around. You mean too much to him."

They bowed their heads together, and Blake asked God for direction for them as a couple and for their problem with Grandpa.

Melina raised her head and smiled at Blake. She felt as if a weight had been lifted from her. Wasn't there an old saying about shared trouble halved it and shared joy doubled it? She felt like that. She'd shared her trouble with Blake and God, and now she felt like sharing Blake's joy in his new sailboat.

"While you're at work, do you need me to run any boat errands for you?" she asked. "Of course any number of people will vouch for you where the club is concerned. Dad will or Tom Brown or Chad. I'm not actually an official member, just a family member hanger-on. But what about the mundane things? Insurance? Getting to the bank?"

They arranged to meet for lunch. Blake would swing by the bank then give the cashier's check to Melina who could deliver it to Mr. Garrison in Seymour.

"I'll see if Grandpa wants to go for a drive," she said. "He doesn't get out that much, and this might give us a time to talk."

"Perfect," Blake said. He kissed her good night, then followed her home to make sure she made it through the storm all right. He blinked his lights as he backed out of her driveway.

The next morning the rain had let up from the gully washer of the night before to a steady downpour. Melina outlined more contractual law before grabbing an umbrella and driving to the Crossland Mooring Cafe where she settled in a booth and waited for Blake.

He arrived five minutes later and handed her a cashier's check and a title transfer sheet which he had already signed and had notarized. "This should do it. I called for insurance and have to drop by the office in a few minutes to sign a paper. You're to meet Mr. Garrison at the tag office in Seymour."

They ordered the blue plate special, and Blake gulped down his food.

"Don't hurry, but I've got to get back to work. We're watching the lake levels. I appreciate your doing this for me, honey." He laid a ten-dollar bill by the check, kissed her on the cheek, and turned to leave. "How about a leisurely meal tonight? Around seven?"

"Sounds great. See you then," she called after his departing figure. Melina didn't dawdle over her meal, but finished and headed out to pick up Grandpa. She hadn't told him the specific nature of her errand. He might have objected to doing a favor for an Allen.

The old man was waiting on the porch, staring out into the rain, when she pulled up to his house.

"It's raining cats and dogs," he said when he climbed in the car. "Sure your trip to Seymour can't wait until tomorrow?"

"No. But I'll drive carefully," she promised.

They talked of nothing important on the way to Seymour.

It was only after she'd turned into the tag office parking lot and parked by Mr. Garrison's truck that she told Grandpa she was delivering a check for a sailboat and had to get a signature on the transfer of title.

"You're buying a boat?" Grandpa asked. "What's wrong with using *Wrinkle in Time*? Your dad thinks of that as your boat."

Melina took a deep breath. "Blake is buying the boat. I'm just the delivery person."

Grandpa snorted and stayed in the car while Melina ran through the rain to the office. Ten minutes later she was back with all papers signed.

"Thanks for riding up here with me, Grandpa."

"It's okay," he grunted. "Now take me over to Seymour

76

Creek. Since we're here, we might as well have a look."

Melina followed the road that led to Seymour Creek and turned in at a pullover place. The flood gauge that stuck out of the creek showed it was two feet higher than when she and Blake had checked it on Monday night.

"It'll be out of its banks by nightfall," Grandpa said. "That boyfriend of yours had better be lifting those gates."

Chapter 8

"But, Grandpa, it's not that high on the gauge stick. It can rise three more feet before it reaches flood level."

"I've seen it before. Those fools at GRDA don't realize how fast it comes up."

Melina turned the car around and retraced their route into Seymour.

"Blake says they've built on a flood plain and concreted areas without proper drainage. That's asking for trouble. The water has to go someplace, so it runs into the creek."

She stopped the car at a filling station and ran in to call Blake. She didn't know the number, so had to call information, wasting precious time.

"Blake, it's Melina," she said when he finally came on the line.

"Are you already back?" he asked. "Any problem?"

"Grandpa says you need to raise the gates. Seymour Creek will be out of its banks by nightfall."

"Did you notice the flood gauge?"

"It's three feet below flood level, but Grandpa says those fools at GRDA don't realize how fast it rises." She gasped. "Sorry, I was just repeating him." Oh, why did she quote Grandpa? Now Blake wouldn't listen to the warning.

"Can I speak with your grandpa?"

"He's out in the car."

"All right. Thanks for calling, Melina. I'll get the sheriff out there to monitor the level, and we'll look at the numbers at this end and see what we can do. I'll talk to you later."

Melina walked back to the car.

"Well? What did he say?" Grandpa demanded.

Melina repeated the conversation.

"He won't listen to a Howard. Allens never have and never will. They only do what's right for them."

"That's not true, Grandpa." Melina swung the car out from the protection of the filling station canopy into the rain and took the highway back to Crossland.

They had only gone a couple of miles when they met a deputy sheriff's car. "See, Grandpa, Blake's already got the sheriff's department on top of it."

Grandpa snorted. "We'll see if Seymour floods."

Instead of turning off at Crossland and taking Grandpa home, Melina stayed on the highway.

"Where are you taking me?" Grandpa asked.

"Gossard Dam. I want you to tell Blake what you've told me. If you have knowledge that will help this situation, you must help him."

Grandpa snorted again. "My knowledge is common sense, not based on some numbers out of a computer. I know what I've seen. That Seymour Creek is the first sign of trouble. It's high long before the lake level sounds an alarm."

The dam was another ten miles and the steady rain took on torrential proportions for five miles of that distance. Twice Melina considered pulling off the road when visibility became so bad she could barely see the dividing yellow line. When she finally parked the car beside the hydroelectric dam's powerhouse, she was a coiled spring waiting to be released.

"Come on, Grandpa. We're going inside," she shouted. The noise from the rain and the roar of the water pouring through the spillways made normal conversation impossible.

She helped him out of the car and kept a protective arm around him as they made their way to the building. They were drenched when they reached the door.

"Melina," Blake greeted her from his position in front of a computer. Two other men stood beside him, examining the screen.

"I've brought Grandpa to tell you what he has observed over the years. Nothing concrete, I mean not specific facts, but he knows the cause and effect of flood control."

Blake stood up and walked toward Grandpa. He raised an eyebrow and said, "Mr. Howard?"

"Now, listen here, Allen. I don't have any fancy degree, but I know when we're headed for flood trouble. Seymour Creek can come up a foot in an hour, and this type of rain can make it quicker."

"Sit down," Blake said in an authoritative voice and indicated two chairs next to the wall. The other men by the computer observed them silently.

"What do you think we should do, Mr. Howard?"

"You should let some water out of the lake."

"Do you know how that affects our generating capacity? We have to make adjustments. People count on our electricity. We're running the numbers now on how long it'll take to lower the level with two, four, and six gates open. We know our electricity customers in Seymour don't want their homes flooded."

"It's better to do it early than have to react late," Grandpa said.

"I agree. If we can prevent a flood, we will."

"They always wait too long," Grandpa said and waved his fist in the air.

"I think he got the picture," Melina said and patted Grandpa on the shoulder to calm him down.

"Mr. Howard, according to the procedure manuals, we are not at flood stage and won't be for some time. However, I believe the procedure needs to be reevaluated. Now what exactly can you give us?"

Grandpa looked down at the floor. "In 1991 Seymour flooded when the lake level was only up three feet on my gauge. When the lake level was up five feet, the flood gates were opened. Too late. In 1995 Seymour flooded when my gauge read two feet nine inches. And now it's reading two."

"Okay, here are the figures," one of the men said. He

tore a sheet from the printer and handed it to Blake.

"We can open seven and eight right now. That should do it, if the rain doesn't continue like this."

Blake studied the page then said, "Let's do it. Open gates seven and eight. Carl, warn them downstream." He stepped to a phone and punched in an automatic dial number.

"Blake Allen of the GRDA. We're opening two gates," he said in a firm voice. "We'd like flood readings every fifteen minutes from Seymour Creek. . . . That's right. Thanks."

"I guess I can take you home now," Melina told Grandpa.

"Do you need to go yet, Melina?" Blake asked. "Mr. Howard, would you like to see the gates opened?"

Grandpa's eyes lit up, but his voice was level. "I suppose I could take a look."

Melina tagged along behind Blake and Grandpa as they trooped through a tunnel to the lower side of the dam.

"Watch through this window. Seven and eight are right over there." Blake pointed across the mile-long dam. "If we need to open more, we'll use fourteen and fifteen to even out the pressure."

It was as if some giant had turned on a hydrant. The power of the water that spurted forth awed Melina.

"At the top of the flood pool, our gates can discharge 525,000 cubic feet per second," Blake said. "But it's doubtful any flood would ever reach that magnitude."

"Seymour Creek is so far north," Grandpa said. "How long will it take before it feels the effect of this?" He waved at the water gushing from the open gates.

"I don't know. Let's check the numbers. We may have to open a couple more." Blake led them back to the room on the high side of the dam and called Seymour. He fed numbers into the computer, then ordered another two gates opened.

"Seymour's still rising, but at a slower rate. This should take care of it."

"We'll get out of your way," Melina said, although she liked watching him at work. His knowledge and his air of authority impressed her. She'd seen another side to a wonderful man. Now if only Grandpa could see past Blake's blood relationship with Claude Allen and respect this fine young man.

Blake held out his hand to Grandpa. "Thanks for sharing your knowledge with me. The citizens of Seymour will thank you, too."

Grandpa grunted, but shook Blake's hand. "I guess you were already planning on opening those gates when I got here."

"We were considering it. Your information decided it for us."

"Well, okay. I. . ." He paused and looked down at the floor.

"Yes, Grandpa? You were saying?" Melina asked.

He didn't glance at her, but looked straight at Blake. "Well, I may have been hasty in my judgment about you," he said. "What your grandpa did has nothing to do with you. And maybe Claude had his reasons."

"Perhaps he saw what hydroelectricity would mean to this area," Blake said. "And maybe he knew his grandson would love to sail on a big lake in the middle of this great country of ours."

This time Grandpa extended his hand. "No hard feelings?"

Melina had never seen her Grandpa appear so strong and noble as when he forgave an injury he had felt for so long.

"Thank You, God," Melina whispered.

"No hard feelings," Blake said as they shook hands. "Does this mean I have your blessings where your grand-daughter's concerned?"

"Depends on your intentions," Grandpa said with a twinkle in his eye.

"Honorable, sir. Mostly honorable," Blake said, and Grandpa chuckled. "Melina, I'll pick you up at seven," Blake said as the phone rang. He picked up the receiver.

"See you then," Melina said and hustled Grandpa out into the rain so that Blake could get back to work.

As soon as they were away from the roar of the dam, Melina turned to Grandpa.

"Thank you for seeing Blake as he is and not as someone's grandson."

Grandpa grunted but smiled at her.

❦

That evening Blake pulled up at her house exactly at seven. They ran out into the drizzle, and he opened the car door for her and dashed around to his side.

"I have your papers," Melina said as he put the car in gear. "Sorry I forgot to give them to you this afternoon."

"We were a little busy," he said with a laugh.

"What's the reading at Seymour?"

"Under control. The water level's going down, but it's far from normal. By morning we should see a major difference."

He drove them to the sailboat club.

"I hope you don't mind, but I had the deli pack some sandwiches. We need to christen the boat with a picnic."

The drizzle was a sprinkle when they traipsed down the hill to Blake's new boat. Once on board, Melina handed Blake his ownership papers.

"I want a special name for her," he said. "I've toyed with *Last Place*."

"*Last Place?*"

"We came in last place in our first regatta together."

Melina laughed.

"But we'll probably come in first a few times, too. What about *Love At First Sight?*" he suggested. He pulled Melina into his arms and kissed her—an unhurried kiss that said he had many days ahead to kiss her, too.

"How about *Forgiven?*" Melina said when they ended

the kiss. "I was proud of Grandpa today."

"He was terrific. How about more kisses?" Blake said.

"*More Kisses* as the name of a boat?"

"No. More kisses for me," he said and lowered his head to hers. "We'll name the boat later."

Veda Boyd Jones is the author of six inspirational romances, including the award-winning *Callie's Mountain* (Heartsong Presents). Besides her fiction writing, Veda has authored numerous articles for popular periodicals. A sought-after speaker at writers' conferences, Veda lives with her husband and "three rambunctious boys" in Joplin, Missouri.

À la Mode

Yvonne Lehman

Dedication

For my two youngest grandsons, Austin and Derek Henslee, both of whom, I'm sure, will grow up to be just the kind of heroes I like to write about. Thanks, Lisa and Mark.

Chapter 1

Heather Willis looked at the clock for the umpteenth time on Saturday afternoon. It was almost three. She didn't want to close a minute early because she needed the business, yet she longed for more time to spend with Molly, her four year old. Maybe. . .someday.

Sighing, she clipped the end off the stem of a silk daisy, placed it into the pick machine, pressed the lever, then stuck the flower in an arrangement she was making for a neighbor who recently had lost her husband. Guilt stabbed her—for suddenly wishing she could sell the arrangement, but only because she could use the money. She really wanted to give too, for she knew only too well what losing a husband was like. She had lost her own, even before his car slammed into a tree, leaving her and Molly alone.

Sunlight glinted on a car pulling into the parking lot. She glanced up. No one paid attention to the "Customer Parking Only" sign in a small town like Highland. Probably someone picking up a worker. But this was Saturday, she remembered. Most businesses were closed. Only the retailers that catered to tourists were open.

A second look told her that no one—at least no one

she knew—drove a car like that. Wow! A white Cadillac —with tinted windows. Must be a lost tourist.

She watched a man get out of the Cadillac and try the door handle to make sure it was locked. Yes, he had to be from out of town. Mmm, and he was wearing jeans, a light-blue knit shirt, and sandals without socks. But his hair shone like silver in the summer sun. He must be old—old enough to afford a luxury automobile. Maybe he's somebody's chauffeur, she thought, trying to see an outline of someone in the back seat of the car.

Then she noticed "Texas" on the front license plate. Concentrating on what celebrity might be out there, she was almost unprepared when he pushed the glass door open and she heard the ring of the silver bell on the handle.

"Good afternoon," he said pleasantly.

A native North Carolinian would have said, "Hi" or maybe "Hello."

He wasn't old at all. He looked like he was in his thirties, maybe early or mid. His hair was silver-white, emphasizing his handsome, tanned face. His expressive eyes, the color of his shirt, were beautiful beneath thick silver-gray eyebrows, and his lashes were long. Mercy, where did they grow men like that? Heather softly cleared her throat. "G-Good afternoon."

"Mind if I look around?" he asked, and smiled.

Ah, he had double-duty dimples! "No, go right ahead," she said.

He walked around the shop. Heather pushed at her short, dark brown hair, as if that would do anything for the unruly natural curls, then wiped her palms on her jeans.

Get a grip, girl. Don't come unglued because a handsome stranger enters the shop. He's probably passing time while his employer. . .does what in this little town?

The "unglued" thought reminded her that she needed to unplug the glue gun. She would be leaving as soon as he did. She resisted the urge to look at the clock, not wanting to hurry someone who probably wasn't, but just might be, a customer. She unplugged the gun, then picked up stems from the floor and tossed them into the trashcan. She reminded herself that looks were deceiving. Her late husband, Rey, had been the world's greatest example. He had been so handsome—tall, dark. . . .

Don't think about Rey, she cautioned herself and rummaged under the counter, open on her side, for a small box for her daisy arrangement.

"Cute," the voice said.

Heather straightened. He was standing right in front of her. "What?" she asked, her dark eyes wide. What kind of guy was this?

His eyes immediately dulled, and the smile left his face. "The daisies," he said. "Cute arrangement."

"Oh, thank you." She couldn't stop the warmth that she knew flooded her cheeks. Surely he wouldn't buy the daisies, not after she had felt so guilt-ridden by wishing she could sell them. But it wasn't just the daisies, *Lord*, she apologized silently. *I just want to sell. . .something!* She should try to be friendly.

"Are you from Texas?" she asked.

He laughed lightly. And it was a very nice laugh. The dimples were terrific, along with the little dancing lights in his blue eyes. With a shrug, he said, "Sometimes." And in the same breath, "Are you the florist?"

"Well, yes and no," she said, feeling foolish. The merchandise was hers, but she rented the building. "I mean, I run the shop, but I'm not a florist. I don't carry fresh flowers. Only silk."

He nodded, occasionally glancing around. She wondered if he were looking at the merchandise or just wanted conversation or. . .what? "Are you a tourist?" she asked. "Or visiting someone here?"

He looked back at her so quickly that her heart skipped a beat. "You might say that," he replied, and she wondered why he was deliberately sidestepping her questions. He seemed to want to only ask his own. But then, she was asking personal questions. She shouldn't do that.

"You're the only silk store in town, right?" he said, with an amused smile.

She nodded, wondering if someone had recommended her.

"I've driven by here many times. Your displays are beautiful."

"Well, thank you," she said, glad that he finally made a statement without hedging. The shop was on a corner with a main road in front and another well-traveled road at the side. Local people and tourists, mainly those attending a conference center farther up the road, passed by all the time—many in fine cars, but she, unlike many other shops, didn't depend upon the tourist trade. She depended upon word-of-mouth from pleased customers and the recommendations of a couple of interior design firms in nearby Asheville that liked her work.

"I like the pink dogwood," he said.

"The pink. . .dogwood," she repeated, foolishly. He didn't seem like the type of man to buy a pink dogwood. Unless a lady in the car wanted one. Oh, this was ridiculous. Why did she have to try to figure out what and why and who?

But she knew why. This was unusual. No matter how much she tried to rationalize, deep inside, she was nervous. She was almost alone in this town on a Saturday afternoon. That's why she closed at three instead of five, like the other days of the week. But this man wasn't what unnerved her. It was something inside that might never trust again. Rey had caused that mistrust.

She drew in a deep breath. "It. . .looks springy, doesn't it?"

He looked uncertain. "I'm not sure it would go with my furnishings. But I need other things too."

"You realize I'm not a licensed interior designer," she said, "although I have studied interior decorating."

"I'm not looking for a designer," he said, "just suggestions. Do you make house calls?"

Chapter 2

Heather felt her mouth open and immediately shut it. She needed to act like a business-woman. But she was accustomed to acting like a friendly retail store worker who knew everybody and would feel out of place wearing anything but jeans, or at least casual clothes, to work. Yes, she did house calls. Had this been someone she knew, she would simply say it was closing time, call her sitter, and they could leave immediately. But she wasn't about to get in a Cadillac with a good-looking stranger. This was the kind of situation she would have to warn Molly about.

"Let me get my appointment calendar," she said, hoping he didn't notice that her hand shook. Where was her letter opener, in case she had to defend herself? "Oh, here. Let's see. I could come any afternoon next week."

"No," he said quickly. "I'm going out of town tomorrow, for two weeks. I would need you to come tonight. I have a dinner appointment but can be home by eight."

"I charge a fee," she said.

"How much?" he asked, and she detected an edge to his voice. She didn't believe this man wanted a pink dogwood and needed her to go to his house to see how it looked. Couldn't he come up with a better line? But if his intentions were honorable, would he come up with a line at all?

"Twenty-five dollars," she said. If she knew someone was serious and would buy, she would waive such a fee. Then she prided herself on the insight of adding, "In advance."

His brows knitted slightly, and she wondered why she had bothered saying that. If he were a pervert, what was twenty-five dollars to get someone to meet him somewhere?

She felt tension crackle between them, and his lips tightened, but he reached into his front pocket and pulled out a roll of bills. He peeled off three 100-dollar bills, laid them on the counter, and looked at her with a sense of finality, as if to say he could afford her fee.

Now what was this? What kind of "house call" did he have in mind? "Twenty-five for a consultation," she said stiffly.

"And 180 dollars for the dogwood," he added.

Heather quickly shut her mouth that had fallen open again. "Oh, you want to buy it?" she squeaked.

"You can bring it tonight. You do make deliveries?" She said she did.

"I suppose there's a charge for that?" he asked.

"Normally, yes, but not since you're paying for a house call. I'll waive that."

His dimples showed again with his slight nod.

"One hundred eighty for the tree," Heather said as

she punched the amount into the adding machine. "Twenty-five for the house call, and six percent tax." The machine ground away. "That's $217.30."

He pushed the bills closer to her.

Now what? She only kept a hundred in the cash register. Was this counterfeit? She didn't know how to check for that. And what could she do anyway? Tell a crook to take his counterfeit bills and leave? She opened a drawer and took out a sales book. "Your name and address, please."

She thought he hesitated before answering. "Tom Smith."

She didn't dare look up while writing the receipt. *Sure*, she thought, *and I'm Jane Doe.*

What else could she do but go along with this? *If he comes around the counter,* she thought, *I'll jump over the top and escape through the front door—if I don't break my neck in the effort!*

"Address?"

"I'll probably need to draw you a map," he said. "Have a piece of paper?"

She handed him a sheet of letterhead stationery and he began to make lines. She glanced at the clock. Three-fifteen! Molly would be expecting her. Jillian would be worried. Well, maybe she would call. At that moment, the phone rang.

"Heather's Silks," she answered.

"You still there?" Jillian said. "Molly's having a fit. Said you promised to let her help you bake cookies."

Heather laughed, picturing Molly's impatience. "Tell Molly to hang on. She can go ahead and count out the chocolate chips. Forty-nine this time." She glanced at the man, thoughtfully looking over his map. "I'm with a customer right now. Hang on a minute." She laid the receiver down, feeling more at ease now that someone could hear if anything went wrong.

He glanced up. "Who's Molly?"

That bothered her. It wouldn't if he were local. She always talked about Molly to local people. "My daughter," she said and thought his face lit up. Why should that interest him?

"How old is she?"

"Four." She forced away a stab of fear. She was being unreasonable. Nobody was out to hurt Molly. This man was just making conversation—almost. Anyway, he might think her husband was waiting on the phone. But if he looked at her hands, which were plainly visible, he would know she wasn't wearing a wedding ring.

"Okay," he said, turning the paper to face her and tapping it with the pen. "My house is on Thomas Lane. You can't miss it."

Her skeptical eyes met his dancing ones, and he added, with dimples, "It's the only one there."

"Mmm," she sounded, nodding. A secluded area? She had never heard of Thomas Lane. He made that up! His name was Tom! At least, he said it was.

"I think you can find it from this." He laid the pen down on the map. "If not, call."

"Okay," she said, not bothering to pick up the paper. "Eight o'clock tonight, you said?"

"Yes. Could I have my change?"

"Change? Oh, I'm sorry." She picked up the bills and opened the register. She hadn't made a single sale all day. "I'll have to give you a lot of small bills." She gave him seventy cents in coins and two ones, then pulled out her only twenty, her only two tens, five fives, and fifteen ones. He could readily see that all she had left were some ones and change. But maybe that's why he was there—to exchange counterfeit bills for all her money. Her glance, as she counted the money into his hand, revealed his raised eyebrows at the wad of bills. He folded the money and had difficulty stuffing it into his front pocket.

"Have a nice day," he said as he turned away.

"You too," she replied, watching him leave without a backward glance. He unlocked the car door, jumped in, backed up, and headed down Main Street toward the interstate highway. "Jillian," she said softly into the phone, while staring at the three 100-dollar bills. You'll never believe this. I either have a very wealthy customer, or I've been conned."

Chapter 3

A few minutes later Heather turned into a long driveway next to a big house and parked in front of what had once been a garage, but was now converted into the small, but attractive two-bedroom apartment that she rented. Molly stood on the couch, framed in the living room window, waiting. Saturdays were long for her since there was no preschool and she had only Billy to play with. Heather rushed inside, fell on her knees with arms open wide, and Molly ran into them. They hugged tightly. "I love you, darling," Heather said.

"I love you, Mommy. What took you so long?"

"I'll tell you all about it while we make those cookies." Molly's big brown eyes widened with excitement and her face glowed. Her mass of dark unruly curls bounced like springs as she jumped. Heather could hardly believe that everyone said she and Molly looked exactly alike. Maybe there was a resemblance, but she couldn't possible be as beautiful as that little girl. *I certainly don't have her energy*, she thought, observing Molly's antics.

Jillian's five year old, Billy, was engrossed in a TV cartoon, but Jillian followed closely on Heather's heels, inquisitive about her remark on the phone.

Heather related the incident with the mysterious stranger while mixing cookie dough, listening to Molly recount the chocolate chips, and responding to Billy's request for a cookie. "We have to cook them first," Heather said, laughing at his impatience.

❧

Heather had refused Jillian's offer to stay with Molly that evening. Jillian, a single parent, was fortunate enough to work at the preschool that Molly and Billy attended. And her Saturday afternoons were like Heather's—catching up on housework, laundry, cooking for the coming week, and spending time with her child. After a quick supper, Heather called her Aunt Mary, who said she didn't mind staying with Molly for a little while. Uncle Bob wanted to watch a TV program anyway.

"Let me speak to him a minute," Heather said.

Uncle Bob had a small auto parts store downtown and kept up with local events. He knew that many Florida residents built new homes in the North Carolina mountains to retire there and that developments were springing up around the area. But he didn't know of a subdivision as outlined on "Tom Smith's" map, and Bob hadn't heard of Thomas Lane. "Seems like I did see a young white-haired fellow in the shop. I didn't wait on him though. I'll ask around if it's important."

Heather said it wasn't, but by the time Aunt Mary

returned to the phone, she was alarmed about Heather's customer. Mary insisted upon accompanying her. "You never know nowadays. I don't like the idea of your going alone to a man's house at night, not knowing what you might find."

Aunt Mary was a composed, middle-aged woman, with her gray-sprinkled brown hair pulled back in a twist and calm blue eyes. Heather had come to recognize her determination. No amount of discussion would change her mind. And frankly, Heather wasn't too keen on going alone.

"We'll all stay in the car," Aunt Mary said. "And at any suspicious signs, I'll call the police on my cellular phone."

They stopped at the shop to place the pink dogwood in the back of the station wagon, then followed the directions on the map as they headed out Highway 70. Heather left the main road, drove through a new development at the edge of Highland, then wound up an unpaved mountain road, growing more nervous when she noticed no places to turn around. She hoped they wouldn't meet another car, for it would be a tight squeeze passing each other. On the other hand, it might be good to have a hint of civilization. Lights glowed far below in the valley but not up on the mountain. The higher they went, the narrower the road seemed, and the thicker the trees.

"Maybe we should go back," Aunt Mary said.

"I can't turn around," Heather answered, trying not

to let anxiety sound in her voice. She didn't want Molly to think she was upset. Molly was guarding the pink dogwood, knowing this was part of their livelihood.

Suddenly, around a curve, they saw the white Cadillac parked on the left side of the road. On the right was a board sign with "Thomas Lane" painted in cursive and an arrow pointing right. The board was nailed to a post stuck in the ground and with rocks.

"It looks like a sign an amateur might make," Heather observed.

"And it looks fresh," Aunt Mary said. Heather braked. The Cadillac started moving. Heather gave her aunt a wary glance. Aunt Mary wiggled her cellular phone, and Heather followed the Cadillac along the road. What would they find, she wondered.

Around the next curve, another long, winding gravel road was lined with mud. A forest of trees almost obscured the starlit sky. Then another turn brought them out under the stars, and on the right was an astounding sight. Perched on the leveled mountaintop was a new two-story house with gables, a big chimney, and a porch. Fabulous views were evident from all directions. The setting was landscaped with rock walls and concrete walks. It all looked recently completed. Imbedded lights bordered the walkways, revealing dirt beds with no flowers. The house looked to be painted a soft gray. The Cadillac pulled into the dirt. Tom got out and walked over to Heather's window.

He greeted Molly by name. Heather had no choice

but to introduce Aunt Mary, who accepted his invitation for them all to go inside. Aunt Mary raised her eyebrows and said, "Why, thank you," as if she had been instantly charmed. However, as they all got out of the car, she stuffed the phone into her purse.

Heather opened the back of the station wagon and Tom lifted out the dogwood. As they followed him to the door, Heather noticed he had changed his knit shirt for a western shirt. She wasn't sure about the jeans, but he was now wearing boots instead of sandals. He must have changed for his dinner engagement. She had changed to another pair of jeans and a different shirt, but only because her clothes had received more than their share of cookie dough and a smear of warm chocolate.

He set the dogwood on the marble floor of the recessed entry that had its own roof and a white railing. Someone designed a beautiful place, Heather was thinking, and inside she would probably meet the lady of the house, who wanted a pink dogwood.

Tom opened the door to the left of the entry and gestured for them to enter. Stepping into a spacious foyer, Heather immediately noticed a wall on her right. Straight ahead a staircase led up. Beside it was a hallway and next to that a massive stone fireplace.

Tom came in with the dogwood, and they all followed him into the living room. An object in the far corner caught Heather's attention. Molly's too—she headed straight for the man-sized cactus. With several cylindrical projections, it was reminiscent of a grotesque giant candelabrum or a narrow hand with enormous fingers.

"Watch the prickles," Tom warned as Molly said, "Ouch!" and jerked her finger back. Tom set the dogwood in the opposite corner, behind a white leather chair. The other corners were separated by a wall of glass with sliding doors and white drapes pulled to the sides.

"What do you think?" Tom asked, straightening.

What could she say? It's okay, if you like a Dr. Jekyll/Mr. Hyde decorating combination? In her head, she heard a bell and an announcer say in a nasal tone, "In this corner, we have a saguaro cactus, weighing 325 pounds, and wearing green prickly trunks. And in the other corner, a delicate dogwood, weighing less than 20 pounds, and wearing pink silky trunks."

Now, if this were a competition, which would possibly win?

Heather glanced at Aunt Mary who grinned and deliberately turned toward the painting over the couch. Apparently, the dogwood would get no help from the referee!

Heather studied the corner for a long moment, while Tom waited expectantly. Finally, she said, "The dogwood goes great with the white chair."

"Does it go with the rest of the room?"

"I haven't really looked yet," she replied, "but it's a definite contrast with the, uh, cactus."

"Ouch!" Molly said again, but looked around grinning

and stuck her finger in her mouth.

"It's the only thing I can keep alive," he said, returning Molly's grin as if the two of them had something in common—a fascination with monstrous cactuses. "It can go a long time without water."

Heather nodded, feeling free to scrutinize the furnishings since he had asked how everything went together. Beyond Molly and the cactus was a room that looked to have cherry paneling on the lower half of the wall and a subdued wallpaper above. Two folding chairs were beneath a card table, and two others, still folded, leaned against the wall. At the end of the fireplace, a stairwell went down. Above it were hanging two baskets of barely living celery-colored vines that she could almost hear gasping for water.

The hardwood floor was beautiful, and a fabulous Oriental rug was spread between the fireplace and the white leather couch. The painting that had attracted Aunt Mary's attention looked western, maybe Indian, definitely colorful with its yellow sandy desert, several cactuses, a bright pink sky, and an orange sun over a distant, purple mountain range.

"Is that Texas?" Aunt Mary asked.

"A very famous artist from Texas painted it," Tom said proudly and gave the name. Both women shook their heads. Tom didn't seem to mind. "Are you an artist?" Aunt Mary asked.

"Artist?" he scoffed, then laughed and glanced away.

"Ah," she said with a laugh. "You're a cowboy."

"That's close enough," he replied.

Another loud "Ouch!" ended the conversation.

"Molly, come here!" Heather demanded. "You're going to look like a pin cushion."

The little girl reluctantly obeyed, and Heather's eyes went to the huge fireplace. On the mantel, several wood carvings looked like some kind of medicine men or voodoo dolls. Heather wasn't sure. Above the mantel, a long piece of weathered wood was draped with a muted pink-brown tweed rug.

"That's interesting," Heather said, for want of a better description.

"From Indonesia," he said. "That's a yoke," he said, and laughed. "Not a joke. A yoke."

"Oh, are you a retired military man?" Aunt Mary asked.

"I wish," he replied, then looked at Molly. "Know what a yoke is?"

She shook her head.

"It's a big piece of wood that's put across the shoulders of an ox." He explained what an ox was, and the various things that one might haul with its yoke. Heather and Aunt Mary's eyes made contact, trying to remain expressionless, but it was obvious to both of them that he deliberately slid by her questions—every time.

"You sound like a teacher," Aunt Mary said, trying again. When he merely displayed his incredible dimples, she added, "I teach kindergarten."

"Next year, I get to be in her room," Molly offered,

her dark eyes flashing.

Tom smiled at her. "You know, I have something I'll bet you'd like. Just a minute." When he struck off down the hallway, Heather took that opportunity to mumble under her breath, "How in the world am I expected to comment on a place like this?"

Before Aunt Mary had time to do anything but snicker, Tom returned with a small box of gummy bears.

Heather said nothing, waiting to see how Molly would react. She had been warned never to take candy from strangers. Apparently she forgot, or didn't consider Tom a stranger, for she took the box and even said, "Thank you." When he said he wanted them to see the upstairs, Molly was right beside him as if she would follow him anywhere.

From the upstairs hallway, he showed them a huge master bedroom. A king-size bed, with a comforter but no spread, dominated the room. There was a bedside table, a chest, and a TV set. The furniture looked expensive, but the room seemed stark. Nothing indicated that either a child or a woman had ever darkened—or brightened—the doors of this place.

"The bathroom is one of the first rooms I'd like done," he said, leading them into a room that could have contained Heather's entire living room. It looked like something from *Southern Living* or *Homes of the Rich and Famous*. A countertop and a mirror surrounded with lights both stretched across one wall. Wow! To have a bathroom like this, Heather thought. It's something a woman dreamed of, but nothing indicated a woman had been near it. Of course, a woman might come later, or perhaps there were enough cabinets, closets, and drawers that a woman didn't have to leave her things on the counter.

Tom drew Heather's attention to the sauna. He wanted an arrangement for the marble ledge. Taking a studied look, trying to decide what sort of arrangement would be suitable, Heather took a mental note of the wallpaper. It wasn't feminine, yet not completely masculine either. It was. . .different—a muted green, maroon, and rose design on a cream background with a leafy border.

"I picked out the wallpaper myself," he said, and Heather wasn't a bit surprised. On the way down the stairs, she could see the living room. What would be suitable throughout the house? His decor was contemporary, Indonesian, western, conservative, ultramodern, weird, intriguing . . .so why not a pink dogwood to bring a touch of the mountains inside?

If she could do this house, she might be able to pay her bills for a while without having to juggle them every month. But on second thought, what on earth could she suggest—western, Oriental, country, what? But, for a man who wanted a pink dogwood, she probably needn't worry.

"The dogwood is too small for the corner," she said, after she had returned to the living room.

"You can make a larger one, can't you? Your sign did say 'two-week exchange.' "

"Oh, sure," she said, "but that will cost a little more."

He nodded, as if that were expected. "When can you have it done?"

"I'll have to get an order in for blossoms, so probably next week."

"That's fine," he said. "I'll be gone for two weeks. Flying out in the morning."

"Oh, are you a pilot?" Aunt Mary asked.

He laughed. "Afraid not," and immediately turned to Molly. "Hey, that's enough gummy bears. Too many will stunt your growth and you never will be big enough to start school."

She moved the box behind her and looked up at him saucily. "I go to school now—preschool and Sunday school."

Aunt Mary seized an opportunity to ask if he went to church. He said he had just moved there. Then Aunt Mary proceeded to tell him they had a wonderful class for singles at First Church on Holly Road. "Heather's in it," she said, and this time it was Heather who changed the subject.

"Do you want me to take the dogwood back?" she asked.

"Yes," he said. "I'll carry it out for you."

Driving back down the mountain, Heather reprimanded Aunt Mary for being so obvious about telling him she was single. "You were along to protect me," she said. "Not reveal my life history."

"But he seems so nice," Aunt Mary rebutted. "And I wanted to know if he was single. Anyway, there's nothing wrong with inviting him to church."

"But he didn't tell us anything, Aunt Mary," Heather reminded her. "He's too secretive."

"He is that," Aunt Mary agreed, then glanced over knowingly. "But awfully good-looking."

"I think Tom's nice," Molly said. "And I like his house."

Heather thought the same thing. But, what if she had gone alone? Did he really live there? It looked as if it had been furnished hastily and not finished. The card table and folding chairs certainly didn't fit the decor of a fine home. Did he work for someone and was pretending it was his house? Or did he have a wife who would join him later? Oh, what did it matter! He seemed to be a customer, and Heather must think of that. His personal life was his own business. Apparently, he thought so too, since he didn't reveal anything about it.

Chapter 4

Almost two weeks later, on a Thursday morning, April showers had subsided somewhat, and the blue sky promised a beautiful spring day. Heather dropped Molly off at the church preschool and pulled into the shop's parking lot at ten o'clock. She didn't like to be late, but she had had to examine the jonquils that the children had set in pots and were now budding.

At least the customer in the pickup was waiting. But, that could be someone using her parking spaces while doing business elsewhere. However, when she got out of the station wagon, the truck door opened and Tom got out. She told herself that skip of her heart was due to surprise. She had expected the white Cadillac, but his jeans were dirty and his plaid shirt was old.

She must have registered surprise for he apologized. "Pardon my work clothes. I've been in the flower beds since dawn."

He must have returned yesterday. But he didn't come to the shop. Maybe he got in late. Or maybe his family had stayed in Texas or elsewhere until the house was built and now he was bringing them here. "Your dogwood's waiting," she said, unlocking the door.

113

"How's that beautiful little girl of yours?" he asked, following her inside.

Beautiful? Her young likeness. Did he think she was beautiful too? But what difference did that make? He was a customer. And he had to be married. Why else would he have such a big house?

He seemed to be interested when she told him about the projects Molly and the young children were working on. The conversation was friendly and easy, until Heather asked, "And how was your trip?"

"Fine," he said and immediately turned his attention to the two dogwoods. "Is this one mine?"

She nodded. He looked it over. It was taller and fuller than the one she had taken to his house. "Looks perfect," he said, and his dancing eyes made her wonder for an instant if he were talking only about the dogwood. She flipped the power switch, and the room brightened. She smiled inwardly, thinking his sunny smile had been enough to do that. *Caution, this is one of the most promising customers you've had. Don't spoil it by being less than professional.*

She told him she felt that ivy in his hanging baskets would be best, since he had such diverse items in the living room, and he agreed. But he didn't think her idea of a bathroom piece was the right color. She wondered how he could draw that conclusion, considering all the colors in the bathroom. "I'll take it with me," he said. "Maybe you could drop by after work and check out the colors."

Heather hesitated, then spoke haltingly. "I wouldn't have much time."

"Another day is fine. I understand if you have an engagement. A lovely young woman like you. . ."

"Whoa!" she said, loving the compliment, but she wasn't tight-lipped about where she stood with men, regardless of how attractive one might be. "My engagement is a Single Parents' meeting at church. We have a covered-dish supper at six, then a special speaker. I could miss the supper, but I need to be there to introduce the speaker since I invited her. And Molly is looking forward to seeing her friends there."

He lifted his hand. "We can do this another time."

She might as well ask. "Would you be interested in coming to the meeting?"

"No, thanks," he said and looked at his watch. "I've got to get back to work." After she made out the receipt and he paid the extra amount, she watched as he put the dogwood in the back of the truck. Maybe he didn't live in that house. Perhaps he worked for a family who planned to move into it.

She was determined to put him out of her mind. However, speculation about Tom Smith abounded that evening at the covered-dish supper. Having already sparked Jillian's interest by telling her about visiting his house, she mentioned that he had returned for his dogwood.

Others overhearing about a young, handsome, well-off stranger in town were interested too.

115

"Heather saw him first," Jillian reminded the other single women.

"He's only a customer," Heather insisted, but it wasn't easy to forget him when everyone kept bringing him up.

She and Molly ate lunch with Aunt Mary and Uncle Bob on Sunday after church. Bob knew everybody and had asked around about Tom. No one knew much; a few merchants had seen him, remembering his silver-white hair. They thought he usually drove a pickup.

Bob said Tom had been asked a few questions. "One fellow even asked him if he was looking for a job, and he said he had one that took him on the road or in the skies quite often. He didn't offer any more information." Bob related it frankly, as if Tom had every right not to talk about how he got his money. "Maybe his folks left him well-off," he said with a shrug, then cut another bite of roast beef.

"Maybe he's an undercover FBI agent," Mary said.

"You don't suppose he's into something illegal, do you?" Heather asked, not wanting to say too much in front of Molly, who might inadvertently blurt out something if they met again.

Bob shook his head. "I doubt there's anything fishy. If he was into something illegal, he'd have a good front. Same if he was with the FBI. You wouldn't need to speculate at all."

❦

116

Tom popped in at the shop on Monday afternoon right before closing time with his baskets and said the dogwood was perfect. While he was there, Jillian called. She couldn't turn off the kitchen faucet. The handle simply made circles when she tried. Would Heather stop at the hardware store and ask Bob what to do?

"Look under the cabinet," Heather told her. "There's a knob under there on a pipe. Turn that to the right. It'll turn the water off. I'll check it out when I get there." She hung up. "It ought to be against the law not to teach girls how to make repairs in a household. We depend on men, then when they're not around, what do we do?"

Tom asked what the trouble was and she explained. "The landlord lives next door, but he always has to call somebody for things like that. Anyway, Uncle Bob fixed that faucet not long ago. But he's got a touch of arthritis now and his fingers aren't working too well." She sighed. "Maybe the faucets weren't tight enough. You can't imagine what we single women have to go through. Everyday, somebody calls with problems—the plumbing, the car, the light switches." She threw up her hands. "You name it—we got it!" She smiled broadly.

"If you have so many problems, why are you so happy?" he asked.

Happy? She supposed she was. She looked at him for a long moment, almost becoming lost in his gaze that seemed to say the question was not a light one. "We call them problems," she said and shook her head. "But they're really just everyday irritations. We complain, but most of these single parents have really had it rough. Some have no family at all to help them. Some have families who don't care to help. Some have never had a husband; others were treated so badly they wish they hadn't had husbands."

She was tempted to tell him more, but reminded herself he was a relative stranger—just a customer, trying to make conversation. And he had indicated she seemed happy, so she decided to keep matters on the positive side. "These everyday problems are solvable. We know the Lord will make a way. Miracle after miracle has happened with this group."

"They call you when they have a problem?" Tom asked. He appeared genuinely interested.

She smiled. "That's my big mission. Another single parent and I started the group. We know there's such a need out there. And it's wonderful to see how many people at church are eager to help."

"Could I?" he asked.

"What?" Heather was taken aback.

"Could I help?" he said. "I have a truck, and I'm a pretty decent handyman. I can put on roofing, saw, hammer nails, rotate tires, change oil. . . ."

"Okay, I get the picture," Heather laughed, delighted with his offer. "We can use all the help we can get." Maybe he was a handyman for wealthy people who owned that big house on the mountain. Maybe he worked for a family or for a wealthy older woman. That would explain his driving the Cadillac. Maybe it was hers and the truck was his.

"You want me to follow you home?" he asked.

"Fol—? What do you mean?"

"I'm offering to fix your faucet," he said.

"Oh, I didn't mean me. I wasn't trying to get you to help me."

"I don't charge for house calls," he said, displaying his dimples.

Heather smiled. "Really, I can handle it."

"But how can you recommend me to others if I haven't proved myself to you? You don't take people at face value, do you?"

She held her breath for a moment. He must have sensed her mistrust of him that first day, and then again when she took Aunt Mary with her on the house call. Not bothering to answer, she looked back at the wall clock, then began her routine of closing up.

About three minutes after leaving the shop, she pulled into the parking area between the big house and the little apartment. Tom pulled in behind her.

Molly ran to him and hugged his leg as soon as he stepped inside the living room, then looked up with the angelic expression she wore when she wanted something. "Got any gummy bears?" she asked.

"You have to come to my house for those," he said.

"Okay," she said, without reserve.

Heather introduced Jillian and Billy, then explained

that Tom had offered to help the single parents with minor repairs.

"You want my list now?" Jillian said, as if she were joking, but she and Heather knew each of the singles could make a long list.

Tom asked Billy what he was watching on TV, then started discussing with the youngsters what they liked about the cartoon and why. Both children quickly said it was funny when the characters got hit on the head, but no, they couldn't do it to people because it would hurt. The TV was just pretend. It was very hard to mistrust a man who children accepted so easily, Heather thought.

Jillian's long look at Heather before she went out the door clearly said, "Call me ASAP!"

While Tom was removing the faucet, Heather asked if he would like to eat supper with them, expecting him to refuse. Instead, he asked what she was having. After a quick look in the freezer, she decided on home-made beef stew.

"Sounds great," he said.

By the time she had supper ready, with Molly helping set the table, Tom had finished working on the faucet and turned the water on beneath the sink. "It should work okay for a day or two," he said, "but it needs new washers. I'll pick some up tomorrow." He washed his hands, then joined them at the table.

Molly, eager to impress him, volunteered to say the blessing, and when he said "Amen" at the end, she giggled delightedly. Being accustomed to telling what happened at school, she dominated the conversation. Tom seemed to encourage her, Heather thought.

Although telling herself he just felt sorry for her, Heather couldn't help but think how nice it was sitting across the table from a man who complimented her on the meal and ate as if he meant it. But, she reminded herself—and the memory brought a pang of hurt—Rey had done that too, early in their marriage.

Molly asked Tom to stay and play with her, but he said he had to leave soon. "Tell you what. If your mom says it's okay, maybe I could stop by tomorrow and put new washers in the faucet. Then you two let me treat you to dinner at my house."

"You don't need to do that," Heather said, while Molly exclaimed, "Oh, yeah! That would fun."

"Honey, if you've finished, watch a little TV while I wash the dishes," Heather said. "I think it's time for 'Loonie Toonies'."

"That's my favorite," Molly told Tom. "Wanna watch it with me?"

"I think I should help your mother with the dishes."

"Okay," Molly said reluctantly as she left the room.

"Don't worry about the dishes," Heather said.

"How else will we know if that faucet works?" he asked, then reached under the counter for the liquid detergent and filled the sink with hot sudsy water.

Heather busied herself with picking up several toys laying on the floor, then swept the kitchen, which really didn't need sweeping, except for a couple of spots where dirt or cookie crumbs had accumulated. But she wasn't about to stand beside him at the kitchen sink. She kept her distance while he washed, rinsed, and stacked the few dishes in the drainer.

Her moment of enjoying the homey family scene was replaced by a sudden fear. *What's going on? This guy looks terrific, has a fabulous house, drives a Cadillac, is Mr. Fix-it, draws children like a magnet, and could charm birds out of the trees—without even trying. Why is he here . . .in my house? For all I know, he may be a serial killer.*

That thought occurred just as she was about to shake the dustpan contents into the trashcan. Instead, she stood like a still-life painting, staring at him just as he turned from the sink and began wiping his hands on a dishtowel—a dishtowel just long enough to fit around somebody's neck. But that wouldn't be necessary. She had already stopped breathing.

"What's wrong?" he said. "You want me to take out the trash too?"

Heather laughed. He looked so innocently boyish, with dimpled cheeks and dancing eyes.

"You have a nice laugh," he said. She quickly emptied the dustpan and propped it with the broom in a corner.

"Thanks for the hospitality," he added. "I've heard it's great in this part of the country."

Then she felt guilty. It must be lonely up there on the mountain—whether he had a family in Texas or elsewhere. And he was just being friendly—maybe. Or trying to help out the less fortunate. After all, hadn't she grumbled about the difficulties of a woman without a man around the house? He probably thought she was begging him to fix her faucet.

She plastered on a formal face, thanked him, and went into the living room.

As soon as he said good-bye to Molly, he left.

Heather did the usual things afterward—a few chores, bathed Molly, and read to her, but a familiar statement kept running through her mind. *If he seems too good to be true, he probably is!*

She needed to remember that.

And she did.

Every time she went into the kitchen and saw the table, the faucet, the sink, or the cabinet under the sink—she remembered that. Even later, after she lay in bed staring through the dark toward the ceiling, and seeing silver-white hair, dancing blue eyes, dimples, smiling lips, and hearing him say, "You have a nice laugh," she remembered that.

Finally, she told herself that she needed to forget to remember that.

Chapter 5

April showers weren't over. The temperature dropped overnight, and so did the rain, as if heavenly buckets were being overturned with an order to douse the humans.

Heather had few customers during the rain, so she finished Tom's baskets of ivy, then worked on hanging baskets of fuchsia for the Asheville McDonald's. The manager had seen what she had done for the local franchise and decided to redecorate. That's how her business worked—please one customer and word got around. She was smiling at the fuchsias when the door burst open, right before five o'clock.

A wet creature with an ineffective piece of flapping orange plastic covering its head stood dripping on the carpet at the front entry. It yanked off the plastic and revealed soaking white hair. "This only works if it rains straight down and the wind isn't blowing," Tom complained.

He waded over to the counter. "Got the washers," he said as if that had been a major feat—and it probably had. Maybe he had to swim for them. "I can take care of that faucet so you won't have to worry about it."

"It's working fine right now," Heather said. "If you're

really serious about helping the singles, Jillian has a major leak around her living room window. She had a puddle on her floor this morning and put down towels to catch the water. This is not expected to let up for a while. If you're serious about helping—"

"I was serious," he said abruptly. "I try to keep my word."

Coming out in this downpour for the washers was evidence of that, she thought. He kept his word. Even kept a lot of it to himself, when the topic got personal.

He liked the ivy baskets but said he would take them another time.

"They're guaranteed not to drown," she reminded him.

He laughed but said he didn't want them to get wet. He didn't mention having supper with him, but after she prepared to leave, he said his gravel road was washing out and he wanted to get it paved as soon as possible.

He followed her home, waved at Molly in the window, then left behind Jillian and Billy.

Later, Jillian called. Tom had torn out part of her window sill to find the leak, had rerouted the steady stream so that it ran to the outside instead of inside, and said he had to wait until the rain stopped before plugging the hole and patching the roof, then replaced the sill. Jillian thought he was special. "Forget who saw him first," she said. "All's fair, you know."

"Did you get any information out of him?" Heather asked.

"I tried. I asked where he learned to do all that stuff, and he said, 'Necessity is the mother of invention.'"

❧

After a week of flood warnings and watches, the sun came out on Friday. Heather kept looking at Tom's baskets and even stayed a couple minutes late in case he came by for them. He didn't. Nor did he show up on Saturday. *He went out of town or is in no hurry for the baskets. He owes me no explanation, and the only reason I care is because he's a paying customer.*

As she arrived home, she slammed the car door with a sense of finality and waved at Molly in the window. Just then, Tom's pickup pulled up. He jumped out, waved at Molly, then smiled at Heather and held out his hand with the washers. "Still got 'em," he said.

Yeah, she thought, in both cheeks and both eyes. Her moment of breathlessness had nothing to do with thinking he might be a serial killer.

By three-thirty, he finished repairing the faucet and asked if she had time to see his bathroom arrangement and make suggestions for his dining room.

"I can tell you now," she said. "For the card table, a bowl of popcorn and a can of soda would be perfect."

"Ah, cute," he said. She had heard that comment before.

It was close quarters riding up the mountain in his pickup, but Molly loved it—sitting on Heather's lap, bouncing with every bump and leaning into every turn.

"Got the potholes filled with gravel yesterday," Tom said. "Good thing. Just in time for the delivery this morning."

"Delivery?" Heather asked.

He just grinned, but as soon as they arrived at his house, he led them to the dining room. A cherry dining room set, complete with drop-leaf table, buffet, and an elegant glass-paned hutch, had replaced the card table. He flipped a switch, and light radiated from a lovely crystal chandelier, centered above the table.

"It's beautiful," she said and wondered if he could read the question forming in her mind. Where does he get his money?

He spread his hands in a gesture of helplessness. "You'll have to tell me if I need a tree in the corner, a centerpiece of flowers, something on the hutch. . . . Oh, let's hang those baskets." He returned to the foyer where he had set them.

She wondered who helped him select the dining room set and the other furnishings, but reminded herself that accessories and flowers were different. Most men didn't seem to have a flair for that. He did, however, she realized when she saw the flower arrangement in the bathroom. He was right. The colors were close, but they were still wrong. She was well aware that colors could easily clash rather than complement. That was one reason she offered a two-week exchange, in case a customer wasn't pleased with the effect.

"Now, where did that girl go?" Heather asked, looking

around. "Molly," she warned, seeing the child trying to open a door in the bedroom, "it's not nice to go snooping around other people's houses."

"It's locked," Molly grumbled, twisting the knob.

Tom walked up behind them. "Let's go downstairs. I'll show you something that might interest you."

Molly's eyes brightened. "Okay," she said and reached for Tom's hand.

Heather glanced at the locked door, realizing there would be space behind it the size of the lower foyer and living room. Was it a dressing room? A walk-in closet? Maybe another bedroom? Being locked, perhaps it was used for storage. She could understand Molly's curiosity and felt a sense of anticipation. About halfway downstairs, the aroma of cooking meat and spices met her.

"What is that?" Heather asked.

"You might call it a family room," Tom replied.

"No, the aroma."

"Oh, just a little Texas spaghetti sauce. Been cooking all afternoon in the crockpot."

She gave him a wicked look, but he just lifted his eyebrows as if he had no intention of extending an invitation again and stepped into a spacious room.

"Tom, this is wonderful," Heather commented, and his smile indicated he was pleased—either with her compliment or the room. It was perfect for entertaining—or just living. The room was huge, but the furnishings were arranged to meet various needs. The back wall boasted a white brick fireplace. On the left were kitchen cabinets and countertops. A small round table with four chairs created a cozy grouping. On the right, an overstuffed, L-shaped couch looked inviting enough to curl up on and go to sleep. The couch, a matching recliner, and a glass-topped coffee table faced a fireplace. In the far right corner was a TV set, and along that wall, bookshelves accented another living room grouping. The walls were an off-white, and the white vinyl floor was spread with several throw rugs.

Heather could readily see the furniture might be moved to accommodate a large crowd or one could feel cozy near the fireplace or among the books. Molly had made her way to the outside wall and was hiding behind the white drapes. Tom chuckled and opened them. The entire wall was glass, and the view was fabulous. Tom unlatched the sliding door, and they stepped out onto a patio that ran along the entire back of the house. The lawn was covered with straw, indicating grass had been planted, and farther away a kidney-shaped swimming pool was covered with heavy plastic. Beyond, a forest of trees on peaked mountains met the blue sky.

"I've wondered how it would look to have baskets of ivy or flowers all along the overhang," Tom said. "You think that would be too much?"

That would keep me in business for several months, Heather thought, but said, "I think that would look great at the sides, but I wouldn't put anything between the house and that fabulous view."

"The silk would hold up better out here than live ones, wouldn't they?" he asked.

"The hanging baskets over the entry of my store attests to that," she said. "They've been there for two years, through rain, sleet, snow, wind, and hot summer sun. Last summer a bird built a nest in one of them."

Molly, who finally stopped jumping and began picking up straw to peek under it, looked around, excited. "There were little tiny eggs and then we had a whole family of birds." In the same breath, she asked, "Can I go swimming?"

"Too cold," Heather told her.

"I've got to get the pool cleaned out before anybody swims in it," Tom added.

Molly, exasperated, put her hands on her hips. "Well, what did you want to show me?"

"As if all this isn't enough," Heather said apologetically, hoping he understood that children were open about their feelings and didn't compare houses and furnishings the way adults did. And too, Molly had grown up in the midst of panoramic views.

Tom laughed, seeming to enjoy her antics, and said, "Come on in."

Inside, he took a video from a cabinet and slipped it into the VCR. This was going to be a disappointment, Heather thought; she had found nothing that intrigued Molly as "Loonie Toonies". Molly's bland expression seemed she say she didn't have great expectations about the whole thing either. Maybe Tom had bought a "Loonie Toonies" video.

However, when the video started playing, Molly giggled. Singing, dancing "cupcakes" were costumed in formal evening wear to uniforms to swimsuits and tutus.

"That's cute," Heather said. One of the cupcakes, a clown named Clumsy Lumsy, slipped and turned upside down, his frosting sticking to the floor and his legs kicking in the air. Laughing, Molly sat cross-legged on the floor in front of the TV, and her little body began to move to the beat of the lively music.

Heather's smile froze as her eyes focused on the bookshelf and on framed pictures of people. She wasn't close enough to see clearly, but one seemed to show a white-haired man, a dark-haired woman, and two young children.

Didn't you tell yourself he has a family? She swallowed hard and looked at Tom. "Where did you find that video? I've never seen one like it."

"Really?" he asked, as if that were weird. "They're the rage in Texas." He walked to the other side of the room and lifted the crockpot lid.

Heather momentarily listened to the cupcakes begin acting out a story, then she pursued the tempting aroma and sat at the small table. "Is that a religious video?" she asked.

"Sure is," he said, opening a cabinet and taking out a package of spaghetti noodles. "They entertain, but there's an underlying Christian message, and some of the songs are about God and Jesus. Humph!" he snorted. "I'm going to have to throw a lot of this away if nobody helps me eat it."

Heather laughed. "You ever heard of freezing left-overs?"

He snapped his fingers as if he had never thought of it, then said seriously, "Will you stay?"

She was about to say no, but other words popped out: "Yes, thank you. We'd love to." At that instant, she decided to ask some direct questions—and get some answers. She believed she and Tom had become friends. And everything was perfectly innocent so far. . .except for perhaps her occasional errant thoughts, rapid heartbeats, and breathlessness. His peculiar charisma was magnetic. *But suppose he's someone's husband? If Tom were my husband, would I like him spending time with another woman?* She knew the answer—she had felt something akin to jealousy when he had gone to Jillian's to look at her leaking window.

How could she just blurt out, "Are you married, Tom?" when he had done nothing more than act like a customer, a gentleman, and a helpful friend. Also, her little girl was giggling and enjoying that video more than she did "Loonie Toonies".

Maybe I'm loonie-toonie for trying to make something out of this. If she asked about his marital status, wouldn't he think she had designs on him? It wasn't as if this were a date or something! The only times they had seen each other, except for his fixing her faucet, was in a consultant/client capacity.

With a decisive nod, she smiled, and asked, "What can I do?"

He tossed the words over his shoulder. "You can start by telling me how you got into the silk flower business."

Heather sat down. Just when she decided this was definitely nothing personal, he got personal. Well, if he could, she would.

While he prepared supper, she told him how she had started her shop.

Having loved flowers, she had worked for a florist to pay her way through a local college where she studied art and interior design. The florist and customers discovered that Heather had an eye for design and a special talent for creating original silk arrangements.

She met Rey during her third year of college. He was tall, dark, handsome, and was studying business. He went to church with her and seemed ideal. He had played football but wanted to get away from that wild crowd and settle down in his final year. He planned to take over his father's real estate business someday, he said. Rey was energetic and fun-loving, and every moment was filled with excitement. He took her to meet his parents. They were wonderful people and seemed to approve of their son's choice. Heather and Rey had met in September and by December they were engaged. Neither could think of a reason not to get married. Since her parents had died in an auto accident years before and she didn't want her aunt and uncle to go to great expense, they had a simple wedding at the church with only his parents and her aunt and uncle present.

As planned, they lived with Aunt Mary and Uncle Bob until school was out, then they moved to Raleigh. They rented a small apartment, and he went to work in the real estate firm, but made very little money. She found a job with a florist, and although it wasn't as satisfying as the one in Highland, she didn't mind at first, because she was in love and never expected to receive anything on a silver platter. By the time she found out that he had been kicked off the football team and out of school because of drugs and that his father wasn't a partner in the firm, she was pregnant. Rey blamed her, claiming she was trying to take away his freedom.

Arguments became more heated, until he finally hit her. Afraid she would lose the baby, she yielded to whatever he said, or wanted. After Molly was born, she threatened to leave him, but he displayed what she now knew were classic symptoms of an abuser—strike out, then convince the victim he was sorry, but each time was worse than before. She felt helpless.

Heather shook her head. "You don't need to hear this."

Tom poured noodles into a colander, laid the pot aside, then sat opposite her. "I'd like to hear it."

After a glance at Molly, still intrigued with the video, Heather met Tom's gaze. She forgot all her questions about him, and saw only a pair of blue eyes that seemed to care about her.

The situation worsened—money got tighter, Rey wanted her to go back to work although she wouldn't make much, after paying a baby sitter. His mother worked and couldn't keep Molly. Once, when Molly was three months old, their fighting woke her and she started crying and wouldn't stop. He threatened to make her stop, and Heather, standing at the doorway, said it would be over her dead body. He slapped her, then left.

Heather packed and drove back to Aunt Mary's. Rey was repentant afterward. He called, asked her to forgive him, said he would never do it again, would go to counseling, would do anything. He came to see them a couple of times and was very sweet. She considered going back, but Uncle Bob told her to test Rey by telling him that she wasn't going back.

Rey threw the worst tantrum Heather had seen. She had been through it many times; she knew what would happen. She saw the blow coming and ducked. He hit the wall with his fist. That enraged him further, and he started toward her. Uncle Bob came into the room and said he had called the police and that if Rey hit Heather, he would need an undertaker.

The police chased Rey. He took a curve at eighty miles an hour and hit a tree. An autopsy revealed drugs in his system. She hadn't known he was on drugs. Looking back, she could see that much of their money must have gone for drugs.

"You didn't ask for all that," Heather apologized.

Tom smiled. "I appreciate your trusting me enough to tell me."

Trust? Did he know she had a lot of difficulty trusting men now? She wondered if others knew that was part of an abuse victim's emotional baggage.

She smiled ruefully and continued with the original story. "Anyway, there was a little insurance money, and it seemed like then or never on trying to make a go of my own business. It's taken a while for the word to get around, but I've made the rent except for one month when we had a blizzard. Aunt Mary and Uncle Bob came through for me. And lately," she said, feeling slightly embarrassed but grateful, "business is picking up."

"I admire your positive attitude," he said.

"It was hard," she admitted. "But the Lord gave me strength through the bad times, even when Rey's parents indicated I might be to blame for his problems. And now with the Single Parents, I see problems everyday worse than mine." A golden light gleamed in her eyes as she spoke softly. "I can't wish it never happened. The most wonderful blessing imaginable came from that difficult time." She glanced at Molly.

Tom nodded, understanding. "I agree," he said. "Family should be top priority—under God."

Was he religious? Or was he saying what he thought she wanted to hear? And why did he have a child's video? "You . . .have a family?"

"Everybody has a family," he said with a wry grin and pushed away from the table. Was he going to answer? Wouldn't silence, in this instance, speak louder than words? He went to the sink and began fiddling with the spaghetti noodles.

She didn't have a chance to find out if he were going to answer. Just then, after a delighted laugh, Molly wailed, "Oh, it's over." She looked back at Tom. "I wanna see it again."

Tom immediately reached for a paper towel and dried his hands. "While it's rewinding, let's have some spaghetti. You can watch another after supper if your mom agrees."

❦

During supper, Heather told herself that Tom's personal story might be more dramatic than hers and perhaps he didn't want to talk about it in front of a child. She was glad that, as usual, Molly was the center of attention. Tom, too, seemed more at ease focusing on the child instead of on anything personal. Molly was enthusiastic about her favorite cupcake, Penelope Peppermint, who had pink frosting and cherry eyes, wore huge red-rimmed eyeglasses, and carried a red-and-white-striped candy cane.

Heather laughed at Molly and Tom's discussion, glad that her daughter had found a friend. Yet, a reserved caution had surfaced, and she told herself that spaghetti, as delicious as this was, shouldn't be so hard to swallow.

Chapter 6

A few days later, Tom stopped by the shop in the Cadillac to say he would be gone for a couple of weeks and asked Heather to make eight baskets of assorted ivy for the overhang outside the family room. He brought a set of four cupcake videos for Molly.

Heather laughingly told Aunt Mary that Tom liked Molly better than he liked her.

Aunt Mary reminded her that just as politicians try to reach the voters by kissing babies at election time, a man often tries to get close to a woman through her children.

He wouldn't have to use such an indirect route, Heather was thinking. Although she had second thoughts about the gift, she decided to allow it. They were Christian videos that taught biblical stories and morals, even through dancing cupcakes. Heather had tried religious videos before, but none had appealed to Molly. And Tom could afford a set of videos more easily than she could afford just one. Where did his money come from?

Heather expected to see him at the shop two weeks later, on Monday. But she wasn't prepared to see him

at the worship service the Sunday before. She saw him
the moment she entered the church sanctuary from the
hallway. He was sitting at the back in the middle section. Her heart did a funny little tap and she warned it
to stop. She spied Jillian sitting near the front on the
left side and slid in beside her.

Whatever the preacher said must have been interesting, but as hard as she tried to pay attention, she kept
losing track of the point of the sermon. She hadn't seen
Tom in a suit and tie before. He looked dignified, so
handsome.

As soon as the service was over, she headed toward
the back to speak to him, but he left before she could
reach him. Aunt Mary had seen him too and asked
Heather if they should invite him to lunch. Heather
said no. If he wanted to see her socially, he should make
the first move.

His next move, however, was to come by right before
five on Monday, to pay for and pick up his baskets
and bathroom arrangement. She helped him put the
baskets on a blanket in the back of the truck and the
arrangement on the front seat. He said, "Thanks," got
in, and slammed the door.

The sinking feeling in Heather's middle left when he
called, "How's your faucet?"

She looked back over her shoulder and smiled.
"Come and see," she challenged.

He followed her home, much to Molly's delight, and
after he washed his hands under the faucet, they both

fixed supper. Afterward the three of them went to his house. The arrangement was perfect and the baskets looked great. Molly unsuccessfully tried again to open the locked door off his bedroom.

When they went downstairs, Molly took off down the hallway away from the family room.

"Molly, come back here," Heather called.

Tom laughed it off. "She can't hurt anything down there. It's just a couple of bedrooms and a bath."

Molly returned and said she was looking for the bathroom. Heather went with her and while waiting, lifted her eyes toward the ceiling. *This is all open, but the room upstairs is locked.*

Stop that, she told herself. Hadn't she already decided the room upstairs was for storage?

Although Molly was interested in the kaleidoscope Tom brought her—from New York, he said—she wanted to see a video. He had some new cupcake ones and she was delighted.

Heather didn't want Molly to have a steady diet of TV, but the videos were teaching tools as well as entertainment. "My favorite's Penel-ope Pep-peppermint," Molly said, stammering along the way. She laughed. "Billy's favorite is Grumpy GumpDrop." Grumpy's frosting was purple, and his eyes and nose were gumdrops. His mouth spread across the front of his face, and multicolored gumdrop teeth always showed when he growled.

"He's really grumpy!" Molly said, screwing up her face.

"Yeah," Tom agreed, "but Penelope Peppermint will sweeten his sour spirit."

"Yeah," Molly agreed, and took her place in front of the TV.

Heather noticed that, while Tom poured coffee, Molly kept looking around at her and Tom and smiling. Having a man around was good for Molly, Heather realized, but she had to keep reminding herself, she knew little about this man. She didn't sit at the table but walked near Molly, pretending to be interested in the video.

As soon as Molly became so engrossed in the video that she stopped vying for their attention, Heather stepped closer to the bookshelf and the pictures. Tom walked up. She asked, "Is that your family, Tom?"

She felt the silence, even with the lively sound from the TV. When he didn't speak for a moment, she looked at him, wondering if this were the time she should leave and not look back. He seemed uncomfortable, then said, "That's my brother and his family. He and my younger brother have a small cattle ranch in Texas." He walked to another part of the bookshelf and took down a picture of another white-haired man with a woman and a little girl, about Molly's age.

"I have two sisters. One married and the other in her last year of college."

Heather felt brave enough to walk to the other side of the couch and look at other pictures. Two confused her. The same man was in each, with different women.

141

"This is my dad's second wife," he said. "My mom was sick for many years and died when I was twenty-three." A wry grin touched his lips. "I was the oldest and had to take over at home when Mom was unable to. The last year, she was completely bedridden."

"I'm so sorry," Heather whispered.

"Like you said, Heather," he said, walking toward the sink, "many blessings come from hard times."

He had opened up a little, and Heather didn't know if he would again, so she asked, with some trepidation, "And you never married?"

He poured the remains of his coffee down the drain. "Came close a couple of times. The first one couldn't wait until I was free of my responsibilities. And the second one—" He rinsed the cup and laid it on the counter, then turned. The dimples dented his cheeks. "I just didn't measure up to the oil man she met."

Heather noticed that his blue eyes clouded and didn't sparkle at all. *He must still be in love with her. And in what way did he not measure up? What more could a woman want? Oops! Watch it. Maybe she knew something I don't! He's probably filling the time with me and Molly, trying to get over her. But if he's really interested in me, wouldn't he ask me out on a date?*

❦

Heather thought she might have the answer to why Tom hadn't asked her for a date when he unexpectedly showed up at a covered-dish supper for the Single

Parents. The speaker's topic was "Dealing With Dating." Tom sat at a table with the three single fathers in the group. It was the first time she had been with him in a group and discovered immediately he was as outgoing and friendly in public as he had been with her and Molly. There was an instant rapport between him and the others. Maybe, she thought, that was because word had already gotten around about him, including his being tight-lipped about personal matters. They also knew he was Heather's customer and had helped her and Jillian. The members of this group, having been though many difficulties, weren't judgmental, but wanted to help others as they had been helped.

However, Tom didn't seem to need any help. During dinner he and the men were involved in animated conversation. During the discussion, after the speech, Tom was outspoken about his feelings on dating. Some of the group voiced their opinions, saying they had dated their future mates for a long time and thought they had known them well—until marriage. Heather had thought that too—although she and Rey hadn't dated for very long.

"I think the ideal arrangement is to see the other person where they live and work—in settings where their real personalities come out," Tom said during the discussion. "Not just at a dress-up affair at a fancy restaurant, although that's okay occasionally."

Heather didn't dare look at him. Had he been doing his kind of dating with her?

Regardless of what it was called, Heather loved the activity of the next few weeks. Tom didn't have to go out of town for a month. She and Molly helped him plant a garden in some of his flower beds. He said that vegetable blooms and leaves were as attractive as flowers and tasted a lot better.

On many days, he stopped at the shop to ask if any repairs were needed. She would give him her list and he would take off. And he wasn't helping only the women. He got together with the men in the group too. On three weekends, they went into his woods, cut the fallen trees with their chain saws, and delivered truckloads of wood to those who would need it next winter. He even took a load to Aunt Mary and Uncle Bob.

Heather had never felt more fulfilled, for herself, Molly, and the Single Parents. People were helping others and being helped, enjoying life, and relating beautifully.

Her business had even picked up. A couple more fast-food restaurants were redecorating, and one of the finest inns in Asheville wanted new trees and arrangements for three of its floors and the lobby. Aunt Mary and Uncle Bob had always helped her pour plaster around her tree trunks, and now Tom helped too. It seemed he had a lifetime supply of limbs of almost every kind of tree anyone would want—except palms—which is what the Asheville Inn wanted. But she could order those. If this kept up, she would have the wonderful problem of having to hire an assistant to run the shop while she handled the finances, consulting, and other arrangements.

Then an opportunity came. Sharon, a Single Parents newcomer with a two year old, couldn't afford a baby sitter but needed to learn a trade. One of the singles offered to keep her child a couple of hours a day if she wanted to take classes at the university, but Sharon couldn't afford the tuition.

In discussing her skills with Heather, she admitted she had been an average student in high school, except she excelled in art. "Maybe you'd be good with flower-arranging," Heather suggested.

Sharon's eyes lit up. "Oh, I'd love that, but I could never be as good you."

"It's the kind of thing that can be learned."

"But yours are much more creative than any others I've ever seen," Sharon said.

Heather thought she could use someone like Sharon. She smiled. "That's where artistic ability comes in. For me, it's more than a craft. So, I can't afford to pay, and I don't know if I will ever be able to hire anybody, but if you want to learn, I'll teach you. That would be considered experience, and you could at least get a job with a florist."

Sharon couldn't wait to start. "You can't go wrong with ivy," Heather said, beginning with that. By the end of the week, Sharon was cutting stems, putting picks on the ends, drilling holes in tree limbs, and learning the names of plants and flowers. Heather wondered how she had ever gotten along without her. *It's another example of how the Lord provides for those who love Him. Sometimes, I feel I take God's miracles for granted—they're so prevalent among the singles.*

And now, it seemed that Tom was a part of God's plan too. He had helped in many ways, including anonymously paying for several hundred dollars' worth of plumbing work for one of the single parents.

Chapter 7

At the end of June, Tom went to California for several days, expecting to return the first part of July. Before he left, he invited the Single Parents to his house for a cookout and pool party on the Fourth of July. Unsure of the day he would return, and just in case he was delayed, he gave Heather a key and more than enough money to put in the fund for the group's needs. If he didn't return in time, she would buy the food, and the Single Parents would have the party without him.

Without him?

The thought made Heather realize how much a part of her and Molly's life he had become.

"I can't allow that, Jillian," she told her friend. "He must be involved in something that's illegal or that he's ashamed of. What could it be?"

They could speculate, but they had done that before, to no avail. Maybe he was a driver for an international celebrity or foreign dignitary who visited the United States. Maybe he was a con man, but Heather didn't have anything he could con her out of. He had about all the silk arrangements he could use. All she had of value was. . .Molly.

On one hand, she believed he was good and decent. But so were mobsters to those who didn't cross them! She even began to wonder if the singles should accept his money, not knowing where it came from.

"Just keep your eyes and ears open," Aunt Mary said, "and your heart guarded."

"My heart learned a hard lesson with Rey," Heather reminded her, with more confidence than she felt. Sometimes the heart behaved like an errant runaway. And because she realized how so much of her happiness now depended on Tom, she would have to get answers to her questions—or back away.

❦

On the third of July, Sharon offered to watch the shop while Heather and others bought groceries for the cookout. After Heather picked Molly up from preschool at three o'clock, they went directly to Tom's. Several of the singles were preparing as much as possible in advance of the big day.

Conversations were lively amid lots of laughter, not to mention mess from preparing for about forty adults and fifty children. The TV was blaring and although the adults managed to keep the children off the furniture, they chased each other and played leapfrog on the spacious floor.

Heather brushed her damp forehead with her forearm. Suddenly, Tom was there. "You're home," she said and hoped he thought that was surprise and not joy.

148

His smile warmed her.

"Now this is what a man should come home to," he said, and she thought that his glance lingered on her, as if she were the object of that statement, but he also looked around at the others.

"They're wreaking havoc on this place," Lottie warned him. "And this is just a preview of what will take place tomorrow."

"Don't worry," he laughed. "Let them have fun. I can always hire someone to clean."

"Hire us!" said three of the women in unison, then ducked their heads in embarrassment and laughed. But Tom glanced back at Heather and lifted one eyebrow thoughtfully as if that were an idea. She knew that at least one person there would be willing to clean his house for free. That thought both thrilled and disturbed her.

After they had straightened up, and the others had gone, Tom asked if she wanted to swim. "I have a feeling we won't have a chance tomorrow."

She didn't have her swimsuit with her. "What's wrong with what you're wearing?" he asked.

She laughed. For a man who had a cactus in one corner, a pink dogwood in another, and grew vegetables in his flower garden, what indeed was wrong with swimming in shorts and a T-shirt?

It was a warm night and the cool water felt wonderful. The swim was refreshing after all day shopping, planning, and preparing. Unaccustomed to a pool, Molly sat on the side and kicked water at Tom and Heather, but she finally grew brave enough to climb down the steps, holding onto the railing. She got into the water up to her neck and even ducked her head a couple of times.

Heather expected Tom to give Molly swimming lessons, but he didn't. He swam across the pool several times with long, strong strokes as if easing all the tension out of his body. Heather hadn't swum in years and had forgotten how relaxing it could be. She got out of the water when Molly picked up a towel.

"I'm c-c-c-cold," Molly said, shivering. After drying her, Heather wrapped her in a dry towel and told her to run inside.

Heather picked up a large towel and before she realized it, Tom had taken it from her, opened it, and draped it around her. For a long moment she gazed at him, at the blue of his eyes as if they were pools and she was in over her head and had no air. He looked wonderful, he was wonderful, and she felt his warm hands on her cold arms. The moonlight seemed to do crazy things. She felt dizzy, her common sense distorted. She could only lean toward him when his handsome face came closer. "Thank you," he breathed.

"For what?" she whispered.

"For bringing so much into my life," he said, and his hands pulled her close as his lips brushed hers. Just as she was about to melt, he moved back, and she wondered if it had even happened. She didn't even get to kiss him back.

She had known loneliness, but in the past weeks, Tom had eliminated that from her life. Had she done that for him? Is that why he thanked her? It wasn't uncommon for men and women to share a hug, squeeze of the hand, or even a kiss on the cheek when they were thankful for help or being able to help others, or were just aware of God's goodness. She shouldn't make too much of this, she warned herself. He even seemed to regret it for he wasn't looking at her now, just striding toward the house. What else could she do but follow him, dripping?

Chapter 8

The Fourth of July dawned gloriously. It was going to be a perfect day. A string of cars followed Heather, Molly, Jillian, and Billy up the mountain. When they arrived, Tom was setting up the grill and men were arranging tables on the back patio. They took lounge chairs that looked new from a room down the hall from the family room. Heather wondered if Tom had bought these things for just such occasions. For an instant, her eyes lifted to the ceiling. What's up there, she wondered. But she dismissed the thought. She couldn't imagine having extra things that needed to be stored.

It was a super day for everybody. The pool was filled with children and adults, frolicking and playing water games. After they had eaten, activity began to wind down. Some played croquet that Tom had set up on the lawn; others played chess or checkers. Some of the adults even napped, a luxury that most, if any, couldn't usually afford. Many sat quietly, drinking in relaxation as if trying to store it in a bottle.

Some of the younger children were sent inside to rest, and Molly insisted they watch the cupcake videos. Seeing the children engrossed in the videos, Heather went outside, relaxed in a lounge chair in the shade of the house, and closed her eyes.

Voices registered, and her eyes opened. The sun seemed lower. Some of the guests were folding chairs; others were saying good-bye to Tom and thanking him. She realized she had been asleep.

Blinking her eyes, she swung her legs to the side and stood up, then went inside. The TV screen was snowy, and a couple of the children were asleep. She didn't see Molly. Jillian came in and asked, "Where's Billy?"

Heather shrugged. "Probably with Molly, wherever that is. Look outside, and I'll check in here."

Heather went upstairs, expecting Molly to be in some obvious place. She checked the deck off the living room, but she barely noticed the exceptional view from there—something was churning inside her. She saw Jillian, down at the pool, talk to a few people, look around, then hurry back to the house. Jillian spoke to others, who immediately stopped their conversations or what they were doing. Heather saw Tom point toward the woods in one direction, then point the other way, and adults rushed in those directions, calling the children.

Hurrying back inside, Heather called Molly and Billy, louder this time. Others began searching rooms and calling. The children were questioned. They knew nothing. Heather had already looked in the upstairs bedroom and bathroom and even peeked out on the balcony. Nothing!

She went downstairs. Tom's face was almost as white as his hair. "Find them?" he asked.

She shook her head.

"Did you look upstairs?"

She nodded.

"We'll search the cars," one of the men said and ran out the front, followed by several others.

Heather began to shake and steadied herself on the stair railing. Tom began looking around the main floor, although she already had. The searchers started to return. "We'd better call the police," someone said.

They all looked as helpless as she felt. Then Tom's eyes widened, and his gaze moved up the stairs. He seemed suspended. Heather looked around. She saw nothing.

"Oh, no," he whispered. "Did you look in the room off the bedroom?"

The storage room? Heather shook her head. "It's always locked."

"I'll bet I left it unlocked."

He looked terrified. Heather wondered what horror lurked in that room. He took the stairs two at a time and she followed, with the others right behind.

Tom turned the knob, and sure enough, it wasn't locked. He opened the door. There were Molly and Billy in front of a large-screen TV screen, pushing buttons.

"Billy!" Jillian screamed and rushed to him. "You scared the daylights out of me. You know you're not

154

supposed to go anywhere without asking me."

Heather was hanging onto the door, so grateful Molly was all right that she didn't even scold her. She had never had such a scare.

"I was right here," Billy was saying. "We wanted to see the video on this big TV."

"Is that okay, Mommy?" Molly asked. Her lower lip began to tremble.

Tom went inside the room. "It's okay," he said. "I should have made sure the door was locked." Heather noticed that he moved to the tables and desks as if checking the papers and magazines laying there. Was he afraid the children had ruined something? She got the distinct feeling he didn't want anyone to see whatever was on those tables.

Jillian told Billy they were leaving and ushered him from the room. After comments and nervous laughs of relief, others began filing down the stairs.

Heather felt too weak even to walk over to Molly. "Come on, honey. We have to get ready to leave."

"We have to go?" Molly protested.

"Do what your mother says, Molly," Tom said. He didn't speak roughly, but his voice contained enough authority that Molly, although she gave a disgruntled sigh, headed toward the door.

Heather put her hand on Molly's shoulder when they turned to leave. A last look at Tom revealed him staring at her. He was backed up against a countertop, holding the edge with such a tight grip that his knuckles were white. What was he so afraid of?

Soon Tom came downstairs, and after a few remarks from others—"Never a dull moment"—they seemed to be putting the scare behind them. It had been a wonderful day and the guests said so as they left. Tom appeared as friendly and lighthearted as usual, but Heather had come to know him well enough to detect he wasn't as relaxed as he seemed. He didn't meet her eyes for a long time and when he did, they held a look she hadn't noticed before—as if he were frightened.

Did he feel the scare of Molly's being lost as she did? Or was he feeling the scare of someone seeing what was in that room, which was supposed to have been locked?

Heather didn't know how she got through the next couple of hours, but went through the motions of cleanup while the men stored tables and chairs and cleaned up outside.

She didn't stay later than any others and left when Jillian did. When she got home, Heather talked to Molly about other people's property, wandering into rooms, and asking before touching anything.

"Tom's got really neat stuff in that room," Molly said.

"Like what?"

She said there was a huge TV screen and some videos and a lot of great pictures. Heather was afraid to question further. She didn't want the horrid thoughts that troubled her mind. She told herself everything was fine and Molly had seen nothing that disturbed her. But some things Molly wouldn't know. Heather knew she could no longer take Tom at face value. That was just too dangerous—for her and for Molly.

Heather wondered how she had allowed herself to slip into a situation in which so much of her time was spent thinking about Tom and their relationship. She believed in honesty and straightforwardness, as much as possible.

After two days of no word from him, she discovered she still had his house key. She called—all day—and got only the answering machine. Was he out of town? Heather debated with herself. Should she go to his house and if he wasn't home, go into that room? It might be locked, and the front door key wouldn't fit the lock. And didn't he have a right to his privacy? And what had he ever done to make her suspect him of anything?

The answer was . . .nothing.

However, if one always suspected ahead of time those who did wrong, then criminals would be apprehended before they struck—wouldn't they? No, I won't turn into a criminal myself and go into his house when he's not there! I'll just back away and leave him to his privacy and his secret job—if there is a job. How many people have as much free time as he seems to have?

I should have had better sense than to get caught up in a situation like this. But it had been so easy. Molly and I have both enjoyed every minute with him. I'll just have to not be so available after this. I'll back away.

Is that what he's doing? Where is he?

When Jillian and Aunt Mary asked about Tom, Heather answered, as if she knew, "He's out of town." She thought they had come to accept that as a job description. His title—Mr. Out-of-town. Hadn't she accepted it. . .almost? Until Molly went into the secret room.

Chapter 9

The singles had planned a hike and a picnic supper on top of Lookout Mountain on Saturday, if the weather were good. On Friday, a fierce but quick summer storm drenched everything with a couple inches of rain. Although the ground was still wet, Saturday was gorgeous. Heather was restless all day, until three o'clock when she could climb the mountain and perhaps blow away the cobwebs from her mind.

Some of the singles had left early, wanting to hike all the way from the bottom. At three, Heather closed the store and went home to change from tennis shoes to hiking boots. After she, Molly, Jillian, and Billy had driven as far as they could up Lookout, they had only a half-mile left to hike. But that was enough for the children's short legs.

Heather tried not to miss Tom, telling herself there had been life before him, and there would be life after him. However, when they got to the mountaintop, there he was, teamed up with three other men, playing horseshoes.

So? He hadn't called. He doesn't owe me a phone call!

But didn't that tell her something? He had spent

time with her but decided he didn't care to confide in her about important aspects of his life. He exercised his prerogative. So, they had had a few good times. Had become friends. That's what this group was all about, wasn't it? Being friends—regardless of the circumstances? She just shouldn't have expected. . . wanted. . .more.

Heather felt he was ignoring her as much as she was ignoring him. Neither was rude and they spoke, but for her the words were stilted and uncomfortable. She thought he felt the same. She prayed that the Lord would help her count her blessings and be grateful for what she had, and that Tom wanted friendship with this group of struggling Christians.

After everyone ate, the children were instructed about what was safe and what wasn't, then they began to play. Heather used to go there with Aunt Mary and Uncle Bob and had played on the huge boulders, away from the edge. She took Molly and Billy to the edge of the rocks. "Nobody is to go past me," she said, perched on top of a relatively flat surface.

She looked up at the late afternoon sky with a few gray clouds that seemed almost close enough to touch. *God knows best, even if I don't. He knows what's best for me, and for Molly.*

"A mudslide!" someone yelled.

Screams pierced the stillness and echoed around the mountainsides. With a crunching, scraping sound, a section of the mountain was disappearing, along with boulders, and Molly was rolling, rolling, rolling.

Heather's scream mingled with the others'.

Muddy children tried to grasp anything and climb up. Hands reached for them and pulled. They were terrified but not seriously hurt. Billy was farther down. Jillian started screaming. He was a little to the right of the worst part of the slide, and one of the men started to climb down to him. As he did, another rock gave way and missed Billy's head by no more than an inch.

The men made a human chain, and the first one was able to grab Billy's arm and pull him up. He seemed okay, except he said his arm hurt. That didn't matter. Not even if it were broken. He was safe. But where was Molly?

"Molly's under there, somewhere!" Heather screamed. "Molly! Molly!" The word seemed to shake the mountains, but there was no answer.

"There!" someone yelled. Far below the mud and rocks what appeared to be a little girl was at the edge of a cliff, behind a boulder that was partially braced by a scraggly tree. The ground was wet. The tree roots could loosen. Other boulders could give way. Molly wasn't moving. She wasn't even making a sound. She looked unconscious.

There was a frenzy of activity. Several adults hurried down the mountain to get help and whatever equipment they could find. They couldn't reach Molly from the top. Mud and rocks had fallen from the huge boulder jutting out over the slide. If more were dislodged, they might fall cover her completely. There didn't seem to be a way to reach her from below since the ledge she lay on looked

161

like a sheer dropoff.

Heather was frantic. The mountainside looked as if it had been scooped out by a huge crane. How could anyone get to Molly? Others were searching for a way. Tom came near, put his hands on her shoulders, and spoke soothingly.

"Stay calm, Heather," he said. "Help will be here soon."

Stay calm? She shrugged him off. He turned away helplessly and leaned his head on his arm, against a tree. Perhaps he was praying. She was. Surely they all were. It would get dark soon, but it shouldn't take more than ten minutes for somebody to come back with. . . something. Surely someone would have a phone and call for help. This wasn't beyond civilization. Surely a rescue squad would be here any minute. Then she heard sirens. Never had an alarm sounded so welcome.

It seemed like an eternity before a team of rescuers reached the mountaintop. They carried all sorts of equipment, including a stretcher, rope, and bags. The team appraised the situation and concluded what Heather and the others had. There was no way to get to Molly from the top. They couldn't drop someone over the huge boulder for two reasons. One, it might come dislodged, since rocks, dirt, and trees had slid out beneath it, and two, it appeared to be too far to the left, and a rescuer wouldn't be able to get a foothold until he was far below Molly.

"She called me," Heather said. "I know she did. Molly! Molly!" She got as close to the edge as the rescuers would allow.

"Tell her not to move," the rescuers said. Heather did, but it looked as if she were wedged between the scraggly tree and a boulder as big as her body. She could be terribly hurt.

Heather heard the rescuers say that a last resort would be to get a helicopter and lower someone to help her, but that might not work. They couldn't tell if she had any broken bones or if the boulder were on her little body.

"You've got to help us, ma'am," a rescuer said to Heather. "It's important that you don't let her know you're scared. We've got to try and get her to put this rope around her body so we can find out if she can be pulled up or if we have to try with a helicopter."

Heather called down to Molly, telling her what the rescuers said they would do. She told her not to be afraid, just do what they said and she would be all right.

The rescuers fastened a rope around a big oak tree, then around the waist of a rescuer who looped a part of the rope around his hand, then lay down and eased himself out on the boulder as far as he could and repeated to Molly what Heather had just told her. He lowered the rope and asked her to grab it.

Heather heard Molly making convulsive sounds. *She'll be okay if she does what she's told. She'll do it. She's a smart little girl. This isn't too hard for her.* Yes, Molly was moving her arm. Then, suddenly, a rock broke loose and tumbled down the mountain, and the tree leaned farther. Some of the onlookers gasped and Heather screamed. She immediately clamped her hand over her mouth, but it was too late. Terrified, Molly began to scream that she wanted her mother.

The rescuer tried again, but Molly made no other move. "Mommy, I want you to come and get me," she said.

Heather moved back from the edge where Molly couldn't see her, long enough to say in terror, "Let me try it. Maybe if I get out on the ledge, she'll do what I say."

The rescuers wouldn't hear of it. It wasn't allowed.

"But it's getting dark," Heather wailed. "And the clouds. It might rain. Oh, it can't rain. It mustn't."

"Let me try," Tom said.

The rescuers were adamant. It was strictly against the rules.

"Then what are you going to do?" Tom asked.

"Call for a helicopter. That's our only choice, and while it's coming, we'll keep trying to coax her into putting the rope around her."

"Okay," Tom said, "you don't have to put that rope around me, but I'm going out on that boulder, with or without a rope, and with or without permission. Now, do you want to fight about it, or try and rescue that little girl?"

Heather fell on her knees. "God, please help my little girl." Others put their arms around her, and several prayed aloud. Heather could hear Tom talking to Molly, who still wailed and called for her.

The onlookers grew silent and watched Tom, leaning over the edge with a rope tied around him. He was doing something weird, Heather thought, but Molly stopped screaming.

Was she listening, Heather wondered. Had she lost consciousness, or did she think Tom had lost his mind?

He was telling Molly a story about a little girl who rolled down a mountain, but he was speaking in the voice of the clown cupcake on the videos. Then in the Penelope Peppermint voice he began to tell Molly what to do with the rope, but Grumpy GumpDrop said she was a scaredy cat and that girls weren't as brave as boys.

Penelope kept encouraging and Grumpy discouraging. Penelope directed Molly to place the rope behind her head, then slowly, carefully get it under her shoulders and slip her arms through. At that point, there was the sound of something falling. Heather heard a catch in Tom's voice, but he continued speaking, louder and in a voice she hadn't heard before on the videos. This was an angel, who sang "Put your trust in Jesus and you can do it."

"No, she can't," growled Grumpy in his deep voice.

"Yes, she can and she will," rebutted Penelope in her high voice. She told Molly how to tighten the rope, then hold on with both hands and not let go.

"It's gonna hurt her, and she'll let go," Grumpy complained.

"She's a brave girl," Penelope said. "She won't let go even if it hurts."

Then the angel began to sing about lifting her up.

Grumpy complained again that the angel was too little.

Penelope said it was growing bigger.

The clown explained, in his funny way, that angels weren't merely little cupcakes but could grow as big as the biggest birthday cake. The clown told Molly that the cake had candles, but she had to close her eyes, make a wish, and not look until the angel told you.

Penelope told Molly to close her eyes and the angel would start lifting her up.

"Pull," Tom commanded. Just then, the rock or the tree gave way, but Tom's angel was singing louder, and the rescuers and Tom pulled and pulled.

Molly's head appeared, and in an instant Tom's arms were around her, and he swung her over the ledge to a waiting rescuer who had the stretcher waiting. Tom was crying and had to be helped off the ledge. It was all Heather could do to wait for the rescuers to examine Molly. She had cuts and was bleeding, and her eyes were closed.

"Molly! Molly!" Heather cried.

"Can I open my eyes now?"

"Oh, yes, yes," Heather told her.

Molly didn't seem to have any broken bones, but the rescuers said they would take her to the hospital to make sure she was all right. Heather looked for Tom, but he was nowhere in sight.

Soon, they were making their way down the now-dark mountain by the circle of light from a powerful flashlight. Heather thanked God with every breath.

Chapter 10

Heather called Aunt Mary and Uncle Bob from the hospital. They were waiting at the house when Heather and Molly arrived. After a bath and a glass of warm milk, Molly talked about the incident until her eyes drooped and she could barely mumble. Heather, with Molly's head in her lap, gently ran her fingers through the little girl's hair and told her version.

She gathered up Molly and tucked her in bed, and Aunt Mary followed. They spoke for a while in quiet tones, then returned to the living room.

Heather picked up the TV remote control. "Sorry to interrupt your program, Uncle Bob, but I've got to check something." She fast-forwarded a video until she got to the credits. Voices: T.A. Smith.

"Aunt Mary! Uncle Bob!" she shouted. "Look. T.A. Smith. Tom! He's a cupcake."

"What in the world?" Aunt Mary muttered.

"It's Tom. He's the cupcake voices. Oh, Aunt Mary." Heather had already told them what Tom had done, how he had persuaded Molly to put the rope around herself and hold on while they pulled her up the mountain. The two women looked at each other in wonder, trying to absorb it. Heather began to giggle. "Tom's a cupcake."

Uncle Bob raised his eyebrows and shook his head. "No wonder he wouldn't tell. Now, can I get back to the fights?"

Heather tossed him the remote. She and Aunt Mary laughed. But tears of relief flowed down Heather's cheeks too. "I've got to go and thank him."

"You might want to scrape off some of that mud first."

"Oh, yes. I'll hurry."

Aunt Mary smiled. "Don't hurry back. I'll be here as long as I'm needed."

❧

It was almost midnight. Heather didn't know if Tom would be home or if he were in bed, but she had to try—now. The imbedded lights glowed along the walkways, but his house was dark, except for a light in an upstairs window. Heather rang the doorbell a couple of times. No answer. If he were out back or in the family room, he might not hear it. She had put his key in her jeans pocket, intending to go inside and leave a note if he weren't home, or wake him up if he were asleep.

She unlocked the front door and headed upstairs, toward the lighted room. She could hear the angel singing, just as it had on the mountaintop, but this time it had vocal backup. She stood in the doorway of the secret room for a long time, watching a cupcake angel on the big-screen TV.

Tom was singing into a machine, switching voices,

from the clown to Penelope to Grumpy to Angelina. He stopped and pushed a button.

"Tom."

He whirled around and stared as if she were a stranger, then reddened.

"I guess you didn't hear the doorbell." She held up the key. "I still had this."

"No, I was. . .yes, uh, okay," he stammered, and stood.

Heather felt tears spill over and run down her face, but she didn't care. "Thank you for—"

"Anybody would have done it."

She shook her head. "I've never heard of anyone doing what you did."

He gave a self-conscious laugh.

"You're the voice on the videos, aren't you?"

"I'm more than that," he admitted. "I'm the cupcakes—the voices, the creator of the stories, and the illustrator. Of course, others help. That's why I have to travel. But it was my idea, and I make final decisions before a tape is released."

"That's what you do for a living?"

He nodded, gesturing toward the paraphernalia on the countertops that surrounded the room. There were papers, computers, machines, art materials. "It's a full-time job, Heather. When I seem not to be working, I'm thinking and absorbing ideas. Would you like to go downstairs, for coffee or something?"

She nodded.

He had a pot made in the kitchen. They took their

cups into the living room and sat on the couch. He took a swallow, then set his cup on the coffee table. "It started when Mom was sick and I had to take over for her as much as possible. My youngest sister was about Molly's age. It was quite an adjustment for a teenager, who'd just gotten interested in girls and wanted to impress them by playing football. There wasn't time for that. I was a lot like Grumpy GumpDrop. Then one day, feeling guilty about my attitude, I made cupcakes for the whole bunch—my brothers and sisters. Every one of them had different tastes, so to please them, I decorated each one differently. They were delighted."

He rose from the couch and walked to the fireplace, then began pacing. "On the way to the table, I stepped on a pencil. My feet flew out from under me, and I had to toss the cupcakes to catch myself, to keep from breaking my neck or my back. I was mad!" He grinned. "But those kids must have known I was at my wit's end. They began to laugh and joke and clean up. Before they'd been resentful when I told them anything. It was a turning point. The cupcakes became a standing joke. I'd always done voices that nobody appreciated, but I began to joke with them, and that got us through a lot of difficulties, where threats and lectures couldn't do it."

Heather set her cup down. "But why do you keep that a secret?"

He paced a while longer, then told her how he had struggled with God's leading him down that strange path. He fought it, particularly when his fiancée thought it was something perhaps to do on the side if he wanted, but she didn't want a joke for a husband and thought it was a ridiculous way to attempt to make a living. "She wanted a husband with more class," Tom said. He looked off in space. "She married an oil man."

"Oh, Tom. I'm sorry—"

"I'm not," he said abruptly. "I know now it would have been a huge mistake. She's not the kind of woman I want or need for a wife."

"I think what you do is wonderful," Heather said. "I've seen how Molly responds to the videos. They're excellent teaching tools and in such a fun way. And it must be very successful."

"More than any of us dared hope," he said. "But back in my hometown, in Texas, I'm still a weirdo, trying to get attention by making funny sounds. This is really serious work, Heather, and I didn't want to start off here by being called. . ." He looked at her sheepishly. "A cupcake."

Heather walked over to him, looking him straight in the eyes. "I don't care if you're Prunella the Prune. You saved my daughter's life. I'll never forget it. How can I ever repay you?"

"Well," he said in a cupcake voice, "you could sign over the rights to Prunella the Prune, and we'll have a whole new series of videos."

Heather smiled. Yes, she could see the wisdom of his wanting to let others get to know him before they learned of his occupation.

"I had no reason to tell the world I was the master-mind behind the cupcakes," Tom said. "I didn't know if I'd stay in this area. I came here looking for a new place and fresh ideas." He rested his hands gently on Heather's shoulders. "I didn't expect to fall so hard for two curly-haired beauties named Heather and Molly. I've been falling in love with you, Heather."

"Me too," she admitted eagerly. "I fought it—tooth and nail. It started for me the first day you walked into my shop."

"Me too," he said. "I knew there was something special about you. I would have bought that shop out if necessary, just to keep seeing you."

"Well," she said coyly, lifting her chin, "you see me now."

"Yes, and I'd like to see you for the rest of my life. Heather, can you love a cupcake?"

She moved closer, and his arms encircled her. She looked up. "I've always had a sweet tooth."

His face came closer. "That's good enough," he said, as his lips touched hers.

Yvonne Lehman is a popular author of inspirational romances, including *Mountain Man* (Heartsong Presents), the winner of the Romance Writers Association's (RWA) National Reader's Choice Award in the traditional category. Yvonne is also the author of the *White Dove Romances*, a series for young adults published by Bethany House Publishers. She and her husband, Howard, have four grown children and four grandchildren, and they make their home in the panoramic Blue Ridge Mountains of North Carolina.

King of Hearts

Tracie Peterson

Chapter 1

Elise Jost stood waiting impatiently at the receptionist desk. Her college advisor, Dr. Cooper, had summoned her, and with only a week left until graduation, Elise couldn't image what she might need to discuss.

"Elise?" a strong but clearly feminine voice called from the doorway.

"Yes?"

"Come on in."

"I have to say, Dr. Cooper," Elise remarked as she followed the older woman into her office, "this comes as quite a surprise."

The trim professional took her seat and motioned for Elise to do the same. "I'm afraid I have bad news. I am partially to blame for this oversight, and that makes telling you the circumstances even harder." Dr. Cooper shuffled some papers nervously before finally settling into silence. "It seems," she finally began again, "you are one credit short of having the requirements for graduation."

"That can't be!" Elise exclaimed and quickly scanned the pages in her hand. "I've calculated all of this to the last detail. I graduate next week. There must be some mistake."

"There was," Dr. Cooper offered sympathetically. "There was an incorrect entry on your elective credits. One of the classes you were given three credit hours for was only a two-credit class. You'll have to take an additional credit or another two- or three-credit class to meet your requirements for graduation. Of course, they'll still let you graduate with your class next week."

"But I can't!" Elise moaned. "I have the possibility of a job that could very well start in June. I'm in the final cut, and one of the only remaining factors is that I complete my degree by summer."

"I am sorry, Elise. I know how much of a shock this is, but it isn't the end of the world. There are several classes offered during the day that should fit in with your schedule."

"You don't understand," Elise began, weariness mingling with anger. She fell back against the chair as though she'd just been given a death sentence. "I had to rearrange my entire work schedule for this semester. I've turned my life upside down so that I could work from three to ten at night and go to school in the day. Now you're telling me it was all for nothing. I can't even complete my requirements without coming back to several weeks of summer school. That's going to put an end to the government job or at least put it off until fall, and I don't even know if my retail job will keep me on."

"I'm sure there's something we can find." The older woman seemed oblivious to Elise's panic and leaned across her desk to pull out her own copy of the summer schedule. Thumbing through it while Elise collected her thoughts, she mentioned several classes that might be acceptable. "Here's a chorus class. It's only one hour three times a week and it would give you the credit you need."

"I can't carry a tune to save my soul," Elise said despondently.

"Okay," Dr. Cooper continued, "how about an art appreciation class. We have several that are for the nonart major. You would surely enjoy learning a little more about the history of art."

"It might work," Elise said scanning the hours. "No, all of these are afternoon classes. I have to work then, and I don't dare ask to change my schedule again. Not with the fact that they know I'm just biding time until a real job comes along."

Dr. Cooper nodded and continued to flip through the few remaining pages. "Here, what about this?" She showed Elise the page. "Renaissance Appreciation."

"What does that involve?"

"It's technically an art credit, but it's a combination class that deals with the historical and artistic values of the time. It leans very heavily toward the history aspect and meets both in the Fine Arts Building as well as the Liberal Arts Building. It all depends on the various assigned projects. Dr. Hunter is the professor, and he's excellent. He used to teach here at the college on a regular basis, but he retired to write textbooks and other projects. Now he just teaches this one class in the summer as a pet project."

"I see." Elise noted the time would work, just barely,

with her already tight schedule. "I suppose it'll have to do. Can I take it pass/fail so that if I don't have an appreciation for the Renaissance, it won't affect my grade average?"

"Of course." Dr. Cooper smiled, happy to see that this was going to work out for one of the university's brightest nontraditional students. "You've worked hard for your perfect record, and the college has been honored to have you here. Now you go ahead and get scheduled for this. Today's the last day for enrollment in this class, so don't waste any time. I'm glad we could catch this before it ruined your plans."

Elise got to her feet, not at all convinced that it hadn't ruined her plans. "Thank you, Dr. Cooper. You've been a tremendous help over the years."

The woman smiled. "I was in your shoes not long ago. It isn't easy to attend college and work full-time."

Elise smiled. She and Dr. Cooper had had this conversation more than once. "I'll let you know how it goes," she said, leaving the office.

Once outside in the busy hallway, Elise wanted to break down and cry. She went to the restroom and blotted a cool towel against her cheeks for a moment. "This isn't working out the way I'd planned," she muttered to herself. She comforted herself with the fact that graduation was in a few short days. I can't let this change anything, she thought while studying her reflection in the mirror. Her cinnamon-colored hair was pulled back into a neat ponytail, making her look younger than her twenty-seven years. Her face, softly rounded and lightly highlighted by makeup, was a bit fuller than she'd have liked, but then so was the rest of her body. For years she'd tried to lose that extra twenty pounds, but it seemed to fall in acceptable places—and since she wasn't trying to look good for someone else, it was easy to ignore.

She continued looking in the mirror for several minutes. It was almost as if she wanted to force some revelation from her reflected image, find the answer to her unspoken questions.

She jumped nervously when the door opened to admit two young, giggling women.

"Daddy said if I did well this semester," one was saying to the other, "he'll get me that new red sports car."

"Not the one you showed me!" the other girl exclaimed.

"Yeees!"

Elise fully expected the girlfriend to break into a high-pitched "Way cool!" but she didn't.

"Then you can drive us to Kansas City and we can meet some interesting men."

"Forget Kansas City. Let's go all the way to New York or California. That's where the really rich ones are."

"Not only rich, but interesting. New York is where all the really interesting men live," the other fairly panted.

Is that so? Elise wondered. Maybe that was why she'd not run across any of the "really interesting" men. Not that she'd been looking. She knew what could happen when a career-driven woman let a man into her life. She would be expected to put her career on the back burner while establishing his, and then if there was time for her job interest, great. If not, it was diapers and bottles and bye-bye career. Who said old-fashioned notions were dead?

"Daddy says the only reason I came to college was to get my M.R.S.," the first one giggled. "I think that's funny, don't you?"

"Sure," the second one answered, sounding unconvinced. Then she chimed in, "Oh, I get it. Your Dad thinks you're here to find a husband. Oh, that is funny!"

Elise rolled her eyes, gathered her things, and went on her way.

Registration passed without much ado. Elise noted with only marginal interest that she had three books to purchase for the class. It was just more money to spend that she'd not planned on having to part with. At this rate, her nest egg wouldn't last until she got a real job.

Passing from the administrative building into the student union, Elise made her way to the bookstore. Might as well get this out of the way now, she thought. With a moan, she pushed past a group of girls who seemed to be holding hands and moving collectively through the store. They should keep us old folks isolated, she thought and watched the girls with a marginal bit of envy. She'd never had good friends. By her own choice, she realized just as quickly.

Nevertheless, the truth hurt. There just wasn't time for relationships in her life. College had taken what little time she had to give, while work and study took the greater portion of her life. How could she possibly give such a precious commodity as time to another person?

Elise juggled her purse and papers and moved to the fine arts section. Over the last few years, searching for textbooks in the union bookstore had almost become a pastime. She glanced around the section, praying silently that the Renaissance books wouldn't be as big as math textbooks. Why someone hadn't found a way to make a math book smaller eluded Elise. She had yet to take a math class of any kind and have the book weigh less than fifty pounds. Or so it seemed.

"*Life in the Renaissance,*" she said aloud, spotting the book. She glanced down at the list. Yes, this was one of the required books. The other two, *Art in the Renaissance* and *Renaissance England*, were neighboring the slots beside the stack of *Life in the. . .* books. Picking up one of each title, Elise noted they were inexpensively priced paperbacks and that the third book had even been written by the same man who would teach the class. "*Renaissance England,*" she spoke softly, "by Ian Hunter, Ph.D."

Turning the book over, she read aloud, "The lifestyles and daily routines of *Renaissance England* are explored in this academically crafted work by Dr. Ian Hunter." The descriptive copy continued, but Elise noted the time and realized she had to hurry in order to get home, drop off her things, and dress for work at the mall.

"I wonder if women in Renaissance England had to worry about schedules the way we do in twentieth-century America," she grumbled to herself. The day was rapidly going downhill.

Chapter 2

Graduation came and went without much fanfare in Elise's life. Her parents were too far away and too busy to make the trip to see her graduate. There had been a sweet card and surprisingly large check, along with a newsy letter about their neighborhood, but other than that, Elise was alone. The government job was given to another person with the promise that they were still very interested in Elise and would have another position available by fall. Fall was months away, however, and Elise brooded bitterly over how she was suppose to survive in the meantime.

"God, sometimes," she prayed, "I just don't get it. I do the things I think I should. I follow Your Word and feel I understand what You want for my life, and then it all seems to fall apart. I don't want to question You on this one, but I could sure use some clarity."

The Renaissance class offered problems from the very first day when Elise missed her alarm going off. She barely had time to shower and braid her hair before hurrying out the door. Trying to save money, Elise had refused to buy a car. Up until this day, it had worked pretty well, but now she questioned her sanity. The twelve-block walk seemed to stretch for miles, and time refused to stand still.

Finally reaching the college, Elise realized she'd have less than five minutes to make it across campus to the Salinger Liberal Arts Building, affectionately referred to as the SLAB. According to the schedule, the class would have its first meeting in the SLAB, but keeping straight which sessions would be held in the SLAB and which would be held in the fine arts building as the course progressed could prove to be a challenge. Elise figured it was a plot to thoroughly confuse and discourage her. She could well imagine showing up one place, only to learn that she belonged in the other.

Remembering the Renaissance Class was on the third floor, Elise made a mad dash for the elevator, only to find a sign taped to the closed doors. "Out of Order!" Elise moaned and realized she'd have to climb three flights of stairs.

The next surprise came when she got in class and found a young man at the head of the classroom. Surely this guy who looked five years younger than she wasn't the esteemed, retired Dr. Hunter she'd heard so much about!

"If you'll take your seats," the man called out, "I have some announcements to make. I'm Jeff Moore," he announced. "I'm a senior here and my major is history. Dr. Hunter was scheduled to be back today, but due to a family illness, he's been delayed. In his absence, I am prepared to walk you through the course requirements and give you your first reading assignment. Hopefully,

Dr. Hunter will be here next Monday and you won't be forced to endure more of my babbling." There were a few muted chuckles, but Elise's was not among them.

"Dr. Hunter is pretty easy going. As you know, this class is a combination history and art class. It's kind of different from anything else you've probably taken, and as you know, it meets four times a week. However, that's just the beginning. There will be multiple projects that will require extra hours during the week to help with a variety of duties related to the festival. And of course, the festival itself."

Elise nearly dropped her pencil. What projects? What festival? She didn't have extra hours to give. Glancing around her, Elise noticed that no one else seemed in the least bit concerned. The young man to her right, in fact, was drawing designs of motorcycles on his class syllabus, as though he hadn't a care in the world.

"Was everyone able to get copies of the three books Dr. Hunter assigned?" A unified mumbling of affirmation rose from the class of some thirty students and died down just as quickly.

"Great!" Jeff said and held up the book entitled *Life in the Renaissance*. "Your first assignment comes from this book. You're to read the first twenty pages, which is actually chapter one. On Monday, be prepared to discuss the material." Jeff put the book back on the table and looked up. "Any questions?"

"When do we start working on the festival?" a dark-haired young woman asked. Elise perked up, wondering again at the festival reference.

"Immediately," Jeff answered. "Dr. Hunter spends a great deal of energy each year on the festival and prides himself in a job well done. This class will of course be responsible, as it is every year, for the foundational planning, coordination, and execution of the festival."

"Do we get to pick what we want to do?" another voice questioned, this time a young man.

Jeff smiled. "For the most part. You are assigned parts to play, but Dr. Hunter always listens to what a person has an interest in. Of course, because of the multiyear involvement by some people in the pageantry, nobles are selected by committee and titles are retained until a person chooses to retire from involvement. Then again, the nobility have more responsibilities. They raise a great deal of the money prior to ticket sales, and they usually sponsor the various activities. Our college is one of four in the state that sponsors a Renaissance Festival, and because of that, we've divided each college according to suits from a deck of cards. Ours is hearts, therefore our king is the king of hearts."

Elise now realized they were speaking of the Renaissance Festival that took place in July on the college campus. She'd heard about it, but in the six years she'd lived in Jacksonville, she'd never bothered to attend.

"Is it true that everybody gets to participate in the festival?" a girl who barely looked old enough to be out of high school asked.

"It's not a matter of being allowed to," Jeff reminded them. "You must participate in the festival or you will not pass the course."

The words slammed into Elise's brain. "What do you mean?" she said aloud before realizing that she'd spoken.

Jeff shrugged and shook his head. "I'm sorry, I guess I don't understand."

Elise eyed him suspiciously. "Do I understand correctly that I have to participate in the festival in order to receive a passing grade? Even if I take the class pass/fail?"

Jeff nodded. "That's right. The class was created by Dr. Hunter and raises a great deal of money to fund projects for the fine arts department. Class participation sees that everything runs smoothly. It's been a most successful way to coordinate the more tedious tasks."

Elise was beginning to feel ill. The day was now officially ruined. "What about those of us with job obligations?"

"A lot of people take their vacations during the actual festival time," Jeff offered. "Otherwise, Dr. Hunter is very flexible and needs volunteers for both day and evening hours. Now, are there any more questions?"

When nobody else spoke up, he dismissed the class with a reminder of the reading assignment. Elise wasn't about to be put off that easily. There was no way she could take a week out to play-act in a Renaissance festival.

188

"Mr. Moore?"

"Huh?" the man looked up rather surprised by her use of his last name.

"What alternative assignment does Dr. Hunter have for those students who can't participate in the festival?"

"Alternative assignment?" Jeff repeated the words like they were some cryptic code.

"That's right. What can I do to get out of the festival and still pass this course?" Elise knew she sounded a bit on edge, but she was rapidly losing patience.

"As far as I know, and this is only from the four years I've attended this college, Dr. Hunter doesn't let anyone out of the festival requirement. There are no alternatives."

Elise felt her ire rise but kept her temper in check. "No other alternatives. Are you absolutely sure?"

"Positive," Jeff said, gathering his things. "Now if you don't mind, I have to get on over to my regular class. I'm sure Dr. Hunter will be back next Monday. Why don't you just wait and discuss it with him then?"

"I think I'll discuss it with someone over at the administrative office today," Elise said and angrily stormed back to her desk to gather her books.

Of all the idiotic things, she thought while marching down the three flights of stairs. King of hearts, indeed!

Making her way to the registrar's office, Elise calmed down a bit. It seemed reasonable that kids would find Dr. Hunter's festival a good way to get an easy credit, but for her it was a complete waste of time.

"May I help you?" an older, gray-haired woman asked.

Elise nodded. "I hope so. I need to talk to someone about a class I'm in. I think I want to change it."

"I see," the woman replied. "I'm afraid you'll have to speak with the department head, but he's out sick with the flu. Why don't you let me pencil you in for an appointment on Monday. If he's still sick, I can give you a call to cancel."

Complete frustration washed over Elise. "Isn't there anybody else I can talk to?"

"Have you spoken to your class instructor?"

"The class is led by Dr. Hunter, and he's not yet made an appearance."

"Oh, yes, Dr. Hunter. Well, we're expecting him back Monday as well. Why don't you talk to him first?"

"I'll start with the department head. Dr. Hunter apparently isn't known for his willingness to work with students on schedule conflicts."

The woman's expression told Elise how incredible she found Elise's words to be.

"Just schedule me early on Monday so that I can still make my class," Elise snapped.

Taking the slip of paper offered her by the receptionist, Elise stormed from the building. "I don't have time to play games!" she said aloud, glad that she was far enough away from anyone so that no one could overhear her. Monday couldn't come soon enough!

Chapter 3

To Elise's surprise, however, Monday came quicker than she'd anticipated. She'd put in extra hours at the department store where she worked in designer clothes sales and was left feeling drained and desperately behind schedule. After a quick shower, Elise realized that once again she was running late. Nothing was going right!

Her long, damp hair wouldn't cooperate in forming a bun, so Elise pulled it back and hoped to do something with it later. Halfway to the school, however, the barrette in her hair snapped from the pressure of the bulky mass and left Elise with a tangled cinnamon mess that the wind whipped at mercilessly.

At the college, the registrar's receptionist sympathetically told Elise that the department head was still out sick. "You can make another appointment, dear, but I can't help you other than that."

"I can't believe this. An entire university staff and I can only complain to one man about one class?" Elise's anger was barely in check. "Look, it's not that I can't work with the regulations and procedures around here, but give me a break. Renaissance Appreciation wasn't my idea, and if I didn't need a single credit in an elective to complete my degree, I wouldn't have even taken it."

The woman smiled tolerantly and nodded, which only made Elise madder. She was placating her, and Elise knew it. "Oh forget it!" Elise exploded. "I can't win!"

"Excuse me," a male voice called from behind a stack of books. It was a very tall stack of books, Elise noted. Probably because it was held by a very tall man.

"Yes?" Elise questioned, thoroughly irritated by the interruption.

"I couldn't help but overhear. Perhaps if you came to my office, I could get the details of your circumstances and help."

Elise calmed a bit. "I would really appreciate that."

"Come on then," the voice called. "My office is half-way down the hall."

Elise followed obediently, and only when her escort stopped and tried to fumble with the door did she speak. "Here," she offered, "I'll get it." She took the keys from his hands and unlocked the door.

"Thanks," the man replied, entering the room. "Just have a seat and I'll be right with you."

Elise was too angry to sit, so she walked over to the dusty window and stared outside while the man momentarily disappeared from the room. Running her fingers through her hair to reestablish order, she sighed.

"There, that's taken care of."

Elise turned and met a pair of chocolate brown eyes and a disarming smile that immediately put her at ease.

She guessed him to be about six-two and maybe in his midthirties. The tweed jacket he wore over a black T-shirt only moderately dressed up the jeans that accompanied them, but Elise liked the look.

"Now what seems to be the problem, Miss. . .?"

"I'm Elise Jost," she finally replied. Her wind-blown hair rippled behind her in a ribbon of cinnamon as she crossed the room and extended her hand. The man took it and gave it a squeeze.

"May I call you Elise?"

"Sure, whatever you like."

"Good," he said with an even broader smile. "Now, I understand you have some problem with the Renaissance Appreciation class."

"You might say that." The anger reappeared in her voice. "I didn't even want the class, but I had to take it so I could graduate with my class last semester. Someone in the transcript department miscalculated my credit hours and I came up on the short end of the stick."

"I see," the man said and sat down behind his desk. "Please, have a seat. I find that people in chairs are less likely to throw things."

Elise smiled at this and sat down. "I suppose it wouldn't have been so bad, but I had to give up a good job offer and I feel as though Renaissance Appreciation has rearranged my entire life."

"What exactly seems to be the problem with the class?"

Elise threw her hands up. "What doesn't seem to be the problem would be easier to answer. I don't know the first thing about the Renaissance."

"Isn't that a good reason to take a course on it?" the man interrupted with a grin.

"It could be, under normal circumstances. But nothing in my life is normal. I have to work for a living, and the man who teaches this class, Dr. Hunter, insists on participation in some rinky-dink festival they have every year."

"I know it well. It's a lot of fun and raises a great deal of money for the fine arts department."

"That's great!" Elise said angrily. "I'm very happy for the fine arts department, but it doesn't do a thing for me. I have to work. I can't very well go to my boss and say, 'Oh, by the way, some clown at the college insists that I play dress-up for a week in order to graduate and leave this hole-in-a-wall job for a better one.'" Elise's voice steadily rose in volume. "I'm sure they'd understand that one."

"So have you talked to this 'clown'?" the man questioned.

"No, he's out on some kind of family emergency. I do plan to take it up with him once he comes back," Elise said, nearly losing complete control. She got to her feet, smiled weakly at the man behind the desk, and began to pace. "I promise not to throw anything, but I'm too mad to sit still. Do you have any idea when Dr. Hunter will be back?"

"Oh," he said, sounding guilty, "I should tell you—I'm Ian Hunter, Ph.D., and clown at your service."

Elise's mouth formed a silent *O*, and she felt as though she might actually faint from the shock. She grabbed the back of the chair she'd just vacated and tried to remember every insulting thing she'd said. "Please tell me you're joking," she finally managed to say.

Ian laughed. "Sorry, I didn't realize you didn't know who I was until you started in on me."

Elise sat down. She had to. Her knees were suddenly jelly, and she had no reserve strength to fall back on. "I'm sorry. I guess I let my temper once again get the best of me. As a Christian, I must say it's one of my biggest crosses to bear." She knew it was a lame apology, but she was completely mortified and had no idea how to set things right. This man was her professor. He would decide whether she could drop the festival requirement. He would have the power to pass or fail her.

"We all have them, Elise," Ian offered. "I, too, am a child of God and quite often, a most childish child. You're in good company, so relax. I'm not the least bit offended."

Elise perked up a bit. "That's kind of you."

"No, not really," Ian said with a shrug, "but it is realistic and will probably work best in our favor. The requirement to participate in the Renaissance Festival was set the first year the class was created. It gives everyone a chance to get a feel for the times and just have a lot of fun. The money raised helps the fine arts department to put on free performances for the community, especially Children's Hospital."

"So trying to get out of it is like saying I don't care about sick kids? Not fair, Dr. Hunter."

"Ian, please." He said it in such a manner that Elise couldn't resist his charm.

"Ian, I appreciate what you're telling me, but I have to work full-time. I'm a nontraditional student, and I've been working to get this degree for over six years. I've already had to rearrange my work hours, and they aren't very happy about that," Elise added.

"Why did you have to do that?" Ian questioned.

"Before last semester, I was working days and attending school at night. In order to take my final business classes, which were only offered during the day, I had to change my hours at work. I work at the mall in retail sales and believe me, they weren't pleased. But, because I had seniority and had a perfect work record, they felt they had to at least try to work with me on my schedule. Now you want me to take even more time away from work and participate in this festival."

"But most of the festival work will take place during the day, so what's the problem?"

Elise felt herself getting angry again. "I promised the store I would go back to days as soon as I graduated."

"Look, Elise," Ian said in a tone that she recognized meant he wasn't going to let her off the hook, "I do appreciate your circumstances, but this is a hard, fast rule. If you absolutely can't work with it, then I suggest you drop the class."

"But I can't drop the class! That's the point. I have to have one additional credit hour."

"There are other classes."

"We tried to find something to fit my schedule. There were other art classes, but they were offered in the afternoon. I can't change it now, because I spent all weekend looking over the schedule and there is nothing else. Please, Dr. Hunter," she paused. "Please, Ian, won't you reconsider this?"

Ian got to his feet. "Look, Elise, this is just the way it has to be. I can't make an exception for anyone, although if I were going to, I'd certainly do so for you."

Elise didn't know what to think about that statement, but she did realize with a heavy heart that she was trapped into a course with this man and she wasn't going to get free of the festival.

"So that's it?"

"I'm afraid so," Ian said, coming to stand directly in front of her. "Don't look so defeated. Once you get into the swing of things, it'll be a lot of fun."

"Fun, Dr. Hunter," she said, stressing the formality of the name, "is something I do not have time for." She picked up her things and stormed out of the room.

Ian watched the vivacious redhead leave his office. She was fire and ice all rolled into one package. With a smile, he crossed to the window and waited for her to come outside. She was an attractive, intelligent woman.

197

When she came into sight, Ian watched as the bulk of cinnamon hair swayed back and forth in the summer sun.

"Beautiful," he said aloud. He watched until Elise was out of sight, then returned to his desk.

Picking up his pen and preparing to write a note to his sister, Ian couldn't get Elise out of his mind. He was just back from his mother's surgery, and even though she'd been quite ill, Ian couldn't help but smile when he thought of their last prayer together.

"And Father," he could hear his mother pray, "please send a good woman to be a mate for my Ian. She'll need to be someone special. Someone with strength and determination and a spirit of love to match my son's."

The words almost seemed to echo on the air. Ian sat back in the chair and thoughtfully chewed on the end of his pen. It looked like his mother's prayers were about to be answered.

"I'm really quite taken with her," he mused aloud. "How about that?" Then posing a more serious question, Ian looked up at the ceiling. "But just what should I do about it?"

Chapter 4

When it was time for class, Elise took a seat as far to the back of the room as possible. Only marginally more composed than when she'd left Ian's office, she was trying hard to figure out how she could work everything out.

"I want to welcome you to Renaissance Appreciation," Ian said as he came to stand at the podium. "I am Dr. Hunter, although I'd prefer you to call me Ian. My office hours are posted in the department if you need help or guidance. I trust you have a copy of the books we'll be using and the syllabus." He paused long enough to acknowledge Elise with a nod.

"What exactly is the Renaissance? The word means rebirth or revival. How's that for dramatic? To me it conjures up vivid images of a group of down-trodden serfs sitting around one day, late in the Dark Ages. Suddenly one of them stands up and proclaims, 'I know, let's have a Renaissance!' Inspired, everyone begins painting and breaking the bonds of feudalism." He paused while most of the class chuckled at this image.

"Well, it didn't happen that way. Few things come into this world fully developed. This especially applies to the Renaissance. The Renaissance is more the result of gradual change than of a spontaneous and dramatic rebirth. The Renaissance is the end result of changes in society and the way people perceived their world and their place in the world."

Elise tried not to care overmuch about the lecture, but the lecturer had a way of drawing in his crowd. Ian was a gifted speaker and teacher, and not only did she find herself wanting to know more, but she was fairly hanging on his every word. The only thing that made it bad was that he seemed to notice her open interest.

"As few things spring into full existence unaided," Ian continued, "all things must have their roots in the past. Essentially, this is why the study of history is important: to give us a better understanding of the present. To understand what has happened to cause or to bring about an event in history is to grasp a better understanding of that event.

"This is why the first topic on our syllabus is the Middle Ages. Before we can talk about the Renaissance, we must have a basic understanding of the Middle Ages. If the Europe of the Middle Ages can be characterized by one word, then that word is *obligation*. In the Middle Ages, nearly everyone was held in obligation to those above him. The peasants had obligations to the land owners. The nobles had obligations to their lord or king, and all of the people had obligations to the church."

Elise watched Ian sit casually on the table beside the

podium. He was definitely in his element, she thought. His teaching style was free-flowing, thought provoking, and easy to follow. What more could a student ask? Before she realized it, the hour was up and Ian was summing up the lecture.

"Therefore, Renaissance is not so much a rebirth as it is a reevaluation of beliefs and attitudes that, when found wanting in terms of what they provided to the enrichment of life, were changed for a better way. Tomorrow's assignment, read chapter two and come to class prepared to discuss your thoughts on the content. I assure you, this will be one of the last classes where I do most of the talking."

The close of his book signaled dismissal, and Elise suddenly realized the time. If she hurried, she could be to work before noon. Maybe if she showed an effort to give the store as much of her daytime hours as possible, they'd lighten up and not be so hard to deal with when the July festival rolled around.

Hurrying from the room, Elise was already to the parking lot when she heard her name being called. Turning, she recognized Ian's lanky form striding toward her with determined purpose. He'd shed the tweed jacket and was juggling it between books and papers.

"Are you rushing off somewhere?"

Elise tried not to be the slightest bit interested in the way the sunlight made his hair turn golden brown. "I, uh, I'm off to work." She struggled into the backpack she'd been carrying.

"How about a lift?"

"No, no thanks." Elise was startled by the invitation but tried to remain reserved. "I walk everywhere, and if I hurry, I can be there to relieve the girls for lunch."

"I can hurry you there faster in the car. I'm parked right here," he said, pointing to a restored classic. The black Chevy gleamed from many coats of hand-waxing.

Elise hesitated. "Surely you don't offer to drive all of your students to work?"

"Nope, just the ones who call me a clown." His lop-sided grin told her that he was working hard to get on her good side. "Come on, Elise, I want to talk to you anyway."

Elise agreed to the ride, hoping that with time to reconsider, Ian would tell her of his decision to let her off the hook. She climbed into the car, admiring the restoration work and then fell silent as the engine roared to life and Ian headed in the direction of the only mall in town.

"Which store do you work at?"

"Gallagher's," she replied, trying hard not to sound too eager for him to continue.

"And what do you do there?"

"Sell women on expensive designer outfits."

"I see," he said, maneuvering through traffic. "And what is the job you had to give up in order to take my class?"

"A supervisory position with the U.S. Customs

Department. I was very excited about the position. It's something I've worked for all my life."

"A customs job?" he asked with a teasing smile.

"Well, maybe not exactly that, but a good solid career. You'll need to turn at the next entrance," she said, hoping Ian would drop the small talk and tell her what she wanted to hear.

"Look, Elise," Ian finally began, "I had a motive in offering to give you a ride to work."

"Oh?"

"Yeah, I know this sounds sudden and maybe a bit out of line, but I'd really like to spend some time with you and get to know you better. You know, away from school."

Elise stared at him open-mouthed. What was it about this man that gave him the power to reduce her to stammers and stunned silence?

Ian grinned and pulled the car up to the store entrance. "Well, what do you say?"

Elise shook her head. "I don't have time for a relationship."

"Seems to me you don't have time for much. First it was fun, now it's a relationship."

"Well," she said nodding, "that about sums it up. I'm driven to see my career off and running. I can't let anything or anyone get in the middle of that. I work full-time, usually going into overtime, and what with college, I don't have the time to give. I'm sorry."

"I won't take sorry for an answer. What time do you

get off so that we can continue this discussion?"

Elise reached for the door handle. "There's nothing to discuss."

"Look, I'm concerned about you. What time do you get off? I'll give you a ride home and then you can tell me why it's so important to keep everyone at arm's length."

"By the time I finish with receipts and counting the drawer, it's past ten. So forget it. I'm perfectly capable of walking."

She got out of the car and as she closed the door, Ian called out, "See you at ten."

He drove off before she could protest, leaving Elise once again dumbfounded by his arrogance and self-confident nature.

"Oh, no you won't, Dr. Hunter," she muttered as the Chevy disappeared from view. "Not in a million years!"

From the first moment Elise stepped onto the sales floor, until she was counting out the money drawer at nine-forty-five, she faced nothing but a myriad of problems. She argued for twenty minutes with a younger employee who thought the display of new silk suits needed more color.

Then two elderly women who were regular customers demanded to see the latest arrivals from their favorite designer. When Elise showed them what had come in, the women were clearly unsatisfied and wanted to know when the next shipment would arrive. Elise spent half an hour running down the schedule that would let her advise them on the line, only to have them grumble about the delay and suggest that they could take their shopping elsewhere if necessary.

Elise wanted badly to tell them to do just that, but instead she calmed them down by showing them a line of sporty clothes that mimicked their favorite designer. And now, she was trying without much luck to get her register receipts to match the cash and charges in the drawer.

"Elise, we need to talk," said a stern-faced, bleached blond. It was Roselle, the manager of the women's designer department.

"Yes, Roselle?" Elise hoped she sounded more sincere than tired.

The woman took a seat at the table where Elise worked. "You promised to return to your original schedule by now. I want to know what happened and why you're still working evenings."

Elise gave up on the money and receipts. "I explained to the store manager that I was one credit hour short. If I'd only known before last semester, I could have worked it out then, but now I find myself in a summer class that I can't get out of without forfeiting my degree."

"I see," Roselle said, not sounding the least bit sympathetic. "Have you considered that perhaps it's time to quit Gallagher's? I mean, you plan to move ahead with your plans and we have many talented people in this department who should have a chance to move up in ranks. If you're going to resign to take another position anyway, why not go ahead and do it now?"

Elise felt mild panic building. "I can't quit, Roselle. I need the money to live on until I have another job. Look, I've been honest and straightforward with everyone here. I've been good to come in when I wasn't scheduled to work, and I've never missed a day."

"Yes, well, it was just a suggestion." Roselle got to her feet. "We'll just have to see how it all works out."

Elise had a hard time concentrating after Roselle left. She counted her drawer out five times before she finally felt confident that it was all there. After hurrying to turn everything in to its assigned place, Elise noted it was nearly ten-twenty.

Grabbing her pack and purse, she hurried to where Marty, the security guard, waited to check each employee out for the night.

"Kind of late this evening, aren't you?" he asked in his grandfatherly way.

"It was a rough one, Marty." She passed through the door stuffing her purse into the backpack. "Hope yours goes better."

Outside, the night was heavy and felt like rain. Elise hurriedly pulled on the pack and started across the dark parking lot toward home. She glanced around nervously as she always did. The can of pepper spray in her pocket did little to reassure her, but this was a small town and the crime rate was very low. Since switching to evenings and walking home in the dark, she'd never once had any problem to concern herself with.

Nevertheless, the nightly walk made her nervous and edgy.

Barely halfway across the lot, Elise heard footsteps behind her. The hair on the back of her neck prickled and her hand reflexively grasped the pepper spray. She could hear her heart beating in her ears, almost keeping time with the footsteps. Glancing around her, she tried to figure out a path of flight. There were several cars she could weave around, but should she head back to the store or make a dead run for home?

"Elise."

She barely suppressed a scream, as a hand touched her arm. She whirled around, spray in hand, but stopped short of depressing its button. Panting for breath, she tried to focus her mind on the image before her. Ian Hunter was looking at her with concern.

"I'm sorry. I didn't mean to scare you," he said, watching the pepper spray intently. "You aren't going to skunk me with that, are you?"

Elise drew her gaze away from Ian's amused expression to the canister in her hands and then back again to Ian. "I should," she finally whispered.

"Come on." He took hold of her arm and led her forward. "I told you I'd be here to give you a ride home. What if I'd been a real mugger or worse yet, a murderer?"

"Then I guess I wouldn't have to take Renaissance Appreciation," she snapped sarcastically. Her fear was quickly being replaced by anger. Pocketing the spray, she jerked away from Ian's hold. "I don't need a ride home. I've been doing this for several years."

"Yes, but as I recall, you did most of those years during daylight hours. Now swallow your pride and let me take you home."

They had reached the car, and Ian stood with a look of resolve that Elise had no doubt was stronger than her own. "Okay," was all she trusted herself to say.

It didn't surprise Elise when they pulled into the driveway of her little rental house. Somehow she'd known that Ian would have looked up her address. But instead of being angry, she was rather touched that he was so concerned for her safety. In six years of living on her own, no one had shown her that kind of concern. Oh, there were those people at church who tried hard to keep her in their circle of activities, and there was her mom and dad, of course, but they were a world away in Washington, D.C.

When Ian shut off the motor, Elise realized he still intended to discuss their dating. She tried hard to steady her already shattered nerves. Ian was a handsome man with a very dynamic personality. It was hard to imagine that he was honestly interested in her, and for once it was hard to say no to the idea of getting involved.

"So have you given more consideration to my request?"

Elise shook her head. "No. There's no room for consideration." She thought the words sounded rather weak and fervently wished she had the courage to open the car door and walk away. Instead, she remained seated, her gaze fixed on the dashboard.

"Elise, don't say no."

She knew it was a mistake, but she couldn't help looking at him. The street light afforded her a good look, and his expression matched his voice. He looked like a little boy who'd been disappointed. Her breath caught in her throat, causing her to cough lightly. Licking her lips nervously, she sighed and tried to find the right words.

"I can't see you outside of school. It wouldn't be right. I don't intend to stick around this town once your class is done, and I don't want to leave any unfinished business behind me. Don't you understand? I've put my life on hold for six years in order to get this degree. I can't mess that up now."

"I'm not asking you to," Ian said softly. "I'm not asking you for anything but a date."

Elise felt her defenses crumbling. She had to do something. No one had ever affected her like this before. "If I date you, will you drop the festival requirement and give me an alternate assignment?"

Ian laughed, and his whole expression turned mischievous. "No, but if you go out with me, I promise you won't be sorry. Come on, Elise. Let some fun into your life."

"Isn't there some rule about professors dating their students?" She knew it was a lame excuse, but she was desperate.

"I'm not a regular professor anymore. I only come in as a guest lecturer for this one class. It's more community service than anything. Besides, you're very nearly graduated. What's six weeks?"

"Then wait six weeks and ask me again." Elise didn't trust herself to remain resolved. "I have to go. I have an early class, you know." She reached for the door handle, but this time Ian quickly jumped out of the car and came around to open the door for her.

"Can't you just think about it?" His voice was almost a whisper.

Elise looked up into his hopeful eyes. She was losing ground, and she knew that she had to get away from this man—immediately.

"Just think about it," Ian said, lightly touching her cheek. "I promise not to take up too much of your time. I know what a bear that professor of yours can be."

Elise smiled nervously. "I wish I had known before signing up for his class."

Ian grew quite serious. "I'm glad you didn't. Now, how about it? Won't you at least consider the matter?"

"All right, Ian," she said, resigning herself to say what he wanted to hear. "I'll think about it."

Chapter 5

For two weeks, Elise faithfully attended Ian's class and waited for him to ask her for a decision on his request. And for two weeks, he very nearly ignored her altogether. On Friday, the only day she had off from both regular classes and work, Elise found herself sorting through festival props. There was everything from armor to velvet gowns and knightly swords. Climbing up and down the long ladder to the overhead storage rooms just opposite the stage, Elise felt hot and very dirty.

Two of the young men from her class were inside the storage rooms handing props out through the opening, while Elise alternated with several other students going up and down the ladder to retrieve the things. Ian was nowhere to be seen, having taken another group of students off to another room for their assignment, and for this, Elise was grateful. She was nervous enough about climbing fifteen feet into the air and juggling props back down a wobbly ladder, but if Ian were there watching, she knew she'd never be able to manage.

She had just made her fifth trip up the ladder to receive a large shield, when two young women came running past the ladder. They were caught up in a game of chase with another classmate, Jason Emery. They laughed at the young man's attempts to poke at them with a wooden sword.

"You will be mine!" he called out in deep, dramatic voice, causing giggles to ensue once again.

Elise was barely halfway down the ladder when one of the girls ran underneath, knocking it just enough to cause the entire ladder to move violently to the right. Without warning, Elise found herself plummeting the remaining eight or so feet, landing with a crash on the wooden floor below.

She had tried to catch herself and land on her feet, but this only caused her to twist her ankle badly and crumble beneath the weight. She cried out in pain, but quickly hushed her complaints when Ian came running through the stage door.

"What happened here?" he asked, coming to Elise's side. He reached out to pull her to her feet and Elise refused to grimace, even though the pain was severe.

"It's our fault," one of the girls replied.

"No, it's really my fault," the young man answered.

"Jason, you want to tell me what happened?" Ian asked.

Jason Emery raised the sword as if hoping it would offer an explanation. "I was kind of chasing after Kerry and Leah and we hit the ladder. We didn't mean to cause any harm. Elise, I feel just terrible that you fell. Are you hurt?"

Ian turned to Elise. "Yes, are you hurt?"

Elise felt Ian's gaze bore into her, demanding the truth. "No, I'm fine. I didn't fall that far, and I think the shield broke my fall anyway." She smiled weakly, and all gazes fell to the broken shield on the stage floor.

"You know horseplay is uncalled for in circumstances like this," Ian said sternly. "Elise could have been hurt severely, not to mention what might have happened if you'd fallen with that sword while chasing after Kerry and Leah."

"Yeah, it was real dumb. I'm sorry, and it won't happen again."

"Hey, what's going on down there?" one of the guys working in the prop room called from overhead.

"Just a minor setback," Ian replied. "Jason, since you've nothing better to do, you take Elise's place going up and down the ladder. Kerry, Leah, do you have something you should be doing?" Guiltily both girls nodded. "Then I suggest everyone get back to work."

"Dr. Hunter!" a voice called from the other room.

Ian let his gaze travel the length of Elise. "Are you sure you're all right?"

"I'm perfectly fine."

"Dr. Hunter, we have a problem in here," the voice materialized into the form of yet another classmate.

"Coming," Ian called.

Everyone went their way, and Elise waited until Jason had climbed up the ladder before she tested her weight on the throbbing ankle. With a muffled cry, she fell to the floor and grabbed her right leg.

"So you're perfectly fine, eh?" It was Ian, and he was standing in the doorway, arms folded in a determined stance. He crossed the room with the same determination in his stride.

Elise looked up anxiously. "Really, I'll be just fine."

"Of course you will be," Ian said, surprising her by easily lifting her into his arms. "After the emergency room has a chance to fix you up."

Elise protested. "I'm not going to the emergency room. Ian, put me down."

Jason was apologetically opening the exit door for Ian. "I'm really sorry, Elise."

"Stop this. I can just put some ice on it and—"

"Nothing doing, Elise. I'm taking you to the hospital, and that's that."

"I can't afford it, Ian," she finally said, giving up any hopes of maintaining her pride.

Ian stopped and looked down at her sympathetically. "You don't have to afford anything. The school has insurance, and if they won't pay, I will."

❦

"I told you it wasn't broken," Elise said later as the nurse wheeled her out from the examination room.

"Yes, but it is badly sprained," the nurse said before Ian could react. "She'll need to be off it until the swelling goes down, and that might take as long as a week. Here's a prescription for painkillers and the phone number for the doctor's office should you have any

214

questions or concerns. She's been given an injection for pain, but she can take the pills in addition to that." The nurse addressed Ian as though she knew him to be in charge. "Oh, and she'll need these." The woman disappeared into a room and returned with a pair of crutches.

Ian thanked her and helped adjust the crutches to Elise's height. He watched anxiously as Elise tried to coordinate the crutches.

"It isn't as easy as it looks," she commented snidely.

"Do you need any more information for the insurance?" Ian asked the nurse, while Elise made her way slowly to the door.

"No, everything is in order."

"Thanks," Ian replied and hurried to where Elise was about to disappear into the night. "Where do you think you're going?" he questioned, scooping her into his arms, crutches and all.

"Ian, put me down!"

"Not on your life. I'm taking you home and seeing to it that you don't get up until that swelling is completely gone."

"I can't do that, Ian. I have a—"

"I know. I know. A job and a class and a life without complications or relationships. Look, I've cut you a wide path these last two weeks. You're going to do this my way, so just get used to it."

Elise opened her mouth, but nothing came out, causing Ian to nod. "Good, I'm glad you're seeing it my way."

Ian wondered silently as he put Elise in the car if there wasn't some way to break through her facade of independent strength. She would never willingly be weak in front of him. It was just too important to her to be strong. Then an idea came to him. Starting the engine he turned with a smile. "I'll fill the prescription after I get you settled in."

Elise nodded and reached for her purse. "Oh, Ian, I left my purse in your filing cabinet at school."

"I'll get it tomorrow."

"But all my money is in it, along with my credit cards and bank card. I can't just leave it there, and I can't pay for the medicine without it."

"All right, all right. I'll get your purse when I go for the prescription, but I'm paying for your medicine and I won't hear any argument about it."

"Okay."

When Elise said nothing more, Ian laughed. "Okay? Just 'okay'? That shot they gave you for pain must have been pretty potent."

"Well, I'm hardly in any position to fight you right now. But, when I get back out of the car and have my crutches in hand, watch out!" She smiled, and Ian thought his heart would melt into a puddle around his feet.

He pulled the car into his driveway and waited for Elise to comment. She looked past him to the Victorian house and then rested her gaze on Ian's face.

"This isn't my house."

"No, it's mine."

"I see, and why are we here?"

"Because you're going to stay here for a few days."

Elise shook her head and reached for the door. "Oh, no I'm not. I told you the first time we met. I'm a Christian. Not just in name, in deed as well."

Ian reached out to stop her. "I'm glad to hear it, but it doesn't change a thing. You're alone, and you need help."

"So you figure that makes it okay for me to move in with you? I don't think so." She was pushing his hand away. "If you're the Christian you profess to be, you'll understand why I can't stay here. What would people think? What would they say?"

"I don't really care, but I do care about you. Besides, I have a live-in housekeeper, a very respectable older woman named Lillian Greer. She's a wonderful, loving soul who is actually a third or fourth cousin to the tenth power or whatever. Anyway, she needed a home and I needed a keeper. It's a companionable relation-ship, and she'll not mind one bit helping me keep you in line."

Once again, Elise stared at Ian with an open mouth, and he raised a single eyebrow, waiting for her to refuse. When she didn't, he grinned broadly.

"Now, no arguments about me carrying you upstairs," he said, reaching to take her in his arms.

"But I weigh a ton," Elise protested.

Ian shifted her lightly in his arms. "I'd say closer to

130." Elise blushed and Ian laughed. "I lift weights at the YMCA. I'm getting pretty good at sizing things up."

His face was just inches from hers, and he studied her expression. She seemed so anxious and concerned about her size.

"I think you're perfect," he whispered against her cheek and lightly kissed her. Whether to hide her embarrassment or because she felt the need to get closer to him, Elise snuggled her face against his chest and didn't say another word. Ian liked her like this, vulnerable and yielding, but he liked her with her fiery speeches and her eyes ablaze, too. She was perfect, he thought as he carried her into the house. She was just exactly what he'd prayed for.

❧

The next morning, Elise awoke to the aroma of freshly brewed coffee. For a moment, she thought she was back home in D.C. It was the sharp jab of pain in her leg that brought her back to reality. With a start, she sat up in bed and tried to focus on the events of the night before. The painkiller they'd given her at the hospital was one powerful drug, she decided, realizing that after the white-haired Lillian had tucked her into bed, she'd instantly fallen asleep.

A quick glance at her watch told her she barely had enough time to get to work. This was Saturday, and a sale day to boot. If she didn't hurry up and get there before nine, Roselle would have a fit. Spying the crutches against the wall, Elise threw back the covers and eased her legs over the side of the bed. Her right ankle throbbed furiously at this change, causing Elise to grimace. Hopping around the room to collect her things didn't make matters any better.

Seeing her purse on the nightstand made her smile for just a moment. Ian had thoughtfully collected it, just as she had insisted. No doubt he was tired and worried, but he'd done the deed, and that somehow endeared him to her just as all his other actions had. Then her mind went back to what he'd said last night and the kiss he'd given her. Maybe she'd just dreamed all of that. Her hand went to her cheek as if to touch the lips he had pressed there.

"You're losing control, Elise," she whispered and pulled the crutches under her. Still trying to master the beasts, Elise made her way out of the room and into the hall. Grateful that the stairs were located directly opposite her door, Elise slowly made her way to the top.

"Just where do you think you're going?" Ian asked, standing in a nearby doorway and wearing a navy-blue velour robe, his face full of shaving cream.

"I have to go to work," Elise protested, trying desperately not to give him her utmost attention.

"Absolutely not. That's why I brought you here. Come on, it's back to bed for you." He reached out for her, but Elise pushed past him.

"I have to go to work. If I don't, I'll lose my job. They're already furious with me for the time I've had off for the festival preparations."

Ian leaned his face down close to hers. "I'm putting you to bed and you're going to stay there. Lillian!" He gave Elise no chance to reply before sweeping her into his arms. The crutches crashed loudly to the polished wood floor.

A woman about sixty years old appeared. She had a brilliant smile that made the wrinkles in her face disappear. "I see our guest is up and about."

"Not for long. Hide those crutches in my room, Lillian."

"You can't," Elise tried to protest, but no one was listening.

"I'll bring her breakfast tray up as soon as you have her settled," Lillian said, retrieving the crutches.

"It may take forever to settle her," Ian said over his shoulder.

Lillian laughed and was out of sight before Elise could say anything about the matter.

"Please, Ian," she said in a pleading tone that stopped him dead in his tracks.

With a grin, he leaned down to touch his lips to her nose, giving her a mouthful of shaving cream.

"Agh!" She spat out the soapy foam. "Stop doing that!"

Ian laughed and deposited her in bed. "Stop being so stubborn, angry, independent, and noble."

Elise wiped the rest of the soap from her face. "I am

not stubborn. I'm determined."

"Call it what you will, but stay in this bed," Ian said firmly. "I'm going to shave, and then we'll discuss your job."

❧

After shaving, Ian took the telephone number Elise had given him and went to his study. If this Roselle were the monster Elise made her out to be, he wanted to have a nice quiet corner from which to make his argument.

"Women's Designs," a voice said on the other end of the phone.

"I need to speak with Roselle Goodman, please."

"Speaking."

"Ms. Goodman, I'm calling on behalf of Elise Jost," Ian said professionally. "Elise was injured at the college last night and is under doctor's care. She severely twisted her ankle and is to be off her feet for at least a week."

"I see, and who may I ask is this?"

"I'm Dr. Ian Hunter," he answered, wondering if the woman would think him to be Elise's physician. Oh well, he thought, let her think what she would.

"Well, Doctor, I'm afraid I can't wait on Elise to return to work. This situation is rather delicate, but Elise was told that should there be any other problems surrounding her work schedule, she'd be terminated immediately."

"But this isn't her fault. She was—"

"It doesn't matter to me whose fault it was," Roselle stated.

Ian barely kept his temper in check. "I would imagine Elise might be able to file a lawsuit of some kind if you are truly threatening her job."

"That, Dr. Hunter, will be up to Elise, although I seriously doubt that she'll have the same notion. She's given her notice to quit by the end of summer, anyway. She hopes for a career in the government, and I don't think she'll want an employment lawsuit hanging over her head for the months, probably years, that it would take to resolve. Please give Elise my heartfelt wishes for her return to health, but also inform her that she is no longer an employee of Gallagher's."

The phone went dead in his ear.

Now he had to deal with Elise, and he worried about how she'd take the news. He had been so confident of being able to smooth things out with Roselle that it never crossed his mind she'd actually fire Elise over the phone. The woman was way, way out of line, but what could he do about it?

The knock on his door gave Ian no choice but to put the matter aside. "Yes?"

Lillian appeared with Elise's breakfast. "I was just taking this up—"

"Let me," he interrupted. "I have to give her some bad news. I might as well see if I can't cushion the blow with your mouth-watering cinnamon rolls."

Lillian frowned, but let Ian take the tray. "Is it her job?"

"Yeah," Ian said with a nod. "They fired her."

"They what?" Elise exclaimed minutes later. "I can't believe this. They fired me? Just like that? After all I've done for them and all the hard work I've given them?"

"I'm so sorry, Elise." Ian sat on a chair beside the bed and reached out to touch her hand. "I tried to reason with Roselle, but she wouldn't hear reason."

"Tell me about it," Elise said, tears threatening to spill. "Oh, this is so awful. Why did this have to happen to me now? I trusted God to work out the details of my life. I trusted Him to keep these kinds of things from happening. I just can't see any purpose in things like this."

Ian leaned closer and smoothed long strands of hair back away from her face. "All things work together for good."

"They can't possibly this time," Elise moaned and put her face in her hands. It had been a long time since she'd cried, but the tears refused to be held back. The last person in the world she wanted to cry in front of was Ian Hunter, but here she was, blubbering like a baby.

Elise didn't stop Ian when he pulled her into his arms to comfort her. Her whole world was spinning out of control, and there was nothing she could do about it.

"It'll all work out, Elise. I'm sure of it. I've had my moments, too, and God always comes through."

Elise looked up and met his tender expression. "But all my plans. . ."

Ian put a finger to her lips. "What about God's plans? Don't you think He knows your heart's desires? Do you honestly think He stopped caring about you?"

Elise shook her head. "I know He cares. But Ian, I'm not a wealthy woman. I have a small savings account that was supposed to help me move and see me through to my first 'real' paycheck. It'll never see me through to fall, and even if it did, what would I move on? What would I—"

"Elise," Ian interrupted, suddenly seeming inspired. "I have the perfect solution."

"What?" She eyed him suspiciously, suddenly realizing she was still in his arms.

"Can you operate a computer?" he questioned, not seeming the least bit disturbed by their closeness. Elise tried to push him away, but he held her fast and grinned. "Can you?"

"Yes, but what—"

"You could work for me."

"Doing what?" Elise's financial fears were being replaced by concern for her racing heart and fluttering stomach.

Ian released her reluctantly. "Typing up my textbook notes. I'd pay you well, and you could come here every day after class to use my computer. It would surely get you through the summer."

"You can't be serious. I'd have to make at least two hundred dollars a week just to keep the rent and utilities paid and put food on the table. There's no way—"

Again Ian silenced her with finger on her mouth.

"I can handle it," he assured her. "Two hundred a

week seems reasonable for a full-time typist. You can get started right away, and can fix things up so that we can keep you off your foot. How about it?"

Elise shook her head and studied his hopeful expression. "I can't believe this. Are you serious?

"Quite."

"Then I'll agree to take the job on, but with one condition."

"Name it."

"When I'm back on my feet, I'll take your notes home and work from my house. I don't think it would be wise to spend so much time here." She knew without a doubt that she'd never be able to hold out against Ian's charms if she had to work with him day in and day out.

Ian grinned. "Chicken," he said, seeming to know exactly what she was thinking.

Elise felt her face grow hot. "I am not. I just don't want this thing getting out of control. In less than three months I plan to leave, and I don't want there to be any regrets."

Ian sobered instantly and got to his feet. "Do you honestly think you can walk away from this 'thing' as you put it, and not have any regrets?"

Elise looked away and swallowed hard. "I can't afford regrets."

❦

"Hey there," Jason Emery said as Ian opened the front

door. "I heard Elise is staying here with you, and I brought her these flowers."

"Come on in, Jason. Elise is typing some notes for me in the study." Just then Lillian appeared, and Ian motioned for her. "Lillian, would you take Jason to the study. He wants to make a more formal apology to Elise." Ian smiled at the young man, but something in Jason's tone set him on edge. With Jason's next statement, Ian instantly knew why he felt that way.

"Guess Elise won't have any trouble passing the course now." Jason's laughter caused even Lillian to stop in her tracks.

"And why would that be?" Ian questioned, barely containing his temper.

"Well, I just figured. . .well, I mean, what with you and Elise. . ." Jason fell silent, seeming to realize he'd overstepped the proper bounds.

"Come along, young man," Lillian said in a disapproving tone.

Jason followed after Lillian, while Ian stood trying to regain control of his temper. The world was so filled with suggestive innuendos and foul intentions that even a simple gesture of kindness was rendered a deed of iniquity.

But Ian had to be honest with himself. He had brought Elise here for more than one reason. Of course he wanted to see her cared for, because he was coming to care very deeply for her. She wouldn't go out with him, yet she was always in his thoughts and passing through his day in one way or another.

He was embarrassed to admit that Jason was probably closer to the truth than he knew. Ian's motives weren't just Christian concern. He had hoped to woo Elise with his presence in her life and make her fall in love with him.

"Well, Lord, I guess I made a mess of this. I'm trying to rush Your hand in the matter, and I know that's never going to work." Ian rubbed his chin thoughtfully for a moment. "She just has to be the one, Lord," he whispered. "She's everything I've ever wanted. She is my heart's desire." Just then Psalm 37:4-5 came to mind: "Delight thyself also in the Lord; and He shall give thee the desires of thine heart. Commit thy way unto the Lord; trust also in Him; and He shall bring it to pass."

"Okay, Lord," Ian whispered. "I'll try."

Just then Lillian appeared with a tray of refreshments. "I'll take those, Lillian," Ian offered, seeing the perfect excuse to interrupt Jason and Elise.

The older woman smiled. "I thought you might."

Ian shrugged with a grin and took the tray. He stood ready to enter the study when he heard Jason ask Elise, "Are you and Ian a couple?" He held his breath. What would she say?

"A couple?" Elise's voice questioned. "No. He's just been very kind to me, and now I'm working for him." Ian felt his chest constrict. She hadn't even played around by joking or teasing about it.

"So then would you think about going out with me?" Jason asked, causing Ian to tighten his grip on the tray. Jealousy wasn't an emotion he was very familiar with, but Ian recognized it as the feeling that filled his being.

"I'm not seeing anyone, Jason, and I don't plan to," Elise answered. "I'm leaving by the fall, and I don't plan to have a relationship to deal with."

"We could just go out for the fun of it," Jason suggested.

"No, I'm just not going to set myself up for that complication. I want to keep things neat and clean. When I leave, I want to know that I have no reason to look back over my shoulder."

When silence seemed to put an end to the conversation, Ian pushed the door open and entered the small study. "We have iced tea and Lillian's famous butter cookies," he said, trying hard to sound lighthearted.

Elise looked up at him and smiled. For some odd reason, Ian thought it to be a smile of relief, but he passed it off as wishful thinking. Jason, who had been standing very close to Elise, moved away immediately and headed for the door.

"I can't stay. I've still got to get the rest of the concession booth inventory done. I hope you're back on your feet real soon, Elise. See you later, Ian."

When Jason was gone, Ian found Elise studying him with a strange expression on her face. He said nothing, hoping she would explain herself. Her green eyes seemed to bore through his pretense at good-natured ease. Licking her lips and slowly nodding, she finally spoke.

"You win, Ian. I already have regrets."

She turned back to her typing before Ian could answer, but it was just as well. She might not have taken too well to the huge grin that spread across his face. It was something to hope on, Ian thought, putting the tray down on a table by the door, and that was more than he'd had ten minutes earlier.

Chapter 6

E lise was trying to get used to being back in her
own home when the call came from the U.S.
Customs Department. The woman advised her
that they had two positions available that were scheduled to begin August 15. The one located on the
Canadian border in Montana was the one she offered
Elise. Floating on a cloud, Elise accepted the position
and immediately called her mother.

"Mom, it's Elise."

"What a surprise. Is everything okay?" Sue Jost asked
her daughter.

"Everything is great. I got the job. I'm going to
Montana at the end of July."

"That's great, Elise! Will you get a chance to come
home first?"

"No, I'm afraid with this summer class I told you
about, I'll barely finish with the obligation to the
festival before having to turn around and move. But I
promise to fly home for Thanksgiving, if I have that
time off."

"That would be wonderful. Your dad and I feel like
we hardly know you anymore."

"I know and I'm sorry. I try to keep up on the letters,

but I know it isn't the same." Glancing at her watch, Elise realized she'd need to hurry or be late for class. "Look, Mom, I need to go. I have class in fifteen minutes. I love you both."

"We love you, too, honey."

Elise hurriedly hung up and grabbed her backpack just as the familiar sound of Ian's Chevy roared into her drive. Her knees felt suddenly weak and her breathing quickened. "This has got to stop," she said aloud but knew it was an impossible demand. Securing a gold clasp to hold back her hair, Elise opened the door just as Ian started to knock.

"Taxi service," he announced.

"You shouldn't have," Elise replied, pulling the door closed behind her. "I had fully planned to walk."

"Give the ankle a break," he said with a smile, "and let me be gallant."

Elise rolled her eyes and nodded. "Okay."

As Ian helped her into the car, Elise suddenly remembered her news and declared, "I've got a job!"

Ian frowned. "Don't you like working for me?"

"Silly, I mean I'll have a job when school is finished. I just got called this morning. I'm moving to Montana at the end of July." But even as she said the words they lost some of their appeal. In little over a month she'd be saying good-bye to him—forever.

Ian didn't take the news well at all. He got into the car quietly and was well on the way to school before he spoke again. "The end of July? But that's only a few weeks."

"Yes, I know."

"I suppose congratulations are in order."

"Aren't you happy for me, Ian?"

He looked at her as though she'd lost her mind. The expression of disbelief pierced her heart. "Happy? For your dreams to come true, I'm very happy." He pulled into his regular parking place at the college and shut off the engine. "But for me, I can't say the same. I don't want to lose you, Elise."

Elise felt emotions surge without warning. Slamming her fist into the backpack on her lap she turned on Ian. "I told you I didn't want this happening. This was why I avoided relationships. This is why I wouldn't date you, and now it doesn't matter!" She jerked open the door and quickly exited. "I can't let this come between me and my dream!" She slammed the door shut and hurried toward the SLAB.

"Hey, Elise!" Jason Emery called out and ran to catch up with her.

Inwardly, Elise wished Jason would be swallowed up by one of the cracks in the sidewalk, but she bid him a friendly good morning.

"I heard you yelling at the professor. You two having a lover's quarrel?"

Elise knew he was trying to make light of the matter, but she was angry. "No! Ian Hunter is nothing more than a teacher and employer to me."

"I'm glad," Jason said, pulling the door open for her. "I don't think he's all that great at teaching, and I sure wouldn't expect him to know how to treat a woman very well. After all, he's thirty-five and he's never been married. He doesn't date anyone, and he doesn't seem to be interested in anyone. I think he's kind of weird."

"He is not!" Elise declared in defense. She hadn't even had a moment to consider her words before continuing. "Ian is a very good teacher, and he's generous and kind. I don't know how you can say those things about him."

Jason shrugged. "He's got the reputation of being too married to his career to have any time for romance and such."

The words stung Elise. "He's just dedicated."

"He's just dead," Jason said with a laugh. "Some people are too busy with the business of life to ever really live it. Give me a good time and a pretty lady, any day."

Elise said nothing more but hurried to take her seat. Was that how everyone saw her? Was that the way she'd turn out, too? Thirty-five and alone?

Ian took charge of the class, but Elise couldn't concentrate. She watched him move mechanically around the room, the joy in his topic clearly ebbing. She'd brought this on him—of that she was certain—and the more she watched him, the more she wished she could apologize for her words.

"Tomorrow read chapter fifteen in *Art in the Renaissance*. Come prepared to discuss three particular pieces of work from the times and why you feel they make important contributions to our society today. Those of you working on the booths tonight, be in my office at five for your instructions. The dry cleaner called and the costumes are ready, so those of you on the costume committee should make preparations to pick them up before Saturday. Thanks."

The classroom emptied out quickly, and Ian headed to his office without another word to Elise. Grabbing her things, she followed him across the campus and without waiting for his invitation, followed him into his office and closed the door behind her.

"Ian, I want to apologize."

Ian turned, pushing back brown hair from his face. "No, you don't have to. You were right to be angry."

"No, I wasn't. I want you to understand where I'm coming from." She tossed her backpack to a nearby chair and went to stand directly in front of him. "There's so much about this that you can't possibly know, but I truly want you to understand it."

"Go on," Ian said, sounding skeptical.

Elise drew a deep breath and sighed. "It isn't easy to explain Elise Jost, but I'll try. I grew up near D.C. My father works for the Smithsonian and my mother. . ."

She paused and looked away. "My mother is one of the real reasons I'm so determined to see this thing through. She was studying to earn a degree in marine biology. It was her dream to work off the coast of Alaska. She met my father in college and they fell in love very quickly. By the time Daddy graduated, he and Mom were talking marriage and family. Mom still had a year to go on her degree, but she quit college and moved to Washington, D.C., in order to accommodate my father's new position. They married in the fall, and I was born the following year. There was never a chance for Mom to go back to school, and certainly never a chance for her to work at what she'd always dreamed of doing."

Elise looked up at Ian, praying he could understand where she was going with this conversation. His warm brown eyes seemed to encourage her to continue. "I was determined not to make the same mistake my mother made. I knew I couldn't go to college full-time and work, so I planned out my hours and figured it would take six years for me to complete my degree. I had every single detail thought through and developed alternate plans in case something went wrong. Coming up a credit hour short wasn't something I'd planned on. Meeting you was definitely something I hadn't planned on. Don't you see, Ian? I can't do this. I can't be like my mother and give up my dream career for the man I love."

Ian's mouth curved into a grin, and a certain knowing came into his expression. Elise's eyes widened and her throat tightened. What had she just said? Had she really declared her love for Ian? Maybe he wouldn't notice. Maybe she could just smooth over the declaration by continuing.

"This job is important to me," she said in a voice that barely croaked out the words. "I think it will be a good adventure, and I like Montana."

Ian just stood there grinning, and she knew she'd lost the battle. Desperate to put the matter behind her, Elise moved to retrieve the backpack, but Ian reached out with lightening quickness and pulled her into his arms. Lowering his mouth to hers, he whispered, "I love you, too."

The kiss was tender and sweet, and for Elise, it was the first time a man had kissed her on the lips. She felt her arms travel upward, almost as though they had a mind of their own, to wrap around his neck. When Ian pulled her tighter against him, she thought surely it must be the most wondrous thing in the world.

"Did you hear me?" he asked, pulling away just far enough to speak. "I love you."

Elise opened her eyes to find Ian's searching, penetrating brown eyes watching her closely. "I. . . you . . .oh, dear."

"Say it," he whispered against her lips. "Tell me you love me."

Elise stared at him in silence. How could she admit it? She could barely fathom that she was standing here in his arms. How could she open herself up for the disappointment that was bound to come?

She felt him tighten his grip, and when his lips fell on hers again, she moaned softly in resignation. *But how can I not admit it?* she thought as his kiss consumed her. *I do love him.*

Again he pulled away, searching her face for the answer he needed to hear. Elise felt a rush of dizzy exhilaration. In spite of her fears, she was overwhelmed with the love she felt for this man.

"Tell me," he said, almost pleading.

There was no other way. "I love you, Ian," she whispered. "I love you, but I don't know what I'm going to do about it. I don't know how it can possibly work out."

Ian laughed, kissed her lightly once more, and released her. "The hard part is already worked out. I thought I'd never get you to admit you loved me."

Elise felt her face grow hot. "I've never been in love before."

"I know."

"How could you?" she asked in disbelief.

"Your agenda would have never allowed it before."

"It wasn't suppose to allow it now, either," she said, feeling very vulnerable under his scrutiny.

"I know," he said softly, reaching his hand up to stroke her cheek. "But I'm determined, too. And I'm very good at rearranging agendas."

"So now what do we do?" A part of her wanted to laugh and throw her arms around him, while the other half wanted to cry in complete misery.

"First, I suggest we be honest with each other. Then I suggest we pray about the entire situation. On second thought, maybe that praying part should come first."

"I prayed for this not to happen and look where that got me. Oh, this isn't fair," she moaned. "I warned you not to do this."

She looked up at him and could have almost laughed out loud at his expression. He was quite satisfied with himself. "You're not in the least bit sorry, are you?" she questioned.

"Nope," he grinned mischievously. "Not a bit."

After dropping her off at her house, Ian drove away

with a smug expression of having accomplished a great task.

Elise wanted to laugh and cry at the same time. "Dear God," she said, closing the door behind her, "how in the world did this happen? I thought I was being so careful. I thought I had guarded my heart so well."

An image of her mother's tender smile came to mind. Suddenly, the only person in the world Elise wanted to be with was her mother. She wanted to be five years old again and crawl up on her mother's lap and be held until the monsters of life had all gone away. Reaching for the telephone, Elise dialed the familiar number and waited for her mother to answer.

"Hello?" The voice warmed Elise from across the miles.

"Momma," she sighed out the word.

"What's wrong? Are you hurt?"

"I'm confused." Elise stated frankly. "I need your advice." With that said, she poured out her heart in a steady stream of words for nearly ten minutes. "I didn't want to fall in love with him. I didn't want to have to give up my career like you did."

"Is that why you've never dated?" her mother asked in disbelief.

"Of course. I didn't want to make all those plans and have to throw them away because my husband's plans took precedence."

"Elise Jost, do you honestly think that your father and I didn't work through all that before we married? Nothing was as important to me as him. I didn't want a life of marine biology if he wasn't at my side."

"I guess, I mean, I just figured that you didn't have a choice."

"Oh, I had a choice. I was even offered a job right here in D.C., in spite of the fact that I didn't have a degree. But I was already expecting you, and marine biology didn't sound half as interesting as motherhood. One thing led to another, and I found a whole lot more to life than studying sea creatures."

"But you had a dream," Elise protested.

"I'm living the dream, Elise. I thought I knew what I wanted, but God showed me another path. I had my priorities all wrong, but God straightened me out. Listen to Him, Elise, and you won't be sorry. Your Ian sounds like a smart man when he says to pray about it. That's exactly what you should do, and what I will do."

Elise smiled. "So you don't have any regrets?"

"Not a one."

Her mother's reply would stay with Elise through the weeks that followed. Ian didn't push his attentions on her, but neither did he keep to a silent corner of her life. As though testing a mine field, Elise gingerly stepped into the relationship, feeling a mixture of giddy excitement and nervous anticipation. Whatever God had planned, she reasoned, she would try to face it with a quiet heart, counting on Him to work out the details.

Chapter 7

The Renaissance festival began with a spirit of community anticipation that was unrivaled. Elise donned her heavy velvet gown, wondering how in the world women of the times ever managed to maneuver comfortably, especially in light of the fact that they wore an additional thirty pounds of undergarments that Elise had opted to leave off.

Farthingales, petticoats, corsets, and such might have been the attire of the Renaissance woman, but Elise would not be hampered by the likes, especially in the Midwest humidity of summer. She chose instead a single-hooped slip to fill out her gown, and even then, moving while carrying the weight of twelve yards of velvet was no easy matter. But by the time Elise put on the matching burgundy headdress with trailing gossamer veil and ribbons, she was beginning to feel swept back in time.

Ian had coached them on speech and etiquette, all to enhance the pleasure of the visiting crowd. Ladies were to behave submissively at all times, curtseying low when addressed by someone playing their superior in nobility ranking, and always they were to be gracious and ornamental. Of course those portraying peasants and household staff faced different challenges. Elise was glad not to have to roam the festival in tattered rags, with theatrical mud smudged all over her exposed skin.

Moving through the still-quiet festival grounds, Elise knew that she was truly happy. The class and festival preparations had proved to be enjoyable, just as Ian had said they would. She'd learned a great deal in the few short weeks of class, and now that it was nearly over, she could honestly say that she didn't regret the change of plans.

She was nearly to the entrance gate, where she would play hostess and sell tickets to those who had not yet purchased them, when Ian popped out from around the corner. He was still dressed in jeans and a T-shirt, and Elise couldn't resist assuming her role and rebuking him for his attire.

"Sire, you will be mistaken for one of peasants," she said, curtseying low, then struggling against the heavy velvet to get back up.

Ian laughed and looked her over appreciatively. "I'm going to my office to change, but there were some last-minute problems with the axe-throwing booth. Seems someone forgot to get the axes out of the prop room."

"'Tis the way of this life," Elise said in mock haughtiness. "Good help is hard to secure."

Ian laughed. "Milady, you are so very right. I would like to remain here to drink in of your beauty, but, alas, if you will pardon me," he said with a sweeping bow, "I will retire from your company for but a short while."

"Very well." Elise curtsied again and this time laughed. "They must have had very strong legs in the Renaissance."

Ian chuckled, handed her into the ticket booth, and gave her a brief salute of parting. Elise had very little time to consider him as he departed, for just then, trumpets blared out and summoned the crowds to their appropriate places. Without any difficulty, Elise was immediately transposed from a modern-day play-actress to a gentle-bred woman of the sixteenth century.

By two o'clock, Elise was exhausted and also frustrated by the fact that she'd not seen Ian all day. When Jason appeared to assist her at the gate, she noted the smell of beer on his breath as he leaned down close to her face and told her how beautiful she was.

"Jason, are you drunk?" she asked, trying not to bring anyone else's attention to the matter.

"Only drunk with love for you, Lady Elise." He leaned closer and tried to place a kiss on her lips.

"Jason! What do you think you're doing?"

"Ah, be nice, Elise. Ian said you ladies are to be submissive. Come on and give me a little kiss," he reached out for her, but Elise managed to dart around him. Twenty pounds of velvet didn't seem such a hindrance after all.

"You watch the booth," Elise said, stepping outside. "I'll get someone else to come and help you."

"But I only want you, Elise!" he called after her with exaggerated flair.

Grimacing, Elise motioned to Dave, one of her classmates, and told him what was happening. Dave immediately agreed to cover for her, while Elise went in search of Ian.

"I haven't seen him since this morning," she admitted to Dave. "He wasn't even in costume yet. Where do you suppose I'll find him?"

"Well, he's probably with his council in the center clearing."

"His council?"

"Sure, that's what the king does."

"The king? Ian is the king of hearts?" Elise questioned in disbelief.

"I thought everybody knew that," Dave laughed. "Since he created the festival and works harder than anyone else to see that it's a big money-maker, he's maintained the privilege of being king."

"I see," Elise muttered the words, feeling herself tremble with unexpected anticipation. "I'll go look for King Ian at the council setting."

She made her way through excited crowds of children and their parents. She watched as couples joined hands and found themselves caught up in the revelry. People without costumes were bowing and curtseying as they found themselves faced with costumed actors and actresses, and all around, the atmosphere was one of pure delight and pleasure.

Why have I never come to one of these before? she wondered, making her way past a jousting tournament.

Armored knights sat atop equally armored horses and demonstrated to the crowds how an honest-to-goodness joust might have taken place. These knights, of course, weren't classmates of Elise's, but trained professionals who toured the country, working at demonstrations and other festivals.

The festival was set on the edge of a woods that encompassed the college on three sides. The enchanting mood the setting created made it very easy to forget the modern world. Elise heard the minstrels and jongleurs singing songs of love and devotion, all while making grandiose gestures of romantic enticement to the ladies in the crowd. It was amusing to watch grown women actually blushing like schoolgirls when the singers took their hands and kissed them ever so lightly.

Laughing to herself, Elise came upon the crowd watching the king's council. She worked her way around the gathering, but still had no good view of Ian. Ducking behind a large cottonwood, she managed to squeeze through a place where the temporary fencing didn't quite reach the stage. From there, she moved forward to a place on the stage itself, where props and painted stage settings would keep her from view but allow her to see.

Her first glimpse of Ian made her breath catch in her throat. He was regal and stately in his black doublet trimmed in gold braid. A voluminous and heavily padded short gown of gold and black came over the doublet, but this garment was also trimmed in red hearts

244

befitting the king of hearts. The long black hose on his legs provided evidence of his devotion to weight-lifting, and his feet were dressed with traditional, square-toed shoes. Elise smiled to herself, noting the simple gold crown on his head. He made a very handsome king.

"The kingdom of Hearts has known peace for many years and prosperity is all around us. There is much to celebrate and—"

"A spy! A spy!" the cry went out from behind her, and before Elise could turn, someone had taken her in hand and thrust her out into the full view of the cheering crowd.

Ian turned a bemused face to her stunned expression. Elise tried to shake loose from the man's hold on her arm, but when Ian came forward, an uncontrollable trembling shook her entire body.

The man was still denouncing her as a spy, and the crowd had picked up the chant. Twisting to break away from the king's guard, Elise was calmed by Ian's touch and reassuring wink. When the crowd saw Ian take hold of Elise, they instantly fell silent and awaited the king's declaration.

Elise stood completely still, and Ian released her to make a full bow. She, in turn, very shakily made a completely floored curtsey, only to find herself too weak to return to her feet. Ian reached out a hand and helped her to her feet, smiling broadly as he did so and seeming to thoroughly enjoy this new turn of events.

Turning to the crowd, Ian led Elise forward. "My

good townsfolk, 'tis no spy who breaks in upon us."

The crowd murmured. Everyone was wondering what the king might do next, but no one wondered as much as Elise. She looked out upon the people and felt her legs turn to jelly.

"If she be no spy, Your Majesty, then pray tell, who is this woman?" one of the council members asked boldly.

Ian laughed and tightened his grip on Elise's arm. "This is Lady Elise, my chosen bride." The crowd cheered in unison, so loudly in fact, that Elise was deafened by the roar. Ian continued when the noise died down. "For many years now, my mother has encouraged me to take a bride, but until now there has been no one worthy of that place. If Lady Elise consents, we will hold the wedding here on the final day of the festival." Again the crowd cheered, and Elise thought she would faint.

Looking into Ian's teasing eyes, Elise couldn't help but wonder if there were something of truth to his statement about searching for a bride. She felt her heart pound faster at the expression of love she read on his face, and suddenly it seemed as though they were completely alone. What might it be like, she wondered, if Ian were asking for her hand in truth? Swallowing hard, she shook the thought away.

"What say ye, Lady Elise?" another councilman questioned when the crowd again fell silent.

"Yea, milady," Ian whispered. "What say ye?"

"My liege does me honor," she replied. "I will quite

happily take the vows with him."

A chorus of cheers rose up from the crowd, and no one but Elise saw the look on Ian's face, a look that strongly suggested he wasn't playing at this—that he was quite serious.

Finally he turned from her and raised his hands. "My good people, if you will be so kind as to return at two o'clock on Friday afternoon, we will hold the wedding here for the pleasure of all."

"Seal it with a kiss!" someone yelled from the crowd. This brought another affirming cheer.

"Yes, kiss the bride!"

"Kiss Lady Elise!"

Ian looked at Elise with a mischievous smirk. "We mustn't disappoint our subjects, milady."

"But Ian," she tried to say, before he swept her into his arms and kissed her soundly. Amid the yells and comradery, Elise lost her will to argue.

Ian pulled away, but not before saying against her ear, "I love you."

❦

By Friday, there was no explaining the exhilaration and happiness Elise felt. She'd seen very little of Ian except in postfestival meetings where progress reports were the focus. Someone had suggested that Elise be fitted with a special gown for the wedding day, and Ian quickly agreed, noting a crate of unused costumes in his office. This extra attention caused Elise to blush scarlet, but when Friday finally dawned, she was fully delighted by her transformation.

Resplendent in heavy, pale blue silk, complete with many of the Renaissance undertrappings she'd avoided with the velvet gown, Elise moved amidst the crowd feeling very much like a bride. With braided hair secured beneath a beautiful headpiece of silver and blue, Elise became a queenly vision.

Her only duty for the day, besides the wedding, came at noon when she was to cover the entrance gate. Taking her place there, Elise daydreamed about what it might be like to become Mrs. Ian Hunter for real. He was everything she wanted in a man. Educated, strong, handsome, and most importantly, a Christian who could share her faith in God. But he didn't live in Montana.

"Oh, Ian," she murmured, grateful that no one else was around. "Why does life have to be so complicated?" She felt a bit of melancholia engulf her. In a few days, she'd be leaving and would probably never see Dr. Ian Hunter again. Putting the thought from her mind, Elise resolved to deal with it later. *I will be happy today,* she declared to herself.

It was growing closer and closer to two o'clock, and still Jason Emery hadn't shown up to relieve Elise from the ticket booth. Glancing again and again at the clock, Elise finally decided there was no other recourse but to close the booth, take the day's earnings, and secure them in the fine arts department safe before taking her place in the wedding procession. The festival had grossed over $600,000 during the week, with Friday already taking in $30,000 in gate receipts alone. Most of that had been shifted to the safe early on, but several thousand dollars were still in Elise's hands, and she couldn't just leave the money unprotected in the booth.

Putting the money in a bank bag, Elise locked the booth and made her way toward the entrance gate. Without warning, a black-cloaked figure appeared before her, and before she could protest, he'd hoisted her over his shoulder in barbaric fashion.

"Help!" she yelled out over and over.

The man seemed momentarily to consider his route of escape, while the crowd clapped heartily. Elise relaxed a bit, realizing she was caught up yet again in the role playing of the festival.

"Are you come to steal the king's bride?" she questioned the man from over his shoulder.

"Yea!" was the grunted reply.

Elise looked out to the crowd. "Someone fetch the king and tell him that his bride has been taken!" Again clapping and cheering rose up while several people moved away to seek out the king of hearts.

Her captor wasted no more time and quickly moved through the remaining crowd, heading deeper into the woods. Elise felt nauseous from being slammed against the man's shoulder and demanded he let her walk.

"We're away from the people now," she cried out. "Put me down or I'm going to lose my lunch!"

The man stopped and did as she asked. His heavy cloak fell away to reveal Jason Emery.

"Jason?"

He smiled nervously. "Hi, Elise. Isn't this great!"

"I agree it's good for the crowd, but you could have hurt yourself hoisting me up like that. I'm a good fifty pounds heavier with this costume." Before Jason could reply, however, Elise noticed the money bag in her hands. "Jason, I need to get this money into the safe. Let's go around the long way and—"

Jason reached out and grabbed the bag away from her. "You don't get it, Elise. I'm taking the money, and I'm taking you, too."

Chapter 8

"**Y**our Majesty! Your Majesty!" Ian looked up to find a collective crowd of festival-goers approaching him. "Your bride has been stolen!"

Ian stared at them in disbelief for a moment. What in the world were they talking about? As if sensing his questions, one of his students approached to explain.

"A hooded man has taken Lady Elise from the ticket booth. He hoisted her over his shoulder and ran in the direction of the woods."

Ian heard other comments of how wonderful this additional playacting was and how it brought real intrigue and crowd participation to the festival, but inside he felt sick at the knowledge that no such demonstration had been planned by his department. Elise was missing, someone had her, and that someone wasn't part of the festival.

"We will go in search of her," Ian announced. But in the back of his mind he wondered at the best recourse. He made his way with the people to the ticket booth where the first thing he realized was that the festival proceeds were missing. It was clear now, Elise had been taken in the midst of a robbery. Security would have to notified and the people kept at a safe distance.

"Good folk of the village, we request that thee leave this area free for our men to observe. There are tracks which lead into the forest and other signs that will be obliterated if thou shouldst traipse about. We beseech thee, therefore, to await our appearance at the inner circle." He made a broad bow, and the crowd clapped.

Motioning to several of the Renaissance students, Ian confided in them that this was no game. He sent one for security and instructed the others on how to maneuver the crowd back to his council stage. With this done, Ian could no longer ignore the sinking feeling in the pit of his stomach. Elise had been taken and could very well be hurt or even dead.

❦

Jason pulled Elise deeper into the cover of trees. Protesting loudly at his treatment, Elise was stunned when Jason produced a gun and threatened her into silence.

"I didn't come this far just to let you blow it for me," he said, shoving the gun into her stomach. "Now be quiet and move that way. The woods end at the river, and I've got a boat there for our getaway."

"But Jason, I don't want to come with you." Elise struggled to steady her nerves. She wanted to sound reasonable and logical. "Robbery is one thing, but kidnapping could get you a life sentence."

Jason laughed. "Only if they catch me. Now move."

He pushed her forward, and fighting against the extra weight of her Renaissance costume, Elise stumbled and nearly lost her balance.

"I'm hardly dressed for a hike in the woods, Jason." She hoped he'd see reason in one way or another. "This dress doesn't allow me to move very quickly."

"Then take it off," he said, glancing around them as they came into a clearance. "Hurry up. Just get rid of it. I know you're wearing a T-shirt and shorts underneath—remember, I was in the dressing room when Kerry was strapping you into some of those contraptions."

"I need help to unfasten the hooks in back," Elise said, hoping it would buy her some time.

Jason glanced around nervously. "No, there isn't time. Just keep moving to the river. We'll cut it off then if we have to, but we're losing time."

Elise had only taken a couple of steps when Ian's voice sounded from behind her. Turning, she saw him step into the clearing. "Let her go, Jason! Take the money, but leave Elise here."

"No way, Ian. She's my insurance policy. If I let her go, there'll be no reason to keep security from coming after me. Elise stays with me."

"No," Ian said, taking slow, determined steps forward.

"Ian, don't!" Elise called out. "He has a gun."

"Yes," Jason said, leveling it at Ian. "I have a gun, and I have no qualms about using it."

The sound of Jason cocking back the hammer of the

revolver caused Elise to forget herself. All she could see was Ian in danger. Rushing forward, she tripped against the weight of her gown and fell against Jason. The gun fired, but Elise had no way of knowing whether it had hit Ian or not. Jason thrust her back violently, and before she could so much as put out a hand to break her fall, Elise hit her head hard against a fallen log and knew nothing more.

❧

Elise struggled to focus her eyes. A blur of images seemed to circle her head, and dizziness made it nearly impossible to think clearly. Where was she?

"Miss Jost?" a woman's voice called out to her through the haze.

"Where am I?"

"County Hospital," the voice answered. "I'm Nancy, your nurse. Can you tell me how many fingers I'm holding up?"

Elise closed her eyes and opened them again. The blurred double image focused into one. "Three."

"Good," the nurse replied. "You have a slight concussion and five stitches in the back of your head, but you're going to be just fine."

"What happened?" Elise questioned, even as bits and pieces of memory came to her.

"You were in an attempted robbery. The assailant pushed you down and you hit your head."

Elise nodded. Yes, that image seemed to be somewhere in her mind. "Your fiancé has been waiting to see you. Should I send him in now?"

"My fiancé?" Elise questioned. Putting her hand to her head, she knew her expression was one of confusion.

"Don't worry," Nancy said reassuringly. "It'll all come back to you in a little while. Your injury isn't very bad, and you'll only have to stay overnight for observation. I'll go get your boyfriend."

Elise nodded and tried to piece everything together, but when Ian appeared at the door still dressed as the king of hearts, all the confusion cleared away. "You're okay!" she exclaimed and grinned. "Forgive me if I don't curtsey, Your Majesty."

Ian's expression changed from gravely serious to one of amusement. "I suppose we'll let it pass this time." He came to her side and lifted her hand to his lips. "I was so worried."

"Me, too," she said, "At least I think I was. The whole thing is still a little fuzzy around the edges, but I do remember Jason and the gun. What happened?"

"When you very stupidly jumped Jason, the gun went off and you hit your head on a log. Jason got caught up for a minute with what had happened to you and it gave me enough time to cross the clearing. By that time, security was there, and they took him into custody."

"So the money's safe?"

"Who cares about that!" Ian exclaimed. "I thought I was going to lose you, Elise. I couldn't stand it."

Elise smiled in spite of the pain in her head. "I felt

the same way. I thought at first it was just more of your playacting. By the time I realized what was really going on, Jason had me too far away to do any good."

"I wish I'd never forced you to participate in the festival," Ian said, releasing her hand. He put his hand to his head and realized he still wore the king's crown. Taking it off, he stared at it for a moment. "Maybe the festival isn't such a good idea."

"Oh, stop it," Elise said with more strength than she felt. "The festival isn't to blame, and you know it." The throbbing in her head caused her to grimace. "I've spent most of my life in relative good health, but since meeting you I've been to the hospital twice. You're a dangerous man to be around."

Ian shrugged and offered her a lopsided grin. "You'd better get used to it if you're going to spend the rest of your life with me. I love a good adventure and can't see giving it up just because we're going to get married."

"Ian Hunter, are you proposing to me?"

He sobered and nodded. "I very much want you to become my wife. I knew it long ago, but when I declared you my bride at the festival and you agreed to the mock ceremony, I so wished we were doing more than acting out parts. Please say yes."

"Yes," Elise said with giggle.

Ian's eyes opened wide in surprise. "Do you mean it?"

Elise nodded, and before she could speak again, he covered her mouth with a very serious kiss that made her tingle down to her toes.

In this glorious moment of ecstasy, a black cloud of despair draped itself over Elise's joy. Pushing Ian away, she asked, "Ian, what about my job in Montana?"

"What about it?"

Elise felt her chest tighten and knew there was no other recourse but to deal with the issue. "I'm supposed to leave next week. You know how important this job is to me—"

He put a finger to her lips. "You worry too much. Yes, I know how important your new career is to you. It made you put up with me and the Renaissance class, didn't it?" He was smiling as though they were discussing nothing more important than the weather.

His expression grew serious, but the soft tenderness in his eyes was not to be missed. "I would follow you to the ends of the earth, Elise. My work can be done anywhere I have a computer and access to the Internet. We can be married as soon as things can be arranged with our families, and then we can move to Montana together."

"Oh, Ian," she said, reaching her arms up to beckon him forward. She let her fingers entwine themselves behind Ian's head. "Just how long have you had this solution planned out?"

"I started packing the day you told me you'd accepted the position."

"But you said nothing."

"I was afraid you'd think me too forward."

She laughed. "You are too forward."

"It got me what I wanted though, didn't it?" Ian's look of satisfaction was firmly back in place.

"Amazing," she murmured. "God had it worked out all along. Your class, which at one time didn't seem to make a bit of sense to me, put us together and in a few short weeks of knowing each other, we feel confident enough to agree to marriage."

"All things work together for good," Ian whispered against her cheek.

Elise released her hold and gently touched his cheek. "I love you, Ian. You'll always be king of my heart. With God, of course, being King of kings," she added with a grin.

Ian kissed her nose. "I'm the happiest man alive and all because you were a credit hour short and had to take my class. God used a simple Renaissance class to create a miracle of love and a lifetime of dreams."

"Speaking of classes, Dr. Hunter," Elise said in a very formal tone. "Have I completed all my requirements?"

"Indeed you have. Summer school is out."

"Do I pass?" she asked, narrowing her eyes ever so slightly.

Ian laughed out loud and pulled her into his arms. "Ah, Elise," he said and kissed her lips very briefly, "you got an A-plus long ago."

Tracie Peterson has written over fifteen inspirational romances including some under the pen name Janelle Jamison. Known mostly for her historical romances, Tracie was pleasantly surprised when *Iditarod Dream* (Heartsong Presents), a contemporary romance, was voted "Best Inspirational" by *Affaire de Coeur* magazine in their annual readers' poll in 1994. Tracie is currently writing an historical series entitled "Ribbons of Steel" with Judith Pella for Bethany House Publishers. She and her husband and three children make their home in Topeka, Kansas.

No Groom
for the
Wedding

Kathleen Yapp

Dedication

To Debby Kline and Wanda Finney, who cheerfully shared their experiences cruising to the Bahamas.

To Mark Mason, pilot and writer, who "flew" me over the Bahamas.

To Mark Burgess, who knows cameras inside and out and answered my many questions with patience.

To my husband, Ken, for his never-ending support and common-sense editing.

Chapter 1

Penny Blake knew he was watching her. Again. Nearly everywhere she'd been that day on the cruise ship, he'd been there, too. Never speaking, and not flirting, just gazing at her with dark, haunting eyes she couldn't forget.

Now here he was in the ship's elegant dining room, watching her nibble on a cracker while waiting for her sister and brother-in-law to join her. "Enough is enough," she muttered to herself.

Determinedly, she rose and strode across the vivid green carpet to where the object of her displeasure sat at his own table, almost directly beneath one of the room's three crystal chandeliers. He was alone, but the table was set for two. His meal had not yet been served.

"Okay, mister," she said, "time to confess. Why have you been staring at me all day?"

Penny plunked her chubby hands on wide hips and glared down at the handsome, dark-haired, thirty-something stranger. She'd first seen him that morning while standing at the rail of the cruise ship photographing the sunrise over the Caribbean waters.

Then, he'd been jogging around the deck, his long

legs and broad shoulders filling out, with impressive size and muscle, black shorts and a sleeveless black T-shirt.

Now, his white tuxedo covered more skin, but those midnight blue eyes, which had so often during the day drawn her attention to him, still lay on her.

At her approach, he had quickly stood up, taller than she'd realized now that she was close. He faced her across the table.

"Have I been staring at you?" he asked in a deep, rich voice perfect for quoting Shakespeare.

"You know you have. Well, actually, not so long the first time as the others." She held up an index finger to indicate one.

"The first time?" One dark eyebrow raised.

"I was on the deck and you jogged by. You slowed down and stared but didn't return my smile."

"You smiled at me."

"Of course. That's the friendly thing to do on a cruise. Then, the second time you passed," she held up two fingers, "you did not return my greeting. I said, 'Beautiful morning, isn't it?' and you said nothing. But again, you stared."

He nodded and, for an instant, Penny thought she caught a gleam of amusement flicker in his eyes. "Would you like to sit down, Miss. . .?"

"I'm not ready for introductions yet but I will sit down, though I can't stay long. I'm waiting for someone."

He moved around the table and gallantly held the

chair out for her, then went back to his own seat, leaving behind the scent of wild musk cologne.

"I'm waiting, too," he said, folding his hands in front of him on the immaculate tablecloth. "So, is that the only incidence of my bad behavior toward you?"

"No. There was this noon, while you were eating lunch at the Windjammer Cafe, and later, in the gift shop, when you were contemplating Bahamian jewelry."

"Interesting. Were there other times?"

Penny looked straight into his eyes. "How should I know? You don't think I was following you around, do you?"

It began as a slow curling up of the right side of his mouth, soon followed by the left. His rigid jaw line relaxed, and Penny detected a twinkle in his eyes. Too late, she knew what she'd done. "You can just stop thinking what you're thinking," she dictated.

He cocked his head and returned to a serious expression. "And what might I be thinking?"

"That I've been watching you all day, too."

"Seems a reasonable deduction," he defended, turning his palms upward.

Penny leaned toward him, her pug nose almost touching the delicate floral centerpiece of pink miniature roses. "I only noticed you because you were gaping at me."

"If you say so." He shrugged nonchalantly.

"I do say so. Then I come to dinner tonight, and here you are, just a few tables away, staring again. And scowling. You scowl a lot. Did you know that?"

"No."

"Well, you do. You almost are now. Anyway, I tried to ignore you tonight, but my patience snapped. Since I'm a firm believer in getting to the heart of a matter," she tapped on the table with a rounded, orange nail, "I decided to find out just what you're up to. Unless you're here to tell me I've won ten million dollars in a national sweepstakes, there'd better be a good explanation for your creepy behavior."

"Creepy?" His chuckle was barely held in check.

Drawing her lips tight against her teeth, Penny nodded, satisfied she'd successfully accosted the man who'd been on her mind all day.

He studied her a moment, which further aggravated her, then said, "I'm sorry I've offended you." He met her eyes courageously and did not look away.

"You made me uncomfortable."

"Point taken."

Penny expulsed a breath. "Is that all you're going to say?"

"What more should I say?"

"How about an explanation of why I have been the object of your scrutiny all day?"

She was close enough to him to notice a subtle two-inch scar along the right side of his cheek. It almost touched the thick but neatly trimmed hairs of his black mustache. *I'll bet he's descended from those pirates who once sailed these Caribbean waters. All he needs is a black eye patch to—*

"You probably thought I was flirting with you," he said.

Her heart began to thud in a most unnatural way. "Oh, no, I knew you weren't doing that."

"Why so?" he probed.

"Because men don't flirt with me."

He grunted. "They don't?"

"Nope." She whisked a hand nervously through her short, curly, apricot-colored hair. "That's saved for my beautiful sister who doesn't mind it. But I do. I don't like being ogled."

He leaned toward her, his large, well-manicured hands spread out on the table. "I wasn't ogling you."

Penny clucked her tongue on the roof of her mouth and shoved two gold bracelets farther up her right arm. They disappeared under the long, loose sleeve of her ivory floor-length dress that had cost her a week's salary.

"If it weren't ogling, what would you call it?"

"Admiring."

He was serious. There was no grin or playful sparkle in his eyes now to make Penny think he was making fun of her. She had to believe him. But admiring her? She couldn't fathom why.

"I think I need to know your name now," she said.

"Good. I'm Doug Ramsey. And you're. . ."

"Penny Blake, and I'm still waiting for a plausible explanation."

267

He held his hand out across the table and she took it, just as an escaped parrot, in the guise of a waiter in black pants, white shirt, and green, yellow, and orange flowered vest and matching bow tie, came to the table.

"Are you ready to order, folks?"

"A tall, cold pineapple juice, if you have it," Penny asked, "but nothing else. I'm waiting for someone at my own table." She started to gesture toward it and realized her hand was still being held by Doug. His grip was firm.

Embarrassed, she pulled away and put both her hands in her lap.

He was frowning when she glanced at him, and he told the waiter, "Black coffee for now." The waiter thus dismissed, Doug looked at an expensive gold watch.

"Is this explanation going to take a long time?" she asked him.

"I think I'd like it to." He didn't exactly smile, but it was close. The formidable eyes gentled and his right cheek exposed a dimple.

Penny swallowed hard.

"I'm waiting for my mother," he said.

"Your mother?" Penny fairly squeaked.

Not wife? Not girlfriend? Why is a man this handsome on a glamorous four-day cruise to the Bahamas with his mother?

"I need to call and see if she's all right," he said. "She complained of a headache earlier, when she returned from shopping in Freeport." He stood to go. "You will

268

wait here for me, won't you? Then I'll answer your question."

"I suppose," Penny agreed, too curious about this somber man who made strange things happen to her heart and cared about his mother.

He returned in a few minutes and sat down. "She's fine. Just tired and wants to spend the evening in her cabin. She hasn't been. . .well, lately."

"I'm sorry. She will be all right, though?"

"Yes. So, where are you from, Penny Blake?" he asked her, taking a long sip of his steaming coffee which had arrived.

"Do you need to know that before you answer why you've been staring at me?"

He chuckled. "I guess not."

"That's good, because this is not get-acquainted time."

"Couldn't it be?"

"No. I'm not on this cruise to make friends. I'm on assignment."

"Assignment?"

"Oh, no. My camera." Penny leaped up and hurried back to her own table where she snatched up a bulky, black bag from one of the chairs.

"I'm the world's worst when it comes to losing things," she explained when she returned to the stranger. "Once I plop them down someplace, I more than likely will forget where I put them."

"There are worse faults."

"Not when it's your livelihood you're misplacing."

"You're a photographer?"

"Yes." Penny took a sip of her icy pineapple juice.

"What's your specialty?"

"Portraits. I have my own small studio. And I emphasize the word small."

"Did the cruise line hire you?"

"No. I'm with my sister, Stephanie, and her husband, Jerry."

"Are they photographers, too?"

"Good heavens, no. They're here on their honeymoon."

Doug coughed on the coffee he was drinking, almost spitting it out. "Honeymoon?"

"Yes. They've never been on a cruise. Can you believe it, living in Florida? So here we are."

"The three of you?"

"Together. I'm on their honeymoon, too. Isn't that a hoot?"

Chapter 2

Doug stared into the lively, emerald eyes of the intriguing woman sitting opposite him and fought the urge to laugh at her last statement. "I'm sure there's a perfectly good reason why you're on your sister's honeymoon," he said.

"Of course, but that has nothing to do with why you've been staring at me all day. I missed a few valuable shots because you unnerved me."

"I'm a bad boy, I guess."

"Yes, you are." Her eyes flashed with determination to get her answer.

He relaxed back in the chair, liking her spunk. *What should I tell her*, he wondered, *so she won't think I want to get involved with her?* That he could not do. His heart was dead; he had nothing to give a woman, even one who'd jolted him aware of his surroundings more than anyone had for the past three months.

He remembered vividly the first moment he'd seen her. She'd been leaning against the rail, focusing an expensive camera at the sunrise. Her copper-colored hair, windblown and almost emanating a light of its own, had caught his attention first, quickly followed by the almost fluorescent shade of her stylish, mint-green pantsuit.

The fact that she was several sizes larger than a Barbie doll, was somewhere in her thirties, and was softly singing some catchy tune held his interest a moment more, maybe because she was so happy compared to his dark moods these days.

Then she'd turned around. The cheeks of her perfectly round face were flushed from the early morning chill. Her huge, dancing eyes looked right at him, and she smiled. Her wide mouth, splashed with lipstick the same vibrant color as her hair, moved over dazzling white teeth. Suddenly, for Doug, the chilly morning air soared to a hundred degrees.

"You told me earlier I scowl a lot," he began cautiously.

"You do, but you shouldn't. You're far too good-looking a man for that."

He blinked at her forthrightness. "You mean I might end up with permanent frown lines on my forehead?"

"Possibly, and why would you want them? Life is meant to be enjoyed and relished. 'This is the day that the Lord has made. Let us rejoice and be glad in it.'"

"This isn't Sunday."

She grinned. "Every day belongs to God."

He nodded his head in agreement. "You're right, but there are a lot of grim days that make rejoicing hard to do."

"It's a choice, isn't it? To be glad or not? I learned a poem when I was young that I really believe in: 'I'm going to be happy today, though the skies are cloudy and gray. No matter what comes my way, I'm going to be happy today.'"

He felt himself scowling. "Don't tell me you never have bad days." He wanted to attack the naiveté of the simple verse, but it was obvious she believed it wholeheartedly. He couldn't bring himself to destroy that childlike faith by reciting for her the many reasons why daily happiness was not possible.

"Of course I do," she answered. "I'm just as human as you are." Her eyes traveled over his face, like delicate fingers searching out bone structure and soft flesh. Doug shifted his weight in his chair, uncomfortable with her scrutiny. His heart skipped a beat when she said softly, "There's a sadness in your soul, Doug."

"I suppose, but just smiling won't make it go away. Tell me, how do you manage to wear your cheerfulness like clothes for all to see?"

"Is it that bad?" she frowned.

"No. No." He sat up straight and leaned toward her. "I like the way you are. Exactly the way you are."

"It's no secret formula," she announced. "I just believe God's promise, 'I will never leave you nor forsake you.' Then the writer to the Hebrews in the New Testament added, 'So we may boldly say: The Lord is my Helper; I will not fear. What can man do to me?'"

It was a powerful verse, and its truth slammed into Doug's conscience. "The Lord is my Helper. The Lord is my Helper," he kept hearing. He made the mistake of looking deeply into Penny's eyes which were filled with compassion so powerful he wanted to pull her into his arms and tell her his whole miserable story of death and guilt.

Instead, he cleared his throat and said gruffly, "Are you still wondering why I was staring at you all day, Penny Blake? Here's the reason: I couldn't help it. You're spirited and vivacious. And, extraordinarily beautiful. It's as simple as that."

Embarrassment mixed with skepticism flooded her expression.

"You're not used to compliments, are you?" he asked her.

"No. I find them hard to believe sometimes."

"Please, believe mine. Earlier, I thought about introducing myself to you," he said.

"But you didn't."

"Because I'm not looking for a shipboard romance. Despite my compliment." The words were harsh, but true. Still, he wanted to know who she was waiting for. Her sister and brother-in-law? Or a man? When he'd held her hand, too briefly, there'd been no marriage ring, but that didn't mean she wasn't committed to someone.

For the first time in months, he felt good inside, and she was the cause. He'd be a fool to let her go. Whenever he'd seen her during the day, his heart had beaten faster watching her joyousness effervesce from her and onto whomever was around. It had even enveloped him as he'd stood at a distance. She was a flame and he a moth who wanted to be near her. But she would soon be meeting someone else.

He took a quick breath and let it out.

"Do you think whomever you're waiting for is still coming?" He nodded toward the empty table she'd come from.

"I was supposed to eat with my sister and brother-in-law, but something. . .uh, must have kept them. . ."

"Yes, something. So, we're both on our own. Shall we dine together?"

The waiter approached and asked if they would like to order.

A long, awkward silence grew. Then Penny stood up suddenly. "I'm not hungry, actually. I think I'll take a stroll around the deck and shoot a roll of film. I haven't had much time for myself since we left Miami yesterday."

Doug stood up, too. "May I join you?" He knew now he couldn't let her walk away from him. She was an unexpected tether to a life he once had relished. Just for tonight, he would let her vigor rejuvenate him. He would smile again, for her sake, and maybe the pain would go away, for a little while.

She hesitated, her eyes following the waiter as he sauntered toward another table, and Doug hurriedly suggested, "Then you can explain to me just why you are sharing your sister's honeymoon."

"I wouldn't say sharing." She picked up her camera bag.

"What would you say?"

"I've been hired to take pictures."

"This has got to be a first." He cupped his hand under her elbow and directed her through the dining room, past the magnificent butterfly ice sculpture and lavish dessert table, and she let him. He held his breath. "I've never heard of anyone hiring a photographer to go with them on their honeymoon."

They strolled along the corridor to the Centrum, the magnificent seven-story lobby glittering with thousands of tiny lights and alive with huge tropical plants and a three-story waterfall. They took the glass-enclosed elevator up to the Sun Deck.

"Oh, it all makes perfect sense," Penny insisted as they got out and walked toward a small musical combo playing romantic tunes by the pool.

"It does?"

"Of course. For instance, on this trip will you be taking pictures of your mother?"

"Yes."

"Will she take any of you?"

"I suppose."

"How many pictures will you end up having of the two of you together?" Penny yielded to a smug smile.

"Well. . ."

"Other than the shots the ship's photographer takes, when you first board and at the captain's party, you'll have to find a trustworthy and capable stranger to accommodate you."

"I'm beginning to see your point."

"I knew you would," she complimented smoothly.

He frowned, then remembered she didn't like it and relaxed his forehead. "Go on," he urged her. They continued past the pool and stopped at a secluded part of the deck where there were no other passengers. Doug leaned one arm on the railing and turned to face her.

"Since I took all the photos of Stephanie and Jerry's wedding," Penny explained, "they wanted me to do the honeymoon as well. You know, unobtrusively be wherever they are on the ship, at the various ports of call. I'm not to yell 'smile' or 'say cheese', but make the shots candid. Sort of tell a story of the first days of their marriage. Now, isn't that logical?"

"I guess I have to say yes, especially when you get a free, relaxing cruise to the Bahamas for your efforts."

"Mmm, no, they don't have much money." Penny turned to face the ocean and the night breeze tossed some curls about her cheeks. Doug almost reached out to brush them back, but fought the temptation. "My sister works only part-time, and Jerry is just starting a business."

"Don't tell me you had to pay your own way, and they expect you to work all the time, too?"

Now Penny was the one frowning. "What's wrong with that?"

"I could give you a few thoughts." Doug looked over Penny's shoulder at the darkening ocean waves. His mind went back to another time, another place. "Sometimes family members ask too much of us."

"I'd do anything for my sister," Penny retorted, raising her chin in the air in a stubborn gesture he fully understood. He had felt the same way about his brother, and it had been a fatal mistake.

"I hope your sister values what you're doing for her," he sighed.

"I'm sure she does."

He wanted that to be true; she shouldn't be taken advantage of, especially by a sister. "So, Penny, where are you from?" He hoped his tone sounded upbeat, like the cheerful melodies of the steel drums and acoustic guitars playing nearby.

"Fort Lauderdale. And you?"

"Miami. We're practically neighbors. Only twenty-five miles apart."

"More or less."

"Is this your first cruise?" he asked her, a bland question compared to what he really wanted to know: *Is there someone special in your life? Why don't men flirt with you?*

"Yes. And you?"

"It's my first, too. I fly everywhere I need to go."

"Are you always in a hurry?"

He paused to contemplate, then answered, "I guess so."

She shook her head from side to side. "Shame on you, Doug. One needs to stop and smell the roses, or in the present case, since we're in the Bahamas, the jasmine and gardenia."

"Is that what you did today in Freeport?" he asked. He hadn't seen her around the capital city of the Grand Bahamas Island, the first port of call on their cruise.

"No. We went on the glass-bottom boat."

"Instead of shopping at the International Bazaar?"

"Well, of course we went there, later, and drooled over the fabulous buys, and had lunch at Admiral Nelson's pub—"

"But didn't buy anything?" He wondered who "we" was.

"A few souvenirs, that's all. Most of my money goes for photographic supplies. I'm on a pretty tight budget."

But you paid your own way on this cruise—for your sister, Doug thought. "So what's on your agenda for tomorrow, when we reach Nassau?"

"Whatever Stephanie wants."

Doug bit back a sharp retort. He wanted to meet this sister—would make it a point to meet her—to see if she really appreciated Penny as much as she ought to.

Chapter 3

"Be sure to take lots of pictures of Jerry and me today," Stephanie instructed Penny good-naturedly. They were standing on the deck of the fifty-six-foot sailboat that would take them on a coastal tour along New Providence Island and later to a shallow-water coral reef. "Especially when we're snorkeling," she added, grimacing a little.

"Are you still going in the water?" Jerry asked.

"As long as you'll be there to protect me, sweetie." Stephanie leaned back into his arms.

What a handsome couple, Penny thought. They were exactly the same height, five feet six inches, and had almost the same sandy, blond hair except Jerry's was short, above his ears ("Appropriate for working in a bakery," he'd told her once), and Stephanie's floated down to her shoulders in a casual, straight style.

"You still have plenty of film, don't you, Penny?" Stephanie asked, turning in Jerry's arms and kissing the tip of his nose.

"Yes, don't worry."

"You know I don't, really, because you always take good care of me." Stephanie came to Penny and gave her a long hug and one of those angelic smiles that showed her to be the sweet girl Penny knew she was.

"You have a husband now, Stephanie, to take over from me," Penny said gently, knowing she and her sister would never be as close again.

Stephanie shook her head back and forth. "You can't be serious, Pen. No one can ever take your place in my life, not even my darling Jerry." She positioned herself between sister and husband and slipped her arms through theirs. "I need both of you in my life forever and ever. That's all there is to it."

Penny's ego warmed under Stephanie's insistence she would always need her, and she watched the happy couple stroll away from her to explore the sailboat.

Yes, she had taken care of her baby sister, ever since their mother had died. They'd only been three and thirteen at the time, but Penny had worked hard at the new responsibility thrust upon her. Of course their father had been there to help, but his work had kept him far too busy to handle the common, everyday needs of a growing little girl—or of a teenage daughter who began to eat more than she should.

"Penny."

She turned from her reverie and found Stephanie and Jerry smiling at her, the captain of the craft grinning between them.

Quickly, Penny flipped off the lens cap of the 35mm camera hanging around her neck and stopped down to f16. She gently nudged the big black bag which sat on the deck between her feet, reaffirming to herself it was still there. She'd brought plenty of 100 ASA film for the outdoor shots, as well as wide-angle and telephoto lenses and a polarizer filter to take the reflection off the water. Stephanie and Jerry were going to have dozens of colorful pictures of their honeymoon.

A pain, almost physical, shot through Penny's chest as she snapped several pictures, but she wasn't concerned. She knew what it was. It had been with her from the very first day Stephanie had announced her engagement.

While, of course, she was thrilled for her sister—and she really liked Jerry, whom she characterized as dependable and as hard working as a man could be, there was a part of her that knew, at thirty-six, it was not likely she would ever be making such an announcement herself, then getting married and going on a honeymoon in June.

"He was just the nicest man," Stephanie enthused, waltzing back to Penny.

"The captain, you mean?"

"Yes. He suggested a wonderful restaurant for dinner in Nassau, on Village Road."

"You're not returning to the ship?"

Stephanie laughed. "Not when there's a tropical island to explore. We—the three of us, Pen—don't have to be back on board till 2:30 A.M., a half hour before the ship sails for Coco Cay. Dinner ashore is okay with you, isn't it?"

Penny hardly hesitated before agreeing, even while she gave up the crazy idea of seeing Doug Ramsey again in the ship's two-story dining room. *This is not your romantic adventure*, she reminded herself.

It's Stephanie and Jerry's.

The contented couple went off by themselves, and Penny gazed out over the sparkling aquamarine ocean, enjoying the balmy eighty-two-degree temperature in this paradise where the monthly highs and lows seldom varied more than eleven degrees, winter or summer.

Down the coast, pristine white sand beaches stretched to meet slender palm or towering banana trees. Above, puffy white clouds meandered over life in slow motion. The Bahamas. It was everything the travel brochures claimed, as the cruise was.

Today was their third day out of Miami, and their ship, the *Nordic Caroline*, had arrived that morning in Nassau, the capital of New Providence, Bahamas, a city of nearly 140,000 people.

Penny had bounded out of bed more quickly than normal, ordered orange juice and a blueberry muffin from room service instead of waiting for the official breakfast sitting, and hurried to that deck of the ship where she'd first seen Doug Ramsey, jogging.

Since she never played mind games with herself, she admitted the reason for her unbounded energy was this stranger who had forgotten how to smile. She was sure, after their getting acquainted the night before, he'd be there to see her again. But he wasn't.

"I'm sorry you had to eat alone last night, Pen," Stephanie said, returning to her, like a delicate butterfly settling again on its favorite blossom. "It was rude of us not to let you know we weren't coming."

"Don't be silly. I hardly expected otherwise."

"What did you do for entertainment, go to the Broadway Revue or the Country and Western Jamboree?"

Penny's breath quickened at the thought of Doug saying to her, "You're extraordinarily beautiful," and their private stroll together along the deck while romantic music drifted on the cool evening breeze around them. Why wasn't he there this morning?

"I did neither, Stephanie," she answered. "I just walked around the Sun Deck, then looked out over the ocean for a while before going to bed."

"That's nice, I guess, as long as you enjoyed yourself."

"Oh, I did. I did."

"Good. Well, I'm going to put on fresh lipstick. The captain says we'll be leaving any minute."

"Okay."

With zeal and concentration, Penny began taking more pictures of the honeymooners, telling their precious story with her camera as though she were writing with pen and ink.

She was good at doing that. In fact, back in Fort Lauderdale, she was building a reputation for her unique style of capturing more than mere form and color on film. She looked for emotion. She wanted her pictures to live. It was art.

She immersed herself in it now: first, Stephanie and Jerry at the bow of the boat, then kissing, laughing conspiratorially at a private joke, and next his hand gently holding back her hair that wanted to blow free.

Penny'd always been envious of Stephanie's glorious

blond hair. No, that wasn't true. How could she be envious of her sister? But she'd always wished she also possessed gorgeous golden locks, or locks of any other color instead of the exploding red bundle with which she'd been stuck. She knew people thought she dyed it that copper-penny color, but she didn't. It was totally natural.

"They look happy."

Penny stopped dead while focusing another shot. She knew that voice. She whirled around, and her heart stopped beating at the way Doug was looking at her. As though he was really glad to see her. As though she was. . .special.

Then his attention was diverted by a lyrical laugh behind her. It was Stephanie's, and Penny watched his gaze move to her sister and saw the familiar flicker of appreciation all men revealed the first time they saw her innocent beauty. Penny's eyes stung with hot tears.

"Is she your sister?" he asked, nodding toward Stephanie, whose gauzy, white dress floated gracefully around her slender figure and clung to her tiny waist. Suddenly Penny felt awkward and big as a blimp in her peach-colored caftan that gave her no shape at all.

"Yes, she's the lucky bride," she forced herself to chirp as she gestured toward Stephanie, not having the courage to look into his eyes and see admiration for something she could never be. She had been heavy-set most of her life, and had long been trying to accept the idea that she would never be the wisp of a girl her sister was. "Isn't she beautiful?"

"Indeed."

Penny forced herself to take a picture of Stephanie twirling round and round, but she felt every movement of the man beside her. He was wearing white cotton shorts that showed off a flat stomach, a navy polo shirt that emphasized wonderfully broad shoulders and equally wide chest, and comfortable tennis shoes and no socks. He still looked like a dangerous pirate to her, with his thick, black hair blowing in the slight breeze, and his mustache touching the firm, wide mouth that rarely smiled. Penny knew he must work out regularly in order to have such a taut physique.

One of these days I must start exercising, she promised herself, as she had for more years than she could remember.

"You're on duty?" he queried.

"I'm not sure that's the proper term, since it's far from a chore in this environment."

"Are they going snorkeling?" He nodded his head toward Stephanie and Jerry.

"Yes. Jerry is pretty excited about it, but Stephanie's a little fearful. This will be her first time, and she's never been very aggressive in sports."

"Do you have one of those underwater cameras?"

"No. I could have bought a disposable one, but since I'm not going in—"

"You're not? Why?"

Embarrassment rushed through her, and Penny hoped she wasn't flushing five shades of crimson. "I rarely wear a bathing suit," she answered simply.

"Why not?"

She stared at him. "I would think that would be rather obvious."

"Because you're not thin?"

"Yes."

"That shouldn't keep you from enjoying yourself," he asserted.

"Oh, I do enjoy myself, Doug. Just not in a bathing suit."

He nodded, and she sensed it really didn't matter so much to him, as it did to some people, that she was not model size. But, she reminded herself, he works out to keep himself trim, so it must matter some.

"Penny, get us now," Stephanie called out as she and Jerry hugged each other. Penny snapped the picture just as a huge catamaran floated into the background.

Her sister pulled Jerry by the hand over to where Penny and Doug stood, and Penny knew Doug was about to fall victim to Stephanie's charm. Men adored her, for she was gentle and wide-eyed, never making sassy remarks or challenging opinions as Penny so often did.

"Stephanie, Jerry, I'd like you to meet Doug Ramsey. Doug, my sister and her new husband, Mr. and Mrs. Ward."

"Oh, Penny," Stephanie groaned, "now he knows we're on our honeymoon."

"Congratulations," Doug said.

Everyone shook hands and Stephanie asked, "Are you snorkeling today, Doug?" Penny sighed in relief that Stephanie thought she'd just met him.

"Yes, I am."

"This is my first time. Will I get bitten by a fish?" Her eyes sparkled, their blue matching a ribbon of water that lay about a hundred yards off the stern of the sailboat. *No wonder she's never had a problem attracting men,* Penny thought. *How many dresses through the years did I buy that matched the blue of her eyes?*

Doug chuckled. "I don't think you have anything to worry about from the fish, Mrs. Ward."

"Call me Stephanie, please."

"Stephanie. They get enough to eat without attacking humans."

"Oh, good," Stephanie cooed.

"Are you on a cruise, Doug?" Jerry asked.

"Yes. The *Nordic Caroline.*"

"Why, that's our ship, too. What a coincidence that we've run into each other today," Stephanie spouted.

"It's no coincidence at all," Doug corrected her.

"Oh?" her lips froze in a perfect circle.

Doug slipped an arm around Penny's waist, to her shock, and drew her against his firm, sun-heated body. "Your sister and I spent some time together last night, during and after dinner. This morning, I checked every excursion list until I found the one she was on." He looked down at Penny, giving her that you-are-special look again. Her legs began to feel rubbery. "So, here I am, shamelessly in pursuit."

288

Chapter 4

Stephanie's eyes widened. Jerry began to grin. Penny tried to pull away from him, but Doug held her tight. Why he'd acted so impulsively, he wasn't sure, but he wasn't sorry he'd done so. He really did want to spend the day with her. And he wanted the beautiful but spoiled Stephanie to know that.

"I think we'd better find a place to sit," he suggested. "The captain's signaling that we're getting underway."

The four of them moved to the bow of the boat and sat side by side on white vinyl cushions while the other six passengers spread out over the deck and the captain started the engine.

The two crewmen, both college-aged, one with long blond hair bleached from the sun, the other with dark hair trimmed neatly about his ears, and both with golden tans, released the braided dock line and hopped aboard. They were barefoot and wore matching navy blue shorts and white T-shirts, as did Captain Jordan. Their names were Mark and David and they urged everyone to ask them any questions.

The boat moved slowly toward the open sea, the engine purring. The captain's hands on the wheel controlled the vessel's direction, and he began to whistle vigorously.

"That was quite a performance," Penny commented to Doug in a ventriloquist voice meant to keep Stephanie and Jerry from hearing.

Doug sat with his arm outstretched on the back of the seat behind Penny, but he knew better than to touch her. The annoyed look in her eyes made it clear he had sailed into dangerous waters.

"I merely stated we'd spent some time together last night and that I wanted to see you again."

"You made it sound like more happened between us than actually did."

"Did I?"

They were out of the channel now, and the crewmen set the sails, catching the breeze to send the sleek craft skimming neatly along the azure-draped coast toward Athol Island.

A burst of wind sent warm salt spray over the four of them. Stephanie screamed and hid her face in Jerry's shoulder. Penny, however, thrust her face into the spray, not afraid to let her flushed cheeks and wild coppery curls get wet. Doug had the wildest urge to kiss those damp cheeks, but he resisted.

"So, Doug," Jerry called out, holding his new wife's hands in his lap, "where are you from?"

"Miami."

"We're from Fort Lauderdale."

"Yes, Penny told me."

Stephanie looked at him and smiled. *She really is a stunning girl,* Doug thought. With nearly flawless features and soft blue eyes that looked as though they'd seen very little of the world's ugliness, she hardly seemed old enough to be married. Maybe part of her mystique was a fragility that played itself out in the way she snuggled into the protection of her husband's arms and gazed at Penny with total adoration. "Have you lived in Miami long?" she asked him.

"All my life. My family has roots there going back generations."

"How interesting. What do you do for a living?"

Penny turned in her seat and gave her sister a certain look that obviously meant she thought Stephanie was asking too personal a question. Stephanie didn't seem to notice.

"I own a charter airline," he answered her.

"Really? What's the name of your company? Where do you fly?"

"Ramsey Air. We charter flights anywhere in the Caribbean and the state of Florida."

"How many planes do you have?"

"Stephanie," Penny interrupted, "pretty soon you'll be asking the size of his bank account!"

Stephanie's eyes grew large, in a guilty reaction to being reprimanded, then she lowered her head and stared at her hands, gripping Jerry's. "I'm sorry, Mr. Ramsey. I didn't mean to be ill-mannered."

Doug leaned toward her and waited until she glanced up at him. "I don't mind your questions, Stephanie," he told her. When she gave him an apologetic half-grin,

291

he tried to reassure her with a broad smile. "If I don't want to tell you something, I won't. So, ask away."

She shook her head no vigorously. "I think I've said enough for now, haven't I, Pen?"

"I guess that's up to Doug." Penny kicked off her straw sandals and tucked one leg under her. She looked at Doug out of the corner of her eye and he bravely winked at her.

Jerry kissed Stephanie on the cheek. "Well," he said to Doug, "I'm curious enough to ask how many planes you have. Your life certainly sounds more interesting than mine."

"Jerry, it's wonderful to be a baker," Stephanie gushed, "to create those marvelous breads and cakes that people from all over the city come to buy." She turned to Doug. "He really is an artist, only he doesn't think so."

"Stephanie's right," Penny averred. "You have not tasted a true cinnamon roll until you've eaten one of Jerry's." She rolled her eyes and licked her lips. "Mmmm! They're four inches high and have the most delectable white icing dribbled over the top and down their sides."

"Sounds like a winner to me," Doug said.

"It's no big deal." Jerry kicked off his thongs and Doug noticed he had huge toes. "Let's get back to your planes. Tell us about them."

"I have seven." Doug answered uneasily, not wanting to think of three months ago, when he'd had eight ..."They're mostly six-to-eight passenger twin-engine aircraft, but I have an ambulance helicopter and a nineteen-passenger Metro as well. We cater mostly to business people and vacationers."

Penny shifted in the seat so she was looking directly at him. "Are you a pilot yourself?"

"Yes, ma'am. I went through Annapolis. Served my required years, then opted to be a private citizen, but I'm still in the Navy Reserves."

"A man of accomplishment," Stephanie praised, her eyes crinkling with pleasure as they darted from him to Penny, then back to him again. "I'm a little puzzled, Doug, as to why you're on a slow cruise when you have your own planes to whisk you anywhere in the Caribbean," she added.

"I'm with my mother," Doug told her.

"Your mother?" Jerry blurted out. "Sorry. I didn't mean that to sound. . ."

Doug waved away his comment. "Don't worry about it. My mother hasn't been feeling well the last few months, and I talked her into taking the cruise, thinking it would be good for her. She loves the Bahamas, and usually goes over every two or three years to stay with a close friend from college days."

"Why doesn't she fly?" Penny asked.

"She's afraid to."

"You're kidding," Jerry exclaimed. "When her son is a pilot and owns a fleet of planes?"

"I know it sounds strange, but that's the way it is. I didn't want her traveling alone, so here I am."

"A dutiful son," Stephanie said.

The words sounded laudable, except that Doug caught the merest hint of disdain in them, too. His gaze met hers, and held while Penny and Jerry began chattering about a nearby fishing boat.

As quickly as the feeling had arisen, Doug dismissed it. There was no reason for Stephanie to dislike him, and her temperament did not strike him as being judgmental. Anyone could tell she cared about Penny's approval and that Penny adored her.

They were interesting sisters. Stephanie was slender and blond, with a perfect oval face and a childlike smile and manner that made a person want to take care of her. While she was sweet in nature, she lacked the energy and excitement of her flamboyant sister who was far from slender, had an unforgettable round face, and a demeanor that announced she loved life and could well take care of herself.

In their eyes, too, there was a difference. Stephanie's expression was almost blank, as if waiting for someone else to bring meaning to her, but Penny's eyes danced with curiosity and a bit of mischief, and were those of a mature woman who understood people and looked out with compassion on those who needed it. He needed it. From her, too, except he would never let her know.

"Have you ever been sailing before, Doug?" Jerry picked up where he'd left off.

"Oh, yes," and he told them a funny anecdote about his sailing days at the Academy, when he had fallen overboard into the ocean. Jerry enjoyed it, as did Stephanie.

"You're not expecting to repeat that episode today, are you?" Penny teased, grinning.

"I don't expect to. You're not planning to push me overboard, are you?"

Penny's eyebrows shot up. "Now there's an intriguing idea."

"Are you enjoying your honeymoon cruise?" Doug turned to the happy couple.

"Oh, yes," they both answered at once.

"Penny, you haven't taken a picture of us in at least five minutes," Stephanie scolded her kindly.

"You're absolutely right. I'm going to be fired if I don't hop to it."

Doug watched Penny wield her camera like the pro she was and take a half dozen shots from various angles. Despite the extra weight she carried, she moved with grace. He couldn't take his eyes off her. She exuded happiness and contentment, two conditions he had not felt for a long time.

He envied her joyous grasp of life. Was it part of her natural temperament, or did it come from her Christian beliefs? She was a living witness that every day came to her from the God she loved, a good God who had promised never to leave or forsake her.

Doug had believed that too, and had tried to live his life to verify it. . .until the accident. Since then, filled with guilt at how he'd failed his brother, he'd questioned why God had not warned him somehow, why the Holy Spirit hadn't spoken to his conscience showing him what to do. He didn't want to think that God had forsaken him any number of times, but that's what it felt like.

He watched Penny laughingly capture on film the captain persuading Stephanie to take a turn at the wheel. "I'd do anything for my sister," he remembered her saying. Would that include giving up her own happiness in order to ensure Stephanie's? he wondered.

He stood up suddenly. "I've intruded on your vacation together long enough," he told the three of them. "I'll leave you now. I see a man over there I need to talk with."

Penny whirled around and stared at him. Stephanie's mouth opened in surprise. Jerry jumped to his feet. "No need to run away, Doug," he countered. "You're welcome to stick with us. None of us mind, do we? Stephanie? Penny?"

"Of course not," Penny answered, "but if Mr. Ramsey and his friend need to plan which Spanish galleon to plunder, we have to understand."

Doug almost laughed. "I told you my family has roots in Miami, not in a Caribbean pirate cove."

"That's what you said," Penny agreed, deliberately sticking her tongue in her cheek.

Stephanie giggled and gave the wheel back to the captain. "I've never known a pirate before. Are you one, Doug?"

"No," he shook his head, chuckling.

"Even if you were," Penny assured, "we'd love to have your company. Of course, we don't want to keep you if you really want to see your friend. . ."

She let the thought hang, and that's when Doug knew: She didn't want him with them. What he didn't know was why.

Chapter 5

"I really do need to see that guy," Doug said, indicating a middle-aged man in khaki shorts with a matching short-sleeved shirt. "But I'll come back later and keep you company while those two," he gestured toward Jerry and Stephanie, "are snorkeling."

"Aren't you going in?" Jerry asked.

"I was, but I'd rather talk to Penny."

"She won't have time for chitchat," Stephanie told him. "She'll be taking our pictures. That's why she's here."

Doug frowned. "Doesn't she deserve any time for herself? After all, she did pay her own way to come on the cruise."

Stephanie spun around and glared at Penny. "What have you been telling this stranger about us, Pen?"

Penny wanted to kick Doug in the shins. He made her arrangement with Stephanie and Jerry sound like they were taking advantage of her, and that's not the way it was at all.

She quickly stepped forward to face Doug. "I'm thrilled to be here taking pictures," she informed him.

"Because Stephanie needs you."

"Yes, and I always want to be available to her."

Penny thought that would end the matter, but it didn't. The frown that creased his forehead and the fire that exploded in his eyes let her know he had a problem with it. She couldn't imagine what that might be, nor did she care. She had always watched out for Stephanie, and she would continue to do so. That's what sisters did.

"Look, I didn't mean to cause a problem," he said, his demeanor relaxing.

"You haven't," Jerry insisted. "Penny's doing us a tremendous favor by chronicling our honeymoon on film, but we want her to enjoy tis trip, too." He slid his arm around Stephanie's waist. "Don't we, honey?"

"Of course."

"So, you join us whenever you want," Jerry invited. "In fact, this afternoon we're going to tour Fort Charlotte. Have you seen it before?"

"Yes."

"Well, come along anyway. You can be our tour guide—and talk with Penny all you like."

"That might work," Doug nodded.

"Just one moment, gentlemen," Penny interrupted, tired of being spoken of as though she weren't on the planet. "Do I have anything to say as to whether or not I want Doug Ramsey's company?"

The two men, and Stephanie, turned and stared at her. Jerry looked sheepish, Doug amused, and Stephanie expectant.

Penny deliberately kept them waiting, not sure herself exactly what to say. Doug had already told her the night before he wasn't interested in a shipboard romance. Why then, this morning, had he announced to them he was pursuing her?

What did he want from her? Was she willing to risk her heart to find out? In her experience with men, she'd had a number of one-time dates where she'd been politely entertained but never called again, which was just as good. She was too busy to date much. Doug was tall, dark, handsome, and mysterious, and she wanted to spend time with him. But she was afraid to. . .

"I think I'll concentrate on taking pictures of my sister's honeymoon," she declared, finally. She saw a flicker of surprise surge in Doug's eyes. "We don't have much time, and I want to make it special for them." She thought he'd scowl at her, but instead, his eyes danced with what could only be called roguery. "I've enjoyed the time we've spent together, Doug, but I'm not interested in a shipboard romance." She caught his mouth quivering at her repeating the exact words he'd said to her, and she knew that if he laughed, she would push him overboard.

He didn't laugh; he calmly said, "Understood. I won't bother you again."

He turned and walked to the other end of the boat so quickly, Penny didn't have time to tell him he hadn't bothered her. Not at all. It was just that—

"Thank goodness he was gentleman enough to know

you aren't interested in him," Stephanie said, coming over to Penny and taking hold of her arm. "Obviously, a tawdry romance is exactly what he's looking for, and you were smart enough to see that."

"Was I?" Penny challenged flatly.

"Sure. Figure it out. Why would a man who's as handsome as he is, and with all the money he must have, owning his own business, be interested in—"

Penny's heart slammed against her ribs and she jerked away from her sister. "In someone like me? Someone past her prime? Someone fat?"

"Penny," Stephanie cried, "I didn't mean that at all. I'm hurt you could even think so. What I was going to say was, why would he be interested in a stranger he's only going to know for a few days? Isn't it obvious he's just looking for a brief fling? You hear stories all the time of that kind of thing happening on cruises. A girl has to be careful nowadays, Pen." She smiled sincerely. "You've always been a role model for me. You have high morals and integrity, and I know you're not interested in a shallow relationship with a smooth-talking Romeo."

"No, I'm not," Penny agreed without expression.

"Then see? You were wise to send him on his way."

Penny glanced over at Jerry, who shrugged his shoulders. "Seemed like an all-right guy to me, Penny, but it was your decision."

Penny looked across the boat to where Doug was having an animated conversation with the man in khaki shorts and a younger woman, who could have been the man's wife or daughter. Either way, clad only in a skimpy bathing suit and see-through wrap, she gave rapt attention to Doug, and Penny felt an unexpected twinge of jealousy.

She turned her attention back to her picture taking and used more film than she'd planned by the time the boat reached its destination and preparations for the water adventures began. Carefully, she'd avoided taking a picture with Doug Ramsey in it.

Everyone on the boat but Penny shrugged out of their clothes, having their bathing suits underneath, and lined up to receive their masks, fins, snorkels, and safety vests. First-timers, like Stephanie and Jerry, were given instructions and a marine-life lecture. Doug went in, too, even though he'd said he wasn't going to, then showed he was experienced and went off on his own to explore the spectacular undersea coral reef.

Penny felt very alone, sitting by herself while all the others splashed about in the crystalline water. It was one of those moments which came to her occasionally, making her regret she didn't work harder to bring down her weight. Not that she was the only woman there with more than a few pounds on her hips. They were enjoying the water; she could have, too. But a natural reticence had always kept her from doing things which exposed her ample size.

"Penny, this is so marvelous," Stephanie squealed in delight when she surfaced after her first time under and swam to the port side of the boat where Penny was sitting, sipping a cold fruit punch. "You can't believe what it's like down there. The colors. The pretty fish."

"Mark's been taking pictures of you underwater," Penny told her. She'd bought an underwater camera from a supply on board and had asked the crewman to take some shots of the honeymooners, which he'd cheerfully done. "I'm proud of you, Stephanie, for doing this."

"I am, too," she giggled. "Jerry's waving to me. I have to go, Pen."

"Have a good time," Penny called as Stephanie swam away.

Penny saw Doug climb up the boat's ladder at the stern and grab a towel which he used to dry off his face and hair. Tossing the damp towel aside, he stood a moment like a colossus, both legs straight, and leaned his head back, closing his eyes against the golden rays of the sun which glinted off the tiny drops of water captured on the dark hairs of his body.

When he opened his eyes, he turned, and saw Penny. He did not smile at her.

Penny wanted to look away. Run away. But there was nowhere to hide, so she returned his gaze to let him know he couldn't intimidate her into playing coy maiden.

He went to where his clothes were and put on his shorts and shirt, then came over to her and sat down close. Too close. Penny tried hard to keep her breathing regular.

"You should have gone in," he announced.

"I'm sure you're right."

"The water's warm."

"Is it?"

Raucous laughter ripped the air as some of the passengers clambered aboard the boat. Penny saw Stephanie and Jerry at the end of the group, waiting to get to the ladder. Doug saw them, too.

Quickly he stated, "I can't be at the fort this afternoon; I have business to attend to. Will you be eating dinner ashore or back on the ship?"

"Well, uh, the captain recommended some seafood place on Village Road in Nassau, and Stephanie wants to go there."

"Samana's. I know the place. I'll meet you there." He stood to go.

"I told you before I'm not interested—"

"That's what you said, but that's not what you meant."

"You don't know what I meant," Penny bristled.

"Penny, we're not kids. There's something going on between us. I promised earlier not to bother you again. I'm breaking that promise."

"You can't."

"Just call me a scoundrel. Maybe I'm descended from a pirate after all." His eyes were pure devilment.

Penny raised her eyebrows. "Why should I want to have dinner with a man who can't keep a promise?"

"What's this about a promise?" Stephanie asked as

she and Jerry joined them. Penny saw the sharp look that passed between her and Doug.

"I've just made a date with Penny for dinner tonight in Nassau."

"We're not eating in town," Stephanie informed him.

"Sure we are, honey," Jerry piped in. "Remember, you wanted to go to that place the captain recommended?"

"I think I'll be too tired after all this swimming and then walking around a big fort all afternoon. We'll just stay on the ship. With Penny."

"Fine," Jerry agreed. "We'll eat in the ship's dining room, but Penny can eat wherever she wants." He turned to face Penny. "Where will you be eating?"

Penny saw the hurt expression on Stephanie's face at Jerry's forceful words and resented the fact that Doug Ramsey was the cause of them. She knew Stephanie did not want her seeing Doug, and her reason was a valid one—starting anything with him would be foolish.

Still, it had been a long time since her heart had raced the way he made it race. When he looked at her, she felt. . .prized. Knowing it was only for two days, not expecting any more, couldn't she allow herself a little fun and a boost to her ego, while still fulfilling her obligation to take pictures? Was he really a scoundrel, or was he a man with a burden that made him frown so much? Could she help him? Encourage him in some way? Perhaps God had intended them to meet for just that reason.

"I think I'd like to eat in Nassau," she announced.

Stephanie's eyes narrowed. "Then Jerry and I will, too."

Jerry took Stephanie's hand. "No, sweetheart, we'll eat on the ship. Penny and Doug can eat alone."

When she started to protest, he pulled her along the side of the ship, away from Penny and Doug.

"I'll pick you up at three o'clock at your stateroom," Doug arranged with Penny.

"For dinner?"

"I'd like to show you Nassau first. If you'll let me."

She hesitated. "If I go with you that early, I can't go to Fort Charlotte with Stephanie and Jerry." The tug of duty to be with her sister squelched Penny's initial excitement at having been asked to dinner by Doug.

"Couldn't they, for a few hours, find other people to take pictures of them?"

"I. . .I suppose I could loan them one of my cameras." Even as she said the words, a feeling of dread stole over her. She was really finicky about her cameras, and never loaned them to anyone. Stephanie was clueless when it came to photography. Penny didn't know about Jerry.

Bravely, she made a decision. It had been too long since she'd had a pleasant evening with a man. Pleasant? Penny almost laughed out loud. When she thought of Doug Ramsey, words such as exciting and intriguing came to mind more quickly than pleasant. And, he was a man of secrets, a man hurting, or angry. She desperately wanted to know which.

Hesitantly, she shook her head yes while adrenaline exploded within her at the adventure ahead.

"What's your room number?" he asked.

"Ninety-one forty-six on the Bridge Deck."

"I'll be there," he promised.

He reached for her hand and lifted it to his lips. The kiss was silent, and devastating. Penny suddenly felt like the heroine in a romantic adventure—desirable, pursued by a dashing hero who would rescue her from—

Rescue her? She shook her head to clear the crazy thought that had popped into her mind. Rescue her from what? The life she was living was just what she wanted it to be.

She watched Doug stride to the stern of the boat, then turned and saw Stephanie watching his every move despite Jerry's attempts to keep her uninvolved.

Penny sank down on the cushion and stared at the sunny beach and some frolicking swimmers. *Oh, dear Lord,* she prayed silently, *please don't let this be a terrible mistake.*

Chapter 6

Doug stood in front of Penny's stateroom, holding a single gardenia he'd bought for her. An inner struggle kept him from knocking on the door.

He'd always been decisive, a characteristic which his mother called a gift and his brother had berated. He'd decided on the sailboat he wanted to see Penny again. Now, he wondered if the decision had been a bad one.

What's the point? he asked himself. *She has her life; I have mine. We'll never see each other again after Friday.*

He knocked on the door boldly. The point was he not only wanted to be with her, he needed to be. She helped him breathe again. She was light to his darkness.

Penny opened the door.

"Hi," he said, and held out the flower to her.

"Oh, thank you." She slowly reached up and took it from him, looking into his eyes with surprise and awed appreciation. "What a thoughtful thing to do!" Her smile put to shame the sunlight flooding through the window into her stateroom, and filled every corner of it.

"This is one of my favorite flowers," she said, lifting the hand-sized, ivory gardenia to her nose and sniffing it. "The scent is so potent. Don't you think? Here." She held it up for him to smell, which he did, then nodded his agreement with her assessment.

"You're right on time," she acknowledged.

"That's me. Mr. Punctual."

"A good trait for a pilot. I'm ready to go, but come in a minute while I put your gift in water."

Doug stepped across the threshold into the stateroom while Penny walked into the bathroom and ran water into a glass. Her room was not as luxurious as his own, but the twin beds covered with vivid multicolored bedspreads and the vanity table, small couch, and tub chair made the room appear better than the average.

She joined him holding the glass and flower. "Thank you again," she whispered, glowing. "I'll enjoy it so much." She sniffed it one more time before placing it on the nightstand by the bed closest to the glass door which led onto a small balcony where there was a table and two deck chairs. "Now I'm ready," she prompted.

"You look very attractive in that outfit," he told her. He could have said knock-dead gorgeous. The pale yellow, short-sleeved pantsuit floated over her body like a benevolent cloud, the softness of the color making all the more brilliant the copper-red of her curly hair.

Gold earrings, each in the shape of a shell, nestled against the soft roundness of her cheeks. Her lips were open, the color of apricots.

He hadn't intended to kiss her, but he did, stepping toward her, gently taking her shoulders in his hands, and leaning down toward those heart-shaped lips until he felt them beneath his own. He lingered there long enough to feel a tremor race through them.

Slowly he raised his head. "I shouldn't have done that," he whispered.

"No?"

"You didn't mind?"

"I didn't mind," Penny affirmed with a shy smile.

Doug smiled, realizing it felt good to do so. He stood up and released her. "Let's go, then. I have a surprise for you."

❦

"We're going up in one of your planes?" Penny exclaimed, when Doug hired a taxi to take them to the Nassau International Airport.

"If you agree. I always keep one or two here."

She grimaced. "How small is this plane?"

"It can hold six to eight passengers. It's a Gulfstream Commander 1200 overwing turboprop, good for sightseeing. You'll be able to see below the wings."

"That's great, but does it have two engines?"

"Two fine, dependable engines."

"Let's go," Penny whooped. "Time's awasting!"

❦

Doug had flown many times over the 100,000 square miles of ocean that encompassed the Bahamas, and he'd transported a wide variety of passengers, but with

Penny, it was like seeing it for the first time.

"Look at the different colors of the ocean," she shouted above the roar of the engines. "How striking they are! It's as though God's paintbrush swept lovingly over the areas, making each unique and captivating."

Through her eyes, looking down through 2500 feet of sunny sky, Doug saw again the pale, pale blue, almost topaz, hue of the water where it climbed up onto the beach. By the coral reefs, it became turquoise. Farther from shore, it was the purest of blues, crystal clear, and sparkling in the sun. Out to sea, where the depths were much greater, the blue was dark, almost black, covering the ocean's many secrets.

"Are those sharks swimming around the coral reefs?" Penny questioned, groaning.

"Yes, ma'am."

"There's so much ocean and so little land. It looks as though the islands could disappear in the wink of an eye."

A brisk puff of wind buffeted the sturdy plane, and Penny looked at Doug with apprehension.

"There's nothing to worry about," he assured her. "Sometimes the air up here is dead calm; sometimes it's a little turbulent."

"Could you please order the calm?" Penny pleaded.

"Would if I could. Has your life always been calm, Penny?"

"Pretty much, except right after Mama died."

"How old were you then?"

"Thirteen. Stephanie was three."

"That must have been hard for you."

"It was. But I liked the fact that my father depended on me to help him raise Stephanie. He's a wonderful man and he loves us, in his own way, but he can be remote, in his own world, and not realize how much he means to us."

"So he's still alive?"

"Oh, yes, and lives not far from us. He's worked for the same insurance company thirty-five years. We have dinner together every other week on Thursday nights, and I fix his favorite meal: roast beef and gravy, mashed potatoes, peas, and pumpkin pie for dessert."

"I think that could be my favorite, too."

Penny turned in her seat to face Doug. "What about your family?"

Doug's insides tightened and his happy mood evaporated. He wasn't ready yet to share the story with anyone. Not even with her. The pain was too fresh, the guilt too stubborn in its hold over him.

"Let's save that for another time," he suggested. "We'll be starting our descent soon."

Penny commented that surprisingly they'd been aloft nearly an hour, then reached over and squeezed his hand as it lay on the throttle and gave him a smile that pulled him out of the doldrums. "This has been one of the most special experiences of my life," she told him. "Thank you for giving it to me."

Her hand was soft, and he wanted to stay connected

to her forever. "I'm glad you agreed to come," he responded.

When she withdrew her hand, he was aware of the coldness left behind. A week ago, he wouldn't have noticed, wouldn't have had such feelings. Penny Blake was becoming important to him.

"How much do you fly?" she asked.

"A lot—maybe two dozen trips a month. From Miami to the Windward Passage at the edge of the Caribbean Sea and everywhere in between."

"Do you ever get tired of it?"

He didn't even have to think before answering. "I do get tired of the never-ending paperwork and the high cost of maintenance and repairs, but never, never of flying."

On the descent, he radioed the airport traffic control and received his instructions: "Seven-zero-Alpha, follow forward traffic."

Back on the ground, they taxied to the RAMSEY AIR hangar, and Doug stopped on the flight line. Carefully he went through a five-minute checklist to shut down the aircraft, feeling like a kid passing his first driving test with Penny watching him attentively.

When the engines' roar finally ceased, she exhaled in a long sigh. "Blessed peace!" Her infectious laugh made Doug wonder what it was about the obvious delight she took in life that made him want to climb out of the dark hole he'd been in for months.

One of his mechanics opened Penny's door and helped

313

her out. Doug jumped down from his own side.

"Good flight, sir?" the burly, red-headed young man asked.

"Great, Mike."

"Yes, it was wonderful," Penny added.

Mike went about his business of refueling the plane and Penny turned to face the huge hangar. "Are you going to take me on a tour of your office?" she asked Doug.

He shook his head no. "You've seen desks and copy machines and computers before. I'm going to be honest with you, Penny. If I go inside, there's sure to be some business I'll have to deal with." His hand reached out to move some errant curls of her wind-blown hair that were falling over her eyes. "I'd rather be with you, in town."

She looked pleased with what he'd said. "I'd like that, too, Doug."

He ordered a cab and, for once, was glad there was a 35-mile-per-hour island speed limit. With Penny chattering away, asking every question she could think of about Nassau, questions he happily answered, he was in no hurry to reach downtown Nassau, or anywhere else, for that matter. Her effervescent enthusiasm stirred his heart, and he found her banter not at all irritating. It showed intelligence, curiosity, and a desire to learn—three traits he admired.

He took her to the straw market where dozens of tiny booths, separated by grass mats, were run by dark-skinned Bahamians wearing brightly colored clothes, though rarely shoes. The lighthearted, loquacious sellers loudly hawked everything from wood carvings to sunglasses to postcards to T-shirts to straw purses and hats and just about any other thing a tourist might need or desire.

"I'm so glad you brought me here," Penny enthused. "I would have been disappointed to miss it."

A barrage of sound, as well as different languages, surrounded them. A kaleidoscope of cheerful colors dazzled their eyes. Little children in bare feet dashed from place to place, and pretty women leaned into Penny's face to say, "Braid your hair? A buck a bead." Then they would point to their own hair which was always artfully done in braids of varying thickness with dozens of different colored beads mixed into the strands.

"No braids. No beads," Penny politely declined.

"You're not very daring," Doug kidded her.

She giggled. "I wouldn't mind kicking over a trace or two, but I'm afraid I'd never get my hair back to normal if I tried that."

Doug placed his arm loosely around her waist and they walked on. "I'd like to be there, Penny Blake, when you kick over those traces," he said.

Chapter 7

He bought her a garish straw hat with an ostentatious yellow sunflower attached to one side and a three-inch ribbon to tie under her chin. Penny laughingly alleged she had never received so special a gift.

The seller, a beanpole of a man dressed in jeans and a flowered shirt, who could have been anywhere from thirty to fifty years old, declared, "Hat is pretty. Lady prettier."

"I agree," Doug said.

Penny peeked out at him from beneath the huge floppy brim. "I could wear this to church my first Sunday back from the cruise, couldn't I?" she teased.

"By all means. You'd turn everyone's head."

"Oh, I don't want to be a distraction. Do you think the flower is too big?" She fingered the monstrosity.

"Of course it's too big. And outlandish. But this is Nassau." He chucked her under the chin "It's supposed to be."

Penny stood in front of a small mirror mounted on one of the grass mats. "It is a fun hat, isn't it?" she said, studying herself.

"It suits you."

316

She whipped it off her head and gave him a perky grin. "What does that mean?" she demanded.

Doug took the hat from her hands and placed it back on her head, arranging it to his satisfaction while she stood still and allowed him. When he tied the ribbon under her chin and his rough fingers brushed against her skin, she unashamedly wanted him to kiss her.

He paused, capturing her gaze with his own, and she saw the same desire she was feeling.

But he didn't kiss her. Instead, he said, "This hat suits you, Penny, because, as you said, it's a fun hat. You're fun, Penny. You laugh. You smile. You make people want to be around you."

"That's not hard to do here in the Bahamas."

"I'd venture to say you're like that all the time, wherever you are."

She shook her head. "I have my moods, believe me."

"I don't."

Then she laughed, and laughed. He did, too. He actually laughed, and his doing so surprised her. Gradually, since those first moments she'd known him, he'd come out of his dark persona. She had no idea of the cause of his sadness, but that he was forgetting it, even for a few moments, made her happy.

An hour later she declared she was finished shopping. Doug had been a patient companion, showing interest in each thing she'd purchased.

"I love the wood carving I got for my father," she raved, "and the leather purse for Stephanie, and the stunning Colombian emerald bracelet for my best friend, Louise. She's getting married in three weeks. I wanted to give her something special." She examined it again. "I just wish the Bahamian dollar was not equivalent to our American dollar. I could buy a lot more, if it were less."

"Are you standing up for Louise's wedding?" Doug sidetracked the conversation.

"Yes. I'm her maid of honor."

"Are you going on her honeymoon, too?"

"What?" Penny scrunched her face incredulously.

"To take pictures," Doug explained.

"No, silly," Penny smacked his arm lightly.

They took a white horse-drawn surrey with white wheels and red seats around town, and Doug paid the driver to keep going until he told him to stop. Penny wasn't used to such extravagance and felt like Cinderella in the golden coach.

"So, Penny, where do you want to go on your own honeymoon?" he asked her.

The question was so totally unexpected, Penny could not think of a witty answer. And, she didn't feel like giving one anyway. Unlike Cinderella, she'd not yet found her Prince Charming, and she suspected she never would.

"Don't tell me you've never thought about it," he goaded her when she remained silent.

"Oh, yes," she said softly, looking straight ahead and sitting very still, "I wanted to get married. I thought three children would be a perfect family, and I wouldn't have cared what my husband did for a living, as long as it was honorable and he was fulfilled doing it."

Doug leaned toward her. "You make it sound as though you've given up on it ever happening."

She sighed deeply and turned to look into his eyes. "I'm thirty-six years old, Doug, and to tell the truth, I've never even come close to wanting to marry anyone."

"Their loss," he said.

"I've never been asked."

"Some men lack intelligence," he offered.

"Well, for whatever reason, I'm still single, and reasonably content. I don't mind being alone, I'm doing work I like, I have my sister and father close by, and I'm involved in my church. That's a pretty rich life, I'd say."

"Except for one thing."

"What's that?"

"Love, Penny. Have you ever been in love?"

"Have you?" She shook off the self-pity that had momentarily grabbed her. She was not going to spoil this magical time she was having with Doug.

"I asked you first," he taunted.

"I'm not telling," she feigned offense.

"Then I don't have to either."

She giggled, and kept giggling, until she was doubled over on the seat. Beside her, Doug was chuckling, too. Oh, it was the nicest sound, all deep and rumbling from that muscled chest of his.

"I will answer one question you asked," she relented. "I'd like to take a honeymoon in England. I'd rent a tiny cottage in the Cotswolds in Gloucestershire. My mother's people are English and come from that region."

"What would you do there?" he asked.

"Oh, my new husband and I would take leisurely walks through the hills on ancient sheep paths, and read to each other by candlelight, and fall asleep in each other's arms."

"And visit London, and see some shows, and tour the museums, and have high tea," Doug finished for her.

"Exactly."

He suddenly sobered. "I hope you do all those things someday, Penny."

She nodded briskly. "All I need is a groom for the wedding."

"Anyone waiting for the honor?"

She cocked her head and gave him a pensive look. "Why, are you volunteering?"

Doug stared at her. The hypnotic clip-clop of the horse's hooves filled the silence that followed. Then he burst out laughing and reached out with two fingersand stroked her cheek. "Am I volunteering? Who knows, Miss Blake? Someday I just might."

Just as quickly as his laugh had come, his expression sobered. Penny looked into darkening blue eyes. "Are you going to kiss me, Doug?"

"Yes, I am," he whispered, and he did, slowly and

tenderly. At first. Then his arm captured her shoulder and a hand moved to her waist, and he drew her closer. His kiss deepened.

A surge of response raced through Penny, surprising her, but she didn't pull away. Instead, she leaned into the kiss, and her hand reached behind his neck and her fingers intertwined with the soft, thick waves of his hair just above his collar. As she caressed those waves, he shuddered and raised his head.

"You'd better stop doing that."

"Doing what?"

"That, with your fingers in my hair."

"Oh," Penny grinned impishly.

"And this." He kissed her again. "With your mouth." They only broke apart when someone hooted at them from the sidewalk.

"I think we'd better go eat," Doug said, but before letting her go, he ran his wide, strong hand gently through her hair. Penny couldn't have cared less if she ever ate again.

Chapter 8

Doug took her to a different restaurant than the one recommended by the captain of the sailboat. Located within walking distance of the downtown area, it was a charming open-air place that specialized in seafood and Italian cuisine. He hoped it would be memorable for her.

"The sunset you promised me is magnificent," Penny approved. She gazed, her chin in one hand, at the sky streaked with jagged, fiery fingers of reds and oranges and purples. "Just look at that great ball of fire hovering over the horizon." The sparkle in her emerald eyes sent Doug's heart spiraling. It was good to bring pleasure to someone again.

Afterward, they strolled along the harbor on Woodes Rogers Walk. Millions of lights from the hotels and nearby shops vied with the sounds of calypso music and the serpentine glitter of the Paradise Island Bridge for their attention. Prince George Wharf, where their cruise ship was berthed, throbbed with life and lights and upbeat music.

Penny said, "I hope Stephanie and Jerry are enjoying themselves tonight."

"You worry about her, don't you?"

"Worry? No. I'm just concerned that everything go well for her."

"What if it doesn't?"

"Then I help her deal with it."

"And if it's too big a problem even for you, then where does Stephanie turn?"

Penny glanced up at him. "This conversation is becoming serious, Doug. Are you trying to make a point?"

They found an empty bench that faced the ocean and sat down on it. The heady scent of fish and tropical fragrances mingled in the refreshing night air. Doug stretched out both arms along the top of the bench. Penny sat up straight, not touching the back of the bench at all. He felt her tension with him, far different from the relaxed, exuberant woman she'd been all day.

"I just want to get to know you better, and under-stand your relationship with your sister," he explained. "Is she concerned about what happens to you, too?"

"I suppose so."

"You seem more a mother to her than a sister."

"As I told you before, I pretty much raised her."

"Is that why she's so demanding of you?"

"Is she?" Penny turned on the bench to face him squarely. Her eyes were narrower than usual.

"From what I've seen, she wants you where she wants you, when she wants you," he said.

"That's ridiculous," she scoffed.

"Okay. Then why do you feel guilty that you're here

with me and not with her, taking pictures?"

"What makes you think I'm feeling guilty?"

"I'm getting to know you, Penny Blake." He traced lightly with one finger a line from the top of her forehead to the tip of her nose. "When you're worrying, excuse me, concerned about something, you get a tiny line that creases from here to here."

"I. . .do. . .not. . .frown."

"Call it what you will. It's probably nothing more than having a hard time letting go."

"Of what?"

"Of Stephanie."

She gaped at him. "What have I done to make you think I'm not totally happy Stephanie is married and will be making her own life with Jerry?"

"Oh, I'm sure you're happy for Stephanie, even to the point of sublimating your own pleasure."

"This is her time, not mine."

"True, but I get the feeling Stephanie doesn't want to let you go either. She wanted you to have dinner with her and Jerry, not to go out with me."

"Shall I tell you why?" she gibed.

"Yes, I want to know." He was concerned for Penny. She was all too willing to do everything to see her sister's dreams come true. What about her own dreams? "Although I already think I know why," he added. "She doesn't want you having a life of your own."

"That is not so."

324

"Isn't it? What other reason would she have for not wanting you to be with me tonight?"

"Are you ready for the truth?" she forewarned.

"Sure."

"She thinks you're a shipboard Romeo. That you're after a one-night stand and, for some crazy reason, you've chosen me."

Doug's mouth dropped open. Then he began to chuckle.

"So you think it's funny for someone to attribute ulterior motives to you?" she asked him tersely.

"I've had worse thought of me."

"Really? Then she's right. I should stay as far away from you as I can."

"No," he suppressed a snicker. "Stephanie's wrong. Very wrong. First, because she questions why a man should be interested in you. Penny, I can give her a whole lot of reasons. Secondly, I'm not at all interested in a one-night stand, and I'm pretty sure you're not either."

"Absolutely not."

"I'm sorry Stephanie thinks I have only evil intent toward you. Where did she get that idea?"

"Probably because we've all heard stories about what happens to people on cruises."

"Tell me."

"Oh, Doug, for heaven's sake." Penny jumped to her feet and gestured while she talked. "It has to do with romance and moonlight and starry nights. People let their passions run free. They do things they wouldn't do back home."

"And Stephanie doesn't want your passions running free, does she? Or enjoying yourself with a man who finds you. . .irresistible."

Penny stopped talking and looked away from him, toward the darkening water. "In her own way, Stephanie's trying to protect me," she explained.

"Did she make you feel you shouldn't expect a man to be interested in you?"

She took a long time to answer. He knew she didn't want to hear what he was thinking, but she had to, before her precious sister ruined her life. "Stephanie would never intentionally make me feel that way. She loves me. She was only reminding me to be careful."

Doug reached out and took her shoulders and turned her to face him. "Penny, what would Stephanie do if you fell in love? If you met a man and moved away from Fort Lauderdale?" He watched her grapple for an answer; he saw her certainty slip into uncertainty.

"I don't think I like that question," she said finally.

"Why, because it makes you wonder whether Stephanie really wants you to be happy?"

"Oh, you are the most exasperating man." She pulled free and stalked quickly toward the ship, the straw hat he'd purchased for her swinging on its ribbon in her hands. "My sister wants only what's good for me. If I moved away from her, she'd. . .she'd get used to being without me. End of scenario."

326

Doug fell into step beside her. "Are you sure your little sister wouldn't do everything she could to keep you close by? You're a mature woman, Penny, but Stephanie's still a little girl in some ways. She wants her second mother always to be there for her, since her first mother was taken away. She never wants you to leave her."

"You are dead wrong, sir."

"Does she live with you?"

Penny stopped walking, and whirled around to face him. "Yes, she does. So what? She did before the wedding, and now both she and Jerry are staying with me—but only for a few weeks—until they find an apartment of their own."

"You told me once she works part-time."

"Yes."

"For you?"

She expelled an impatient breath. "She's a receptionist at my photography studio, if you must know, but she goes to school as well. She'll be an accountant one day."

"Did you graduate from college, Penny?"

Penny's back straightened and her lips tightened over her teeth. "There wasn't enough money for both of us to go to college," she said fiercely. "My father's job always provided the essentials of home and food, but not much else. I never minded giving Stephanie a good life. Besides, I wanted to be a photographer and didn't need a college degree to be one."

Doug wasn't sure whether he was facing a saint or a

fool. Either she was the most self-sacrificing woman he'd ever known, or she was deluded into thinking it was her duty to be sure her sister got all the good things in life while her own dreams disappeared one by one.

Anger roiled through Doug's body, but he wasn't sure with whom he should be angry: Stephanie or Penny.

Penny plopped her fists on her hips. "Why am I being given this third degree, Doug? What's more, why am I answering all your questions, when I'm more than sure they're meant to disparage my sister?"

"I'm sorry, Penny. I don't want to argue, but I am wondering if you're creating a problem by always being there to help Stephanie and not letting her learn the consequences of her own actions. Maybe she could have earned part of her own way through college, so you could have gone to school, too. And maybe she could have gotten her own job and helped you in some way."

Penny glared up at him. "What a bunch of psychobabble. You don't know my sister, and you certainly don't know the depth of our relationship. Besides, she's the one who found a husband—without my help, I might add—while I'm still. . ."

"Available. And I don't understand why, unless—"

"I think I would like you to keep any further opinions to yourself, Mr. Ramsey." Frustration contorted her face. "It's late, and I'm tired. I'm going back to the ship."

"Okay," Doug consented easily.

"You don't need to accompany me."

"Yes, I do. Right to your door."

Penny groaned and strode away from him. Doug was frustrated, too, with her inability to see what he perceived the truth to be. He was also intensely stirred by her loyalty to her sister and her ability to defend herself. She was one glorious woman.

At her stateroom, they heard the phone ringing, and Penny hurried to unlock the door and get inside.

Doug decided to wait. He didn't want the evening to end on this sour note. He didn't want Penny angry with him. He leaned up against the open doorway and watched her pick up the phone.

Chapter 9

"Penny, where have you been?" was Stephanie's anxious question when Penny scooped up the receiver.

"I've been having dinner with Doug Ramsey. Why? Is something wrong?"

"Look at your watch and you'll know what's wrong."

Penny did so, and was shocked to see it was nearly 2:00 A.M. Before she could say anything, Stephanie plunged on.

"What have you been doing together all this time? He picked you up this afternoon. This afternoon, Pen."

"Yes, well, before we went to dinner, he took me up in one of his planes. Oh, Stephanie, it's incredible to look down on so much water and land. The colors are spectacular. Did you know there are more than seven hundred islands in the Bahamas?"

"No, I didn't. It sounds like you had a wonderful time."

"I did." Penny took a much-needed breath.

"Unfortunately, I can't say the same. Jerry and I couldn't find anyone to take our picture at Fort Charlotte, or at dinner, or coming out of the musical revue, or eating chocolate at the late-night dessert buffet."

"Why not, Steph? I gave you my camera."

"Yes, and we lugged it around all the time, but neither of us really knows how to work it, and we couldn't remember all those quick instructions you gave us about aperture and lenses."

"I'm sorry. You should have asked someone to help you."

"And risked a stranger running off with your camera? We weren't going to take that responsibility. So, the whole afternoon and evening were lost. Our honeymoon story is incomplete."

"Stephanie, please don't try to make me feel guilty about tonight."

"Oh? You don't think you should feel guilty because you left Jerry and me all alone this afternoon and tonight to go off with some dark-eyed stranger you only just met?"

"Stephanie, you're on your honeymoon. I would think you'd want to be alone."

"Well, sure, but I was too worried about you to have a good time myself. Have you been to his cabin already? It is two o'clock in the morning."

Penny gasped into the receiver. "No, Stephanie, I have not been to Doug's cabin. How could you think such a thing?"

"Because I know you're vulnerable."

"Vulnerable?" Penny ground her teeth.

"Yes. You haven't dated a man for. . .how long has it been. . .nearly a year? So when Doug Ramsey smiles at you, it's understandable you fall into a romantic fantasy—"

"Stephanie, stop right there." Penny could not believe the words she was hearing. "Are you saying I'm incapable of controlling my own feelings, or that it's unlikely a man as handsome, sophisticated, and successful as Doug Ramsey could be interested in me?"

The minute the words were out of her mouth, Penny whirled around, praying Doug had left already. He hadn't. He stood there, jauntily leaning against the door, arms comfortably folded across his chest, one ankle casually crossing over the other, the most annoying grin on his lips. She wanted to slap it off.

"I rest my case," he said.

Penny turned her back on him and gripped the phone so tightly her fingers began to hurt. "Stephanie, thank you for calling. Your concern is duly noted, your chastisement received. I'm back now, safely where you want me to be, with honor intact. I'll see you in the morning."

She set the phone down harder than she should have, angry with her sister, but ready to take on Doug Ramsey in a verbal battle.

But when she spun around to face him, he was gone.

❦

Penny saw Doug come into the dining room the next morning and wondered if he'd come to her table. She wouldn't blame him if he didn't. What man would want a relationship with a woman he thought hung on to her little sister for emotional fulfillment?

Hard as it was to accept, he was right about Stephanie. At least partially. She was spoiled and too dependent on her. Penny knew now she herself had fostered the situation, not realizing that keeping her from learning to stand on her own could hurt her sister as much as help her.

But Stephanie was also loving, and not deliberately manipulative. Penny would declare to the heavens that her sister had a good heart.

She looked down at her plate to avoid Doug's eyes and stabbed with her fork a lump of scrambled eggs that were stone cold.

"Penny?"

She looked up into a face that struck her as being more cheerful than it ought to be. Hadn't he thought about her through the night, as she had him? Hadn't he lost sleep because of the way their evening had ended—with frayed feelings between them? A tiny molecule of resistance surged through her blood.

Without invitation he sat down. "Good morning to you, too." His voice rang with. . .confidence. Another molecule of resistance joined the first. "Thank you for yesterday and last night. I enjoyed it."

She waited a minute before saying, "I did too, until you decided you know my sister better than I do and accused her of manipulating my life."

"I don't think I went that far."

"I do." She placed her fork on the plate.

He poured himself a cup of coffee from the silver carafe sitting to his right. "Penny, I don't want to cause trouble between you and Stephanie. Just forget what I said if you want to."

"Oh, I plan to." She took a quick drink from a squat glass of orange juice. She knew she should admit to him that he'd been partially right about her sister, but she felt disloyal doing that. After all, she'd never see Doug Ramsey again after tomorrow, so why should she confess her shortcomings to him now?

"Where are you off to today?" she asked in a way that sounded as though she didn't really care if he dropped off the face of the earth.

"You tell me." He leaned toward her, and his eyes, so intent on her, started her heart racing. "I was hoping to spend the day with you."

She shook her head no. "I'm sorry. I can't."

"You'll be with Stephanie?"

"And Jerry. The cruise will end tomorrow. I want to make the best of it for them."

"I admire you, Penny, I really do, for your devotion to your sister."

"Even though it's misguided? Siblings take care of each other, Doug. I don't know if you have any brothers or sisters, but if you do, you'll understand why you naturally want to help each other."

She raised her eyebrows in question, expecting an answer, but Doug gave her none. In fact, a haunted look spread over his handsome features and his eyes looked beyond her into a space she knew nothing about.

Stephanie and Jerry arrived. Silently they seated themselves. Stephanie looked about to cry and Jerry was grim as he greeted them with, "Hi, Penny. Doug."

The four of them sat there, as though teetering on a precipice waiting for one of them to fall over the edge. It was Stephanie.

"Oh, Penny, I'm so sorry I was mean to you last night," she cried. She leaned over toward Penny and threw out her arms, and Penny quickly accepted them. They hugged each other a long time. "I shouldn't have made you feel guilty for being out with Doug just because Jerry and I didn't do a good job taking care of ourselves."

Doug stood up. "I should go," he said. "You folks have plans to make for the day."

"You don't have to leave," Jerry spoke up. "Have you had your breakfast yet?"

"No."

"Are you waiting for your mother?"

"She's no longer on the ship. I took her in to Nassau early yesterday afternoon." He turned to Penny. "Before I picked you up. She's staying with that friend from college I told you about."

"So you're on your own," Stephanie stated. "Why don't you have breakfast with us, and then you and Penny can tell us about your exciting day yesterday?

Especially that plane ride."

Doug looked at Penny and she shrugged her shoulders to show she didn't care whether he stayed or went. *Liar,* she accused herself, *you know you want him with you.*

"Since you insist," Doug said, sitting down again.

As they breakfasted together, the atmosphere among them relaxed. Jerry suggested they spend the day together in Coco Cay. Stephanie did not object, and Penny was glad. *I only have one more day with him,* she thought, but she never would have admitted to her sister that she felt that way.

"We can look for Blackbeard's treasure," Doug said.

"Pirate treasure?" Penny asked, smiling, relieved that the friction between herself and Stephanie was resolved. At least for the time being.

"Yes. Bahamian waters were a haven for pirates in the early 1700s, you know. They preyed on Spanish galleons laden with gold which passed this way. Some of Blackbeard's treasure is believed to be buried in Coco Cay."

"How exciting," Stephanie squealed. "Where should we look?"

Doug's eyes met Penny's. They were vibrant again.

"Come on, where should we look?" Penny pleaded.

"Let's start with glass-bottom paddleboats."

They all shrieked and laughed together, and after breakfast took a tender from the ship to the shore, being reminded by one of the crew that the last boat would leave Coco Cay at four-thirty that afternoon.

"Could you imagine being left behind?" Stephanie questioned as they walked along the dock "I wouldn't know what to do." She clung tightly to Jerry's arm.

"You could perfectly well take care of yourself," Penny assured her. She put down her camera bag on the dock, took a wide-angle lens off the camera, and replaced it with a polarizer filter to take the reflection off the water. She snapped two pictures of Stephanie and Jerry with the cruise ship and the ocean in the background, then turned toward Doug. "Hold still, Mr. Ramsey." She aimed the camera at him.

"Don't waste your film on me," he protested, but Penny took a picture anyway. At least she would have a way to remember him.

Chapter 10

They walked through Coco Cay's marketplace, browsing amongst Bahamian arts and crafts. Penny took pictures of the honeymooners. They all watched agile young native men in a limbo contest on the beach. Doug got a great shot of Penny applauding the performance.

They ate barbecue at Bahama Jack's Café, then sat in lounge chairs by the ocean. Jerry started feeling sick right after he took a photo of Penny and Doug together.

"Possibly too much sun," Doug suggested.

"Yeah, you're probably right." Jerry moaned. "I should've worn a hat."

"Do you want to go somewhere cool and get something to drink?" Penny inquired.

Jerry looked from one to the other of them, dismay saddening his features. "I don't want to spoil your fun, but I think I'd like to go back to the ship and lie down. If I feel better later, I'll come back."

"Oh, sweetheart," Stephanie lamented, "we're going to miss you while we're sightseeing."

Penny put her arm around her sister's shoulder. "Stephanie, you go with him. He needs you."

Confusion clouded Stephanie's Wedgwood blue eyes

338

as she looked from Penny to Jerry and back to Penny. Then, straightening her shoulders, she brightened, "You're right, of course. A husband needs his wife when he's ill. Come on, sweetheart." She and Jerry walked arm in arm toward the tender that would take them to the ship.

"That was good," Doug said after they were gone.

"What was?" Penny asked.

"The way you pointed out to Stephanie that she needs to be the caretaker for a change."

"It was just common sense."

"Not for Stephanie. She's so used to having you around, she thinks you'll always be with her, even in her marriage."

Penny raised a warning finger. "Don't start on that again, Ramsey." She dropped her head and stared at the ground a moment. "I'm sorry. You didn't deserve that."

"Yes, I did. I told myself last night I'd never bring the subject up again, but here I am, with both feet in my mouth."

Penny looked up and began to smirk.

"What's funny?" Doug asked.

"The mental picture you just painted. You'd better sit down before you fall down."

"Don't get sassy now."

"I've been that all my life. That may be one reason men have shied away from me. I'm too opinionated, too sure of myself. Maybe if I'd learn to be more helpless—"

"Then you wouldn't be the unique, independent,

339

intelligent, feisty, unpredictable woman you are." He grinned. "Add to that adorable and tempting."

The fact that she hadn't mentioned her weight as a reason she was not yet married made Doug respect her even more than he already did. In a world obsessed with being thin, she accepted herself as she was and didn't apologize. He found that remarkably refreshing.

"I hear music," Penny said. "I think there's a steel band concert at the bandstand. Do you want to listen?"

"Sure, and while we do, you can tell me about your life, starting with Day One."

Penny sighed. "That's easy. I was born. Here I am."

Doug draped an arm around her shoulder. "It's all those years in between I'm interested in," he coaxed.

"Boring stuff. Besides, you haven't told me about your family yet. I know you have a mother, but you never mentioned a father."

They started walking toward the music.

"He died in Vietnam. He was a helicopter pilot."

"Oh, I'm sorry. That didn't keep you from wanting to be a pilot?"

"No, it didn't. In a way, it was keeping his memory alive by doing the thing he loved—flying."

They reached the bandstand and found two empty seats. About seventy-five people were listening to the talented musicians who were clad in wild colors. It wasn't long before both Penny and Doug joined everyone else in swaying back and forth, clapping their hands, and tapping their toes to the catchy rhythms.

"Your mother never remarried after your father's death?" Penny posed during a short intermission. They were sipping lemonades Doug had gotten them from the nearby cafe.

"No. She was a working mom, a high school teacher. She often told my brother and me that my dad was the only Mr. Right in her life."

"You have a brother? Where does he live?"

Doug squashed his empty lemonade cup and tossed it in a nearby trash bin. "I had a brother. He's dead."

Penny was stunned. "I'm so sorry, Doug. He obviously meant a lot to you."

"He did." He kept his face turned in profile to her, hoping she couldn't see the sudden tears in his eyes. "He was killed in a plane crash. It was my fault."

Penny inhaled a breath and held it. "Why was it your fault? Were you with him?"

"No, but I should have prevented it."

Doug leaned forward then and rested his elbows on his knees. He covered his face with his hands. He felt her hand on his shoulder, but she sat quietly and asked no further questions.

When he finally sat up, he grasped her hand tightly and kissed the top of it. "I know you resented my saying anything to you about Stephanie and the dangers of not letting go. Well, I spoke from experience."

"What do you mean?" Penny's voice was a whisper.

"I didn't let Greg grow up and take responsibility for his actions. I was always there for him, getting him out

341

of trouble, trying to understand his bad attitudes, listening to his excuses, being the strong rock he could count on."

"I think that's called love," she smiled gently.

Doug grunted. "It may have been done with love, but it wasn't good for him."

"Was Greg older or younger than you?"

"Three minutes and forty-two seconds younger. We were twins."

"Oh, Doug." Penny laid a sympathetic hand on his arm.

"We may have been the same age, but we were as different as catsup and mustard. I was the one who enjoyed homework; Greg would do anything to get out of it, even cheat. I didn't like chores any more than the next kid, but I did them to help my mother; Greg never got around to doing half of his. We both took our first drink at a friend's house when his parents weren't home. I gave it up when I became a Christian; Greg made it a way of life."

"What about your mother?"

"She tried. Again and again, with so much patience. We both prayed Greg would grow up and become responsible one day, but he never did. He was a perpetual kid. He needed a father, but ours was gone. I tried to be what he needed, but all I did was exacerbate the problems he had. He laughed off my lectures, ignored my encouragement to try to change, to do better. I never found the secret for reaching him."

"Doug, you can't blame yourself for Greg's mistakes. He had a mind of his own, that's all."

"Sure, but I wasn't tough enough." He placed his hand on her cheek. Her effort to find excuses for his ineffective behavior with his brother touched him. "What if I hadn't bailed him out of the trouble he got in?" he said. "What if I'd made him take the consequences of his own actions?"

"I'm sure you did what you thought best."

Doug jumped to his feet, took a deep breath, then let it out fast. Agony and guilt over what had happened to his brother swept over him. He began to shake. He was suddenly cold. "Greg's drinking is what killed him. He was drunk when he was flying one of our planes. Thank God there weren't any passengers with him. If I had made him get help—"

"Stop it, Doug." Penny stood up and grabbed both his arms and shook him. "Family members try to be caretakers. Sometimes their efforts have results, but much of the time the person bent on his own destruction won't listen to anyone, even to someone who loves him."

Intermission had ended and the band was regrouping to perform again. Penny and Doug exited the bandstand and walked to the beach, where they took off their shoes. The clean, white sand felt good squishing between Doug's toes, and he took Penny's hand. They meandered along the water line, letting the gentle waves lap over their feet.

"Do you remember those words from Hebrews I quoted to you once, Doug?" she reminded. "'The Lord is my Helper; I will not fear.' You tried to help your brother, but his problem was deeper than human love. He needed a Savior."

They sank down on the cool sand. In the distance, their gleaming, white ship lay at anchor. Close by, people were swimming in the crystal aqua ocean, laughing and having a good time.

"I guess I kept my brother from fully trusting in God, didn't I? From letting God be his Helper instead of me?"

"Maybe I've been doing the same with Stephanie."

Doug turned to her. "We're a pair, aren't we?"

Penny returned his gaze. "Looks that way."

For a long time, they sat there, silently holding hands. Music from the bandstand wafted on the breeze. Waves gently ran up the gleaming white sand and retreated. Sea gulls, the determined flap of their wings and their raucous calls punctuating the tranquil tropical paradise, soared through the sky searching for dinner in the water below.

Doug wondered why he and Penny had been brought together at this point in time. Maybe for no other reason than to share the innermost secrets of their hearts and begin a healing on this remote beach.

"Penny?" Doug murmured, looking straight ahead.

"Yes?" she answered, not moving.

He looked over at her. Her beauty took his breath

away. Her soft, moist skin, her vibrant copper hair, the twinkle in her eyes, the warm smile that melted his very heart—that was her beauty.

More than that, though, she was beautiful in soul and spirit. She loved people. She wanted to understand what they were going through. She made a difference in lives. In just three days, she'd found his heart, buried in darkness and guilt, and exposed it to the light again. Her light. God's light, the same God who'd said, "I will never leave you nor forsake you." What an unfathomable promise that was!

"Penny," he repeated, now looking not at her, but at the ocean in front of them, "I think I've fallen in love with you."

Penny sat very still, afraid to move, afraid that motion would cause him to vanish, along with this beach, this ocean, this sapphire moment. She had just heard the words she'd always dreamed she would hear from a man she could love in return.

"For the first time in three months, I've smiled," he confessed. He slowly turned to look at her. "That's because of you. For the first time in three months, I've enjoyed living again. Because of you."

He raised her hand to his lips and kissed each finger. "I know it's too soon. I've only known you for hours, but it seems like forever. I think you're my soul mate." Penny leaned toward him, tears forming in her eyes.

"I. . .have feelings for you too, Doug." She saw in the vibrant blue of his eyes a softness, a tenderness she had not seen before. He portrayed the image of a tough man, a strong man always in control, a man able to solve any problem. But she saw in him now a gentle side, a nurturing way, which he must have honed on his brother.

He kissed her, then, for a long time, with emotion that took the place of words but told her how much he cared. Really cared. But love? Could he love her already, as he'd professed?

"Stay in Miami for a while," he said, when they separated. "We need time to get to know one another. You can't drive off to Fort Lauderdale and out of my life."

Penny's mind began to whirl. "Stay in Miami? How could I do that? I have my work. Stephanie is newly married—"

"Stephanie has Jerry. I need you. We need each other. I'll get you a hotel room not far from my house." His hands moved down to encircle her arms. "Say yes, Penny. Give us a chance."

She wanted to. She wanted, for once in her life, to be daring and to do something unexpected. She didn't want to leave Doug. Could they have a future together? Oh, it was crazy! Changing her life for someone she'd met on a cruise? It must be the ocean breezes and the palm trees playing with her mind. Could she trust him to be telling her the truth about his feelings?

"Or I'll come to Fort Lauderdale," he amended.

"But your business?"

"As long as your town has computers, modems, and

faxes, I can adjust. The one thing I know is, I need you, Penny, for all the reasons a man needs a woman, and for the spiritual discernment that is your gift."

He kissed her again, sending her head spinning.

"We shouldn't rush into anything," Penny cautioned.

"You mean like marriage?"

Was he proposing? It was outrageous, if he were. "Yes," she quibbled, "we don't know each other well enough."

"How long will it take you to know me well enough?" Doug wiggled his eyebrows, his eyes dancing with mischief.

Penny puckered her mouth and studied the sky. "I'm not sure. Two years, maybe."

"Three months," he dickered.

Her eyebrows shot up. "It couldn't possibly be less than a year."

"Six months," he negotiated.

She paused, trying to keep from laughing. The man was persistent, as well as charmingly, wonderfully crazy. And she was crazy, too. In love with him. "We'd have to spend lots of time together," she stipulated.

"Yes, we would."

"It won't be easy, juggling both our lives, in two different cities."

"I will if you will," he cajoled.

"I will."

"Great!" He jumped to his feet, grabbed her around her waist, and whirled her around and around until

347

they were both dizzy. "Let's go back to the ship and tell Stephanie and Jerry that we're engaged."

Penny pulled back. "But we're not engaged. We've only just agreed to get to know one another."

"Same as engaged to me." He pulled her forward.

"Doug. . ."

"What, Penny love?"

She danced along beside him, chattering nonstop, making rules by which they'd have to abide.

Doug just smiled and held her hand tighter. She was his. That's all there was to it. Whether it took her six months or two years to find that out, he'd be patient.

Then he'd marry her, and fly her, himself, to England, where they'd rent a little cottage in the Cotswolds, and take leisurely walks through the hills on ancient sheep paths, read to each other by candlelight, and fall asleep in each other's arms.

Especially fall asleep in each other's arms. Doug grinned at the thought. *Thank You, God, for bringing us together.*

Kathleen Yapp is the author of more than eight inspirational romances, including *A Match Made in Heaven*, and most recently, *Golden Dreams* (Heartsong Presents). Kathleen writes inspirational fiction because "the love between a Christian man and woman is like no other love in its depth, fulfillment, and excitement." She and her husband Ken have four grown children and seven grandchildren, and make their home in Gainesville, Georgia.